Kira Metzger is a mother of four. Writing has always been her passion. She works besides studying in a college. She wants to be a role model for her kids.

# Kira Metzger

# A Luna's Dark Past

## Book 1

AUSTIN MACAULEY PUBLISHERS™

LONDON • CAMBRIDGE • NEW YORK • SHARJAH

**Copyright © Kira Metzger (2021)**

**Ordering Information**
Quantity sales: Special discounts are available on quantity purchases by corporations, associations, and others. For details, contact the publisher at the address below.

**Publisher's Cataloging-in-Publication data**
Metzger, Kira
A Luna's Dark Past

ISBN 9781647505158 (Paperback)
ISBN 9781647505141 (Hardback)
ISBN 9781647505165 (ePub e-book)

Library of Congress Control Number: 2021911743

www.austinmacauley.com/us

First Published (2021)
Austin Macauley Publishers LLC
40 Wall Street, 33rd Floor, Suite 3302
New York, NY 10005
USA

mail-usa@austinmacauley.com
+1 (646) 5125767

I would like to thank my boyfriend, Steven Gill. And also to Nikki Main at Austin Macauley Publishers.

# The Beginning

I had awoken to a rustling sound just beyond my window. As I slowly approached the window, I was surprised to see a long, dark figure staring back at me with bright white eyes. I stared for what seemed like hours till the figure disappeared back into the dark. I walked back to my bed, and there I sat for a while before I lay back down; the next thing I knew, the sun was up. So, I started to stretch and yawn to hopefully get myself to wake up enough that I could get out of the bed. I had remembered the night prior, thinking it only to be a dream. *Why was I so worried about a dream?* I shrugged it off and chuckled.

As I got ready for school, looking at myself in the mirror, my dark black hair was a mess, and my blue eyes were shining brightly. As I fixed my hair, my mother yelled up the stairs, "Artemis, are you awake?"

I rolled my eyes before shouting downstairs, "Yes, Mother, I'll be down in a minute." So, I grabbed my bag. Opening my door and walking into the long hallway toward the stairs, I suddenly got a shiver that ran down my back as if someone or something was watching me. I started to run down the stairs, not paying attention to where I was going, I ran into something that felt like a brick wall. I looked up, only to see my older brother scowling at me, and all he said was, "Watch it, Squirt." So, I stood up, fixing my clothes before going into the kitchen; right before entering the kitchen, there was a pleasant aroma swirling around the kitchen door.

I walked into the kitchen to find my mother at the stove, and a pleasant cinnamon smell was floating in the air. I noticed that my mother had been making me French toast for breakfast.

"Artemis, why did you wake up so late this morning?" I hung my head at the sound of that; I didn't like disappointing my mother.

"I am sorry, Mom, I didn't get much rest last night." She just nodded at me, so I grabbed a couple of slices of French toast. Recalling what I had seen last night as I dismissed it out of my mind, reminding myself that it was just a dream.

I got up and thanked my mother before grabbing my things and rushing out the door and down to my bus stop. As I stood in the fresh morning air, waiting for the bus, a slight breeze sent shivers up my spine; why was I getting this cold feeling when it is not that cold. As I stood there staring down the road, I couldn't help but wonder where Genius was, and he was slightly late even for him. I shrugged it off. *He will be here; he never misses the bus.* Right as I started walking toward the street to see if I could see the bus, I began to hear some rustling from behind me in the bushes, and my heartbeat began to speed up; I was terrified. At first, a small bunny came from behind the bushes. I started laughing at myself because I allowed myself to get scared of a small animal. *But I have this feeling like someone is watching me.* I moved toward the bushes, kneeling down to see if there were any more animals in there, but I didn't see any, so I turned around, focusing on the road once more.

Then, suddenly, out jumped Genius; I let out this blood-curdling scream that was so loud, it could have woken the dead. He just looked at me and proceeded to fall over, laughing, and I kicked him.

"Genius, what are you trying to do, give me a heart attack?" He stood up, wiped his face, and smiled.

"I'm sorry, Princess, I couldn't help myself." After a moment, I realized that he was joking around with me. I was just on edge from my dream the night before. But Genius had this bad habit of scaring the living crap out of me because he thought it was funny. I told him one of these days, he was going to give me a heart attack. So, as we waited there for the bus, Genius just kept looking at me, and I couldn't understand why.

"Why are you staring at me?" He just smiled.

"I can't believe you screamed that loud; you almost blew my eardrums." I smacked his arm.

"Sorry, I have just been jumpy today."

I turned back to the road and noticed that the bus was approaching our stop. When the bus arrived, we climbed the steps. We started looking for a place to sit when we noticed that the back two seats were open; we walked to the back of the bus and took our seats. The moment we did, the bus driver closed the door and proceeded on his way to our school. Genius let me get the window seat because he knows I like to look out the window on the drive to school.

*The scenery is just so beautiful, but I never seem to notice what is going on around me, as I admire the scenery.*

Suddenly, the bus came to a sudden stop, so I looked up and realized we had already arrived at school. Genius was looking at me, and he had a worried expression on his face.

"Are you okay?" I nodded my head. We got off the bus with the other children when something caught my attention from the corner of my eye. When I looked over, I noticed the same figure from the night before; the one with the bright white eyes was watching me. Genius noticed I had stopped behind him and approached me to ask if I was okay.

"Yes, I thought I had seen someone over there by the tree." He grabbed me gently by my shoulder and rushed me along to class; the first bell had already rung. Had I been standing there that long that I hadn't noticed the bell?

The first period seemed to last forever; I kept watching the clock, hoping that it would just move faster. Mrs. Phoenix was going on about the history of the phoenix. Odd, I know; she was talking about her last name. I finally was able to focus on the last thing she said about the phoenix being able to bring itself back to life from its ashes. The next thing I knew, the bell was ringing, so I got up and walked out of class. I was walking toward my locker where Genius was already waiting like he usually was.

"Hey, Princess, what are you doing for your birthday this weekend?" I shrugged my shoulders.

"I'm not sure why?"

"Well, don't plan anything. I have something I want to show you for your birthday." He kissed my forehead. "Bye, Princess, I'll see you after class." He just disappeared into the crowd of students.

So, I closed my locker and walked to my next class. As soon as I walked into the classroom, I noticed the most popular jock of them all sitting on my desk, and I couldn't help but wonder what he was doing sitting on my desk. Oliver King was sitting on my desk, and I had no clue why. I slowly started making my way to my desk; he looked up at me.

"Are you Artemis Cage?" I shook my head yes; I couldn't seem to get my mouth to form the words that I needed it to. "Well, you're my new tutor, so that I will see you after school today." Then, he just walked away, leaving my mouth wide open. So I took my seat by the window; I was trying to pay attention to what Mr. Dew was saying, but I couldn't focus.

*How could he drop in here and tell me that, then leaving without letting me respond?* I had been talking to myself for so long, I hadn't even noticed that the bell had rung. My classmates had already left, and so had Mr. Dew. So, I got up and started to walk toward my locker. Once I turned the corner, heading toward my locker, Genius was already there and waiting. Genius looked so worried; no, it wasn't worried that was on his face; he looked pissed.

"Genius, what's wrong with you?" He stood straight up and came and stood right beside me.

"I can't believe you agreed to tutor Oliver."

"Well, Genius, I didn't exactly have a choice; I wasn't aware of it until I walked into class. But I am okay with it, and I don't know why but I have some pull toward him even though I don't think he notices it."

The moment those words left my mouth, Genius's eyes went from green to straight black, and he started growling at me like a dog; no, not a dog, something else. Through his teeth, he growled, "YOU'RE MINE."

I slowly started to back away. "Genius you're scaring me." I wasn't sure what was going on; I just kept backing up because he was scaring me; *I have never seen Genius like this before.* His growling got louder, so I turned around and started running toward the school entrance, not knowing if he was following me when, suddenly, I ran into someone and bounced right off. I looked up to see that it was Oliver that I had just run into.

"I'm sorry, I didn't mean to." He helped me up off the ground when we suddenly heard a loud howling coming from inside the school. Oliver grabbed my hand and started running, and I didn't understand what was going on; I'd just seen the man that I had known basically my whole life slowly turning into something I had never seen before here…

# Something Strange

Once we were some distance from the school, Oliver finally let go of my hand. I was trying to catch my breath from all the running we just did. I was still so confused about why we were running. "Oliver, why did you just grab me and run?" He just stared at me in shock like he couldn't believe I even asked that question.

"You don't know who you are, do you?"

"What are you talking about, Oliver? I'm a 15-year-old girl that lives in Tennessee, and there isn't anything to know about me." Oliver just shook his head.

"Let's get you home before your mom starts to worry." Luckily, my house wasn't too far from where we stopped.

We didn't speak the whole way home, not a word; when we got closer to the farm, I noticed my mother was standing on the porch, looking around.

"O man, I am in trouble; I didn't even call her to let her know I was going to be late."

When I got to the porch, my mom instantly started freaking out, "Artemis, where have you been? I heard howling, are you okay?"

Before I could speak, Oliver said, "Yes, ma'am, I am sorry that I have Artemis home so late; we were studying; she was appointed my tutor for the semester." My mom looked just as shocked as I did but not for the same reason. I had never had any boy over before; well, except for Genius. I, on the other hand, was shocked because that was not what just happened. Why wasn't he telling my mom what happened? My mom and Oliver had a conversation on the porch, which, in any case, was weird to me because he just met my mother.

After what seemed like forever, my mom went into the house. She left Oliver and me outside to talk alone. "Oliver, will you tell me what is going on? Why did my best friend growl at me?" He just stood there and stared at me, almost like he was confused about why I didn't know the answer to the question. After a brief pause, he just smiled and looked at me.

"Artemis, don't worry about that for now. I think you should go inside and speak to your mother." He left me with that sentence, and he just left me standing there with my mouth wide open. I finally got the courage to go inside, afraid that my mother was cross with me for being late and bringing a boy home with me.

But when I walked inside, my mom was sitting on the chair in the living room; she honestly looked upset. *I hope I didn't cause her to be upset,* and I hate seeing my mom upset. I have never liked my mom being mad or upset with me. "Mom, what's wrong? Are you angry with me for being late? I am sorry, I just lost track of time." She just looked at me with tears running down her face.

"Baby girl, I am so sorry for everything. I have kept so much from you, trying to protect you. But I see now that maybe that wasn't what was best." I just looked at her with astonishment. What could she be talking about? *We have never hid anything from each other.*

"Mom, what are you talking about? I am sorry for being late. I didn't mean to upset you at all." I was shocked. I wasn't sure what was going on. My mom just started crying more; I couldn't make out anything she was saying to me. "Mom, where is my brother? Where is Zeus?"

My brother could always get my mom to smile no matter if she was upset or angry. Even when she was cross with him, he still managed to get a smile out of her. My mom just looked at me with such sadness in her eyes. "He isn't here right now, sweety. He went out with his friends; he won't be home till around 5–5:30 a.m., but let's just head to bed for now. We can talk more tomorrow when your brother is home." Then, she got up and went to her room, and I just kept staring at the stairs. How could she say that, then leave without explaining anything? I shook my head; I approached the stairs, hoping to see her waiting on me, but she wasn't there. She had already gone into her room and closed the door. So I walked up to the stairs, went into my room, and threw my stuff on the bed. I went straight to the bathroom to take a long, hot shower, hoping that maybe I would feel better after I took a shower.

When I got out of the shower, I put my pajamas on and went to lay down on the bed; I needed to finish clearing my head before I could fall asleep. Or so I thought, I don't even remember falling asleep, but when I woke up, it wasn't because it was time to. I woke up because I heard a blood-curdling scream. I was scared. I thought it was coming from outside, but, suddenly, I heard it again, coming from my mom's room. I looked at the clock, hoping it was 5:30 a.m. already because my brother would be home and I wouldn't have to search by myself, but it wasn't; it was only 4 a.m. Then, again, I heard another scream, so I jumped out the bed. My feet barely touching the floor, I flung my door open and started running down the hall to my mother's room. When I opened my mother's door, all I could see was blood. It was everywhere; piles of it on the floor, streaks of it on the walls and ceilings. There even was a handprint made of blood on the wall, then I looked to the corner and, there, my mom was sitting with her chest ripped wide open, stomach slashed open to the point her organs were leaking out onto the floor. I wanted to scream. I tried to scream, but the moment I opened my mouth to cry, I heard a growl coming from my mom's closet.

I heard the deepest growl I had ever heard come from her closet when this big, black wolf came out of the closet. It had bright white eyes like the figure I had seen outside my bedroom window and again at school. I slowly started backing up, trying not to give it any reason to attack me. I backed up so far, I hit my back on the handle of the door. The wolf kept getting closer to me, but, somehow, I managed to get myself out the door and slammed my mother's door shut. I took off, running down the hall to my room. I rushed into my room and slammed the door. I started piling anything substantial that I could lift or push with my legs in front of the door. I jumped over my bed, landing hard on the floor.

I reached on the bed and grabbed my cellphone. I dialed my brother's number; it just kept ringing and ringing, but he didn't answer. I pressed the end-call button and immediately dialed 9-1-1; it was buzzing when the operator answered suddenly, "9-1-1, what's your emergency?" I was still shaking from what I had just seen, and the wolf was trying to get into my room.

"Yes, ma'am, there is a wolf in my house. It has attacked my mother, I am home alone, and I believe my mother is dead." The operator took a second to realize what I had just said.

"What's your address, ma'am?" The wolf was getting louder and louder as it tried to force itself into my room.

"1641 Wolfsbane Drive, Gatlinburg, Tennessee. Please hurry, the wolf is starting to split my door." I was freaking out. *What in the world is going on?*

"Ma'am, we have police, ambulance, and wildlife services on the way; you should be hearing them now. Please stay with me on the phone till they arrive."

At that moment, I was petrified; the wolf with the bright white eyes had already splintered my door enough to get his muzzle in. *If they don't hurry, there isn't going to be anyone alive here to help them.* I heard the sirens.

"Operator, I hear the sirens, and I see the lights. They're pulling up the driveway now."

"Okay, thank you, ma'am. I will stay with you until the officers get you out safely." The moment the wolf had heard the sirens, it took off; it quit banging on the door and disappeared.

But I didn't dare move until the officers got inside; I was scared for my life. I heard the officers come inside. I informed the 9-1-1 operator and she hung up with me. I saw the officers through the hole in my door; they went to the door and asked for me to open it. I got up off the floor and moved everything from in front of the door and met them outside my bedroom door. The one officer I recognized because he had mentored my brother for a while, Officer Jacob. He immediately came to me, and before I could even say anything, he asked, "What happen, Artemis? You said there was a wolf here; where did it go? Where is your mom? Where is your brother?"

He asked so many questions before I could even process the first question he asked me, so I took a big breath in so that I could try to answer them as best as I could without crying. "The wolf was here. As soon as it heard the sirens, it just took off. My mom is in her bedroom; there is a lot of blood; please help her. My brother should be home in a few minutes; he was with his friends." As soon as I finished, I started crying. I dropped to the floor and just sobbed. Officer Jacob bent down beside me and hugged me.

"Artemis, it's going to be okay. You're safe now, you're safe." He walked me outside, and he made me sit down on the back of the ambulance. That was when my brother's car pulled into the driveway. I don't even think my brother put the car into park before he jumped out and ran to me.

"Artemis, what happened, are you okay? Is Mom okay?" I just started crying again, and I couldn't look at my brother; I was scared, not sure what was going on. Everything just hit me at once, and my mom was dead; a wolf killed her. Wolfs don't go into people's houses and eat them.

That's when Officer Jacob pulled my brother off to the side and, from what I could only assume, started to explain everything that had happened. The next thing I knew, my brother took off into the house, yelling for our mom like he didn't believe Officer Jacob. Officer Jacob ran in after him. Once Zeus saw Mom's room, he came back down; you could see he was upset and angry. But when he got back to the ambulance, all he did was hug me.

"I am sorry, Art, I should have been home so I could protect you and Mom." He was blaming himself for something that was out of his control, and he couldn't have protected us from the wolf. "Big Brother, it's not your fault; you couldn't have protected Mom or me from the wolf. You would have just gotten hurt too." Zeus just stared at me like I was stupid, but then he just looked down sadly like he wanted to say something but he couldn't right then.

Officer Jacob came back over. "Artemis, are you ready to go down to the station so we can you can fill out a witness report on what happened?"

"Zeus can come with you, and, Zeus, you're 18 now, right?" Zeus just stared at him blankly; he was trying to figure out why he was asking such a silly question, but I knew why he was asking.

Zeus looked at me before answering, "Yes, I am, but what has that have to do with what's going on now?" Officer Jacob shook his head in disbelief.

"Really, Zeus, you have to come down to the station to talk to child-protective services, since your mom was the only parent. They are going to want to know if you want to take care of Art, and then they will explain everything you need to do." Immediately, my brother got angry.

"Of course, I will take care of my sister. What kind of question is that? I am not just going to let anyone take her. We are all we have now."

I touched Zeus on his shoulder to calm him, and I had never seen my brother get this angry about anything, especially when it came to me. "Zeus, it's okay, nobody is going to take me away from you. I am your sister, after all. I don't want to be with anyone but you." Zeus wrapped his arms around me.

"Come on, Art, let's get you down to the station so we can get this day over with." And with that, Officer Jacob drove us downtown to the police station. Zeus and I didn't speak the whole way there; I laid my head in his lap and cried the entire way there. My brother kept playing with my hair to try and soothe me because that was what my mother used to do when I was upset or not feeling good. I knew he was trying to help, but that just seemed to make it worse. I saw my mom torn apart, and what was worse was the wolf almost had me if it wasn't for the police. I decided to go to sleep because the drive to the

17

police station could take a while to get there, especially with the traffic that was up ahead.

# Reality

We were in the car for what seemed like forever, when, suddenly, we came to a complete halt. I thought we had made it to the police station, but that wasn't it, I sat up to see what was going on, and it was the wolf with the bright white eyes. The one that had attacked my mother. I squeezed Zeus's arm to the point I was drawing blood. Zeus just looked at me. "Squirt, what's wrong?"

"Zeus, that's the wolf that attacked Mom and tried to attack me." Zeus sat up and immediately started growling which I did not understand why he was growling. *What in the world is going on; first Genius, and now Zeus?* But the wolf immediately took off. Officer Jacob just shook his head and started driving again.

Within a few moments, we were at the police station and being ushered into Office Jacob's office. My brother and I sat down in the chairs that were stationed right beside the desk when Officer Jacob came and sat down in his chair.

"Now, Artemis, could you please explain what happened? I know it is hard, but please explain as much as possible." I kept looking down at my feet like they would protect me from this conversation, when I suddenly felt a gentle squeeze on my hand. I looked up, and Zeus was smiling at me.

"It's okay, Squirt, just tell them what you remember so we can go to the hotel for the night."

I nodded; I didn't understand why my brother was being so nice to me; he usually ignored me. I took in a deep breath and looked at Officer Jacob. "I got woken up around 4:30 a.m. to screams. I assumed they were coming from outside until I heard the second scream that I realized it was coming from my mom's room." I started crying, but I continued. It was essential to figure out why this happened, and Zeus deserved to know as well. "So I jumped over my bed, ran down the hall to my mother's room. When I opened the door, all I saw was blood everywhere, and my mother's lifeless body in the corner. When I went to scream, I heard growling coming from the closet when this big wolf with bright white eyes came out of the closet, causing me to back up till I reached the door." I realized that after I had mentioned the wolf, Zeus seemed more agitated in a way, and I wasn't sure why. But nonetheless, I continued the story, "So I managed to get out the door. I started running down the hall back to my room. I started placing everything that I could in front of it, hoping that it would stop the wolf from getting to me, but it was almost through when you guys got there, but as soon as it heard the sirens, it disappeared."

Officer Jacob arched his eyebrow at me, surprised to hear what just came out of my mouth. "Artemis, are you telling me that a wolf attacked your mother, went after you, then just disappeared when we showed up?" I nodded, acknowledging that that was what happened. Officer Jacob was typing away on his computer when he turned and looked at Zeus. "Zeus, can I speak with you a moment, then, after that, child-protective services would like to speak with you. Artemis can sit in my office until you are done. The wildlife officer would like to ask her some questions about the wolf if that's okay." Zeus stood up from his chair and looked at the officer.

"I do not have a problem talking to you and child-protective services, but my sister will not be talking to anyone else tonight; she has been through enough, and I just want to get her somewhere safe."

That seemed to shock Officer Jacob because we were at a police station, why wouldn't I be safe there. My brother walked outside the office with the officer to where child-protective services were, and then they went into another room where I could not see nor hear them. I sat in the office for a while when, suddenly, I heard Genius asking for me, which was shocking because I haven't heard from him since the incident at the school. But nobody knew what had happened because Oliver didn't tell anyone. An officer brought Genius to the office where I was, and I immediately stood up and backed away from him. Genius thanked the officer, then turned to face me.

"Princess, are you okay? I heard what happened." I stood there, frozen, unsure of what to do. "Princess, I am sorry for the other day at school. I shouldn't have acted like that."

I just kept staring at Genius. Unsure of what to do or say, I finally worked up the courage to speak, "Genius, what are you doing here? I didn't call you, how did you know where I was? Why were you growling, what's going on?"

He just hung his head. "Princess, there is a lot you don't know about; you won't know until your birthday, but I never meant to scare you." I was still so confused on what was going on, I had forgotten all about my birthday. With everything going on, I just realized that I turned 16 today. What was he talking about? *It's just my birthday, there isn't anything special about it.* He tried to inch closer to me, but I kept backing up until I backed into the desk behind me. That's when my brother came into the office. He looked at me, then looked at Genius. I think he just realized I was up against the desk.

He immediately started going toward Genius. "What are you doing here? Nobody called you. Why is my sister backing away from you? Genius, what did you do?" Genius just looked at him and laughed, then walked out. What the hell was that about?

Zeus walked over to me. "Are you okay, Squirt? Did he do something to you?" I shook my head no, afraid to speak. My brother just hugged me. "I am so sorry I wasn't there to protect you and Mom, but I will not make that mistake again. Let's get you to the hotel." Zeus walked me out of the building, and there was a car already waiting on us. Zeus had called his best friend, Daniel, to come to pick us up. Daniel was as tall as Zeus, but he had blonde hair, and Zeus opened the door for me, then we both got in. I didn't speak the entire way to the hotel. Zeus just kept watching outside like he was waiting for something or someone. I wasn't sure of what was going on; I just wanted to go to sleep and wake up, and this all be a dream. This couldn't be real, and I couldn't have just lost my mom, especially before my birthday.

Before I knew it, we had arrived at the hotel. My brother thanked Daniel, then got out of the car and went inside the office to pay for the hotel for the night. Daniel just kept looking back at me like he wanted to say something but was scared.

"Artemis, are you okay?" Was I okay? I really couldn't feel anything; I was numb.

"I honestly don't know, Daniel. I am so confused on what's going on. Nobody is telling me anything; they just keep mentioning my birthday." Daniel looked down after that like he knew what was going to happen.

"I am sorry that all this is happening, but maybe you should go get some sleep. I am sure Zeus will explain things, but Happy Birthday, Artemis." I got out of the car and walked over to where my brother was standing, waiting for me.

"Come on, Squirt. Let's get you to the room so you can sleep." I just nodded following him to our room, and he got us one with a double bed. That way, we weren't sharing the same bed. I went and sat down on the bed; Zeus sat across from me.

"Zeus, what is going on? Why does everyone keep mentioning my birthday?" Zeus just looked at me.

"Squirt, let's not worry about that right now. I want you to get some sleep, then we will talk about everything." I nodded and lay back on the bed; my brother came over and sat on the edge of the bed and started running his hands through my hair. "I am so sorry, Art, we never meant for any of this to happen. Happy Birthday, Squirt. Get some sleep, and we will talk a little bit later today, okay?"

I didn't even realize I had fallen asleep when I woke up; the sun was shining, and my brother was in the shower. I realized we were in the hotel, so that wasn't a dream; *Mom is gone.* I scrunched my knees to my chest. What was I going to do; my mom wasn't here for me to talk to; I wanted answers. The shower stopped, Zeus opened the door, and steam just came rolling out.

"Hey, Squirt, come to get in the shower and freshen up. I am going to take you to breakfast, then we have some stuff we have got to get done for Mom's funeral." I just nodded and went into the bathroom; I looked at myself in the mirror. *What is going on? Why is all this happening?* I pushed it out of my mind and jumped into the shower. Once I was in the shower, I was able to relax some. When I got out of the shower, *Zeus must have put some new clothes in here while I was in the rain,* because on the toilet sat this beautiful, red, flower top with some cute high heels to go with it. *When did my brother get so good at picking out clothes,* I laughed to myself.

After I got dressed, I walked out of the bathroom; my brother just turned around and started to smile. "Squirt, you look beautiful, do you like it?"

I shook my head. "Yes, but when did you get so good at picking out clothes?"

He just started laughing. "I'm not; it's the dress that Mom and I picked out for you for your birthday." At the mention of my mom, I hung my head; I missed her; why did this all have to happen to us? My brother walked over to me and lifted my chin up. "Art, I know this is hard, but we're going to get through this; it's just you and me now." I hugged my brother. I had never seen this side of him before. He pulled me back a little away from him. "Come one,

Squirt, let's go get Mom's ashes, then we can decide if we want to have a funeral or just spread her ashes at her favorite spot, okay?" I nodded and followed him out to the car that was there.

The drive to the mortuary was silent; my brother nor I spoke the whole time. When we pulled up, I looked at the building; *this isn't the one I have seen in town before.* My brother noticed that I was looking strangely at the place.

"This is one that only our family has, nobody else is allowed to use this one. Mom's parents purchased it a long time ago." I looked at him, confused, and I didn't even know my grandparents; they died when my mom was pregnant with me. Zeus looked at me. "All right, Squirt, I will be back out. You sit here till I come out. If anything happens, I want you to lay on the horn till you see me, okay? Do not open the windows or doors for anyone who got it." I nodded yes; I didn't know what to say, he was acting so strangely now. He got out the car and walked inside but not until I locked the car doors; he wouldn't budge till he made sure I locked the doors.

*Why is everyone acting so strange to me now? Nobody cared this much before; nobody cared what happened to me until now.* I looked at the building in front of me. It was ancient; the outside was made of marble, there were beautiful angel statues on the very top of the building. The more I admired it, the more attractive it became. *This is our family's, but how? We never seemed to have that much money.* I sat in the car for about 30 minutes before my brother came back out holding an urn. I unlocked the door; he opened the door and got in.

"Well, Squirt, what do you think Mom would want us to do?" I just looked at him, and the answer came to me so quickly; *I know exactly what Mom would have wanted.*

"Let's take it to her favorite spot and release her there." Zeus just smiled and nodded before starting up the car.

I sat back in the seating, watching the scenery. My mom's favorite spot was about a half-hour drive from there. She used to take my brother and me there every summer, and it was only right that she be put to rest there. When we arrived there, it was beautiful; her favorite oak tree with the pretty, pink flowers on it stood tall; the flowers in the grass were beautiful. Zeus put the car into park and turned to me.

"Are you ready to say goodbye to Mom, Squirt?" I shook my head up and down, so we got out of the car. We headed over to the tree. As we were walking

23

up to the tree, a breeze started blowing, like the tree knew why we were there; it was soothing to me. *I always loved coming here with Mom and laying on the grass, watching the clouds.*

We finally made it to the tree. We just stood there for a moment, taking in everything around us. My brother spoke, "Mom, your time was cut short. We will miss you. I will protect Artemis with my last breath. She will know who she is by tonight. I am sorry, Mom, this shouldn't have happened like this. We love you." I started crying as my brother opened the top of the urn and slowly dumped the ashes into the wind. The wind took my mother with it; it swirled around her favorite tree, then back around my brother and me. Like my mom was still with us, letting us know it would be okay and everything would work out. My brother came to me, wrapped his arms around me, and squeezed me. "Art, I think we need to talk. Do you want to sit down here?" I shook my head yes. *This is what I have wanted since everything that happened with Genius and Oliver.*

My brother let out a long breath before speaking, "Artemis, before I start explaining everything, I want you to know that the only reason Mom didn't tell you any of this before is because she was trying to protect you." I was shocked. *Why did Mom have to protect me? I never did anything for anyone to want to hurt me.* Zeus just stared at me, waiting for me to say anything before he started speaking at.

"Zeus, I don't know what is going on." Zeus just shook his head.

"Art, this is not your fault. Mom was going to tell you everything tonight before the full moon, but unfortunately that isn't going to happen, but do you remember the stories about the werewolves that Mom used to tell you when you were little?" I nodded, encouraging him to continue. "Well, Art, we are those wolves; Mom had to run away after our father was killed. Mom was the pack's Luna/Alpha, Dad was also an Alpha. But Mom wasn't like the rest of the wolves; she was special, unique." I just stared at him with disbelief.

"So you're telling me that Mom was a werewolf?"

He nodded. I went to speak, and he held his hand up, signaling me to stop so he could finish before I asked questions. "Mom was the strongest out of us all; she had special abilities that made her different from other wolves. One of the powers she had was the power to change into her wolf form even when the moon was not full. All of those who were a part of the pack had this power as well because Mother performed a ceremony with Father. That way, we were all protected from turning strictly on full moons.

"I was four when Mom was pregnant with you. She and Dad were really happy when they found out they were having a little girl. Well, during the first war between a rival clan and us, when Mother was still pregnant with you, someone had tried to hurt Mom and you, and that's when Grandma and Grandpa died.

"They died to protect you and our mom. After the war ended, everything was going good. Mom had you, and boy were you loud when you were born. You made sure we all knew that you were alive and well. Now we are going to jump to when you were four and I was eight, okay?"

I nodded, not wanting to interrupt him. "Well, we were playing outside one day when you started to show signs that maybe you had inherited some of Mom's many gifts. We were playing by a tree with some of the other children. One of the boys had bitten your leg. I went to beat him up, but before I could get to either of you, you had somehow managed to lift him by his neck; the boy started to catch fire. I raced over to you and was begging you to put him down, but when you turned to look at me, Art, your eyes were a deep purple. I had not seen that before except when Mom was fighting in the war, but, even then, Mom's eyes were not that dark." I was shocked. *What is he trying to tell me? Is there something wrong with me?* I wouldn't be able to find out unless I let him finish the story. I urged him to continue.

"Well, I started yelling for Mom because I didn't know what to do. Art, you were way too strong for me at that point. Well, Mom and Dad came running over when they both stopped dead in their tracks. They both saw your eyes. The moment they saw your eyes, they rushed over to you and pulled you away from the boy; they rushed you and me into the house. All they told me at the time was that they were going to contact this witch. They had to bind your powers and your wolf form until you reached 16. That way, they had enough time to prepare you for it."

Now I was confused. "What do you mean prepare me? For what?" He just looked at me. "I'm sorry, Zeus, please continue."

He just chuckled before continuing, "As I said at the time, I didn't know what that meant, and I didn't ask them questions. Well, about a week after they had your powers bound and your wolf-side bound, a group of wolves came to our home, looking for the child that had the deep purple eyes. Naturally, Mom and Dad denied the claim, but the group was not listening to them. Once Dad noticed they were not taking no for an answer, he turned toward Mother and told her to grab you and me and take the secret entrance out and not to turn back. That was the last time I saw our father. Once Mom got us out, she traveled here because it was such a small town and so far away, nobody would have looked for us. But once we got settled in and I hit about 16, when I first shifted, Mom sat me down.

"She started to explain why they had to bind your powers and your wolf form till you were 16. You were born the queen of all wolves. You are the leader of every pack in this world. You are stronger than any of us. They bound your powers because they feared if other packs heard about this that they would revolt and hurt you. But Mom did say that once you find your mate, he will become Alpha with you."

Finally, Zeus stopped and just stared at me. I was left speechless. What was I supposed to say to that? I finally took a deep breath. "Zeus, am I supposed to believe all this? Why would you guys hide all of this from me?" Zeus looked down at his feet. He was sad; you could see it.

"Squirt, we couldn't tell you till your birthday for your protection. If it got out that you were still alive, then all of this would have happened a lot sooner." I lay back in the grass, just staring at the sky, trying to process everything he just told me; I turned to him.

"Zeus, so does this mean I am going to turn into a wolf tonight?"

Zeus smiled at me. "That is exactly what I am telling you, Squirt. We are going to Daniel's tonight. That way, we are surrounded by some of the pack. That way, we can protect you while you shift." I was somewhat happy, and I just thought something was wrong with me.

"But why? Daniel's the part of our pack?"

Zeus just started laughing. "Art, you have a lot to learn; there are at least two people in our pack that I know and you know. One of them is Genius, and the other is Daniel." That shocked me. *That explains why Genius was growling at the school that day.*

"Zeus, is it okay if we just lay here awhile at least until it gets closer to time for us to head to Daniel's?" Zeus nodded yes, so I lay back, looking at the clouds, trying to process everything that I had just learned about our family. I wasn't sure if he was telling the truth, lying, or just losing his mind, but he was my brother, and he was the only family I had left.

# Full Moon

Zeus and I lay under the sun for an hour before heading over to Daniel's house; when we got there, everyone was waiting. It was weird because I just lost my mom the day before. Today, I just found out I am the queen of all wolves and that I am about to have my first shift. Once we finished pulling into the driveway, Daniel, Genius, and a female were all waiting for us to get out. Once I got out of the car, Daniel came over and hugged me. "Did he tell you who you truly are?" I nodded and smiled at him. With that, he gave me a big hug. "Thank the heavens. I was truly tired of hiding what we were, who you truly are."

He sat me back down on the ground, and I started to chuckle, then came Genius with his head hanging low; Daniel and my brother gave us some space. "Hey, Princess, I am sorry for not telling you all these years, but I was sworn to secrecy by your mom and my parents."

I just looked at him. "Genius, it's okay. I understand why you were acting the way you were, and I don't understand how Oliver knew what was going on."

Genius got angry at the mention of Oliver's name, but, soon, he calmed down before speaking again, "Oliver knows who we are because he is from a rival pack; he made it his mission to try and take you away."

I was shocked. "Why would he take me away, Genius? This is my home; I will not leave." That earned a smile from him.

"Princess, I am relieved to hear that, but there is still much to learn about being a werewolf, especially one as powerful as you.

"You can't guarantee that you will leave because you have not yet found your mate."

I was curious now. "What do you mean mate?"

Genius shook his head. "Your mate, the one that you are meant to spend your life with, the one that the ancient ones have picked just for you. Princess,

27

I am not going to lie. I hope I am your mate. I have yet to find one yet, and it would be the best thing if you and I were meant to be together. But I won't know until after you shift, and same with you." I was not shocked by his answer because Genius and I had always talked about getting married and having children when we got older.

"Genius, I do have a question. Is it possible for one to have to soul mate?"

He looked shocked. "Normally no, but since you are our queen, you are stronger than most and have powers. It is possible that it may happen. I believe your mom had two; she had to choose between them." I was shocked by that response, and my brother never told me that.

"Genius, my brother never brought that up."

He laughed. "That's because he didn't know; your mom only told me this because I told her I was going to marry you when we got older. Now, enough talking, time to come meet your pack." Genius led me back to the forest where there was a group of people waiting, and I noticed that Daniel and my brother both had females standing close to them. My brother and the girl were the first to approach Genius and me.

"Artemis, I would like you to meet my mate, Dream."

I was shocked. My brother had not mentioned he found his mate either. "Nice to meet you, Dream, I am Zeus's sister."

She just smiled. "I know who you are, Queen, and your brother has talked very highly of you." My brother started to blush.

"O, has he?" I started chuckling.

Then there came Daniel and the girl that was standing by him. "Artemis, I would like you to meet my mate, Jade." I was amazed. Daniel got such a beautiful girl.

"Nice to meet you, Jade." She smiled as well.

"Nice to meet you. Zeus, Genius, and Daniel speak very highly of you; I am grateful you are our queen and alpha." I blushed after that. One after one, the other members of the pack came to me and introduced themselves.

That was until Zeus, Daniel, and Genius all told everyone that was enough. It was time; they led me over to this big open patch of forest where everyone surrounded us.

Zeus turned and looked at me. "Artemis, I want you to know I love you, but this is going to hurt. This is your first shift since you were bound with magic. But everyone has been instructed not to shift till yours is done.

"Genius and I will stay right by you until your shift is complete. I am sorry we have kept this from you for so long; it was only for your safety."

I hugged him. "It's okay, Zeus. I understand why." He smiled at me, but then I got a sharp pain in my stomach that made me bend in half. I started to panic. *What is wrong with me? There is no reason I should be in pain right now.*

Zeus and Genius exchanged looks. "Princess, it will be okay. Just don't fight it, it will only make it worse." I tried to smile, but then the next wave of pain came. This time, it was in my back. I started freaking out. No, what was happening?

It made me hunch over on my hands, and my feet began to crack. My hands started to transform into paws along with my feet, then the skin started to peel off my body, and this purple-tinted fur started appearing where my skin used to be. What was happening? Please, God, what was happening? My little nose elongated into a snout, with sharp teeth in my mouth; finally, the pain had subsided. I started turning around when I noticed my tail, and I looked at both my brother and Genius. Their mouths were wide open; they were shocked at what they saw. But then I heard a voice in my head, "Finally, you can listen to me, can't you?"

I tilted my head to the side; I was confused. My brother was trying to talk, but I couldn't hear him.

"Who are you?"

"I am your wolf, my name is Violet, and I have been trying to reach you since we were little."

"O, hi. I am sorry; Mother put a spell on us because of something that happened when we were younger." But then this aroma hit my nose; it smelled like musk, forest, something I couldn't describe. I approached Zeus, the smell wasn't his. Then I turned toward Genius; the smell was coming from him. I heard Violet yell something. I finally tuned the smell out for a second to listen to what she said.

"MATE!" The next thing I knew, I was jumping on Genius and licking him. He started laughing before he pushed me off and started shifting into his wolf. Once he shifted, I noticed how amazing his wolf looked. He was pure black with purple eyes too, but once he shifted, he lifted his snout and took a long sniff in the air before coming over and licking me.

By this time, everyone else had shifted. We had run for what seemed like hours before we all went back to Daniel's house for clothes. Once Genius caught up with me, he swept me off my feet and twirled me around.

"Princess, I was right. You're my mate; you're my mate."

I just smiled. "Yes, Baby, I am." He embraced me into his arms and gave me the biggest kiss ever, until my brother walked over.

"Artemis, you are more beautiful than I could ever imagine, and I see Genius was right; you are his mate."

I just smiled, then Daniel came over. "Artemis, you are beautiful. I am glad you're our queen."

When Genius heard Daniel call me beautiful, he let out a low growl. "She's mine."

My brother and Daniel laughed. "Bro, it's all good. I have my mate, but I understand. I was the same with Jade. Artemis, he is going to be protective till you mark each other, but even then, he still is, but you can help control it then."

I was confused. "What do you mean mark each other?"

My brother and Daniel laughed. "He will explain it." Then they walked off.

I turned toward Genius. "What are they talking about?"

Genius started to blush. "Well, Princess, for us to complete our mate bond, we have to have a little intimate ritual. Umm, we have to have sex, then while we are having sex, we have to bite each other over our mark spot.

"Once we do that, we will be linked as one. We will feel each other's emotions, help control the other's anger, help heal each other; we will be one." I had my mouth open. I have never had sex, which made me nervous. I put my head down because I was blushing.

"Genius, I have never had sex before."

Genius walked forward and placed his hand on my shoulder. "Princess, we can wait until you're ready to complete our mating bond. I will not rush you. You're new to all of this. Let's just enjoy the rest of the night before we make those decisions, okay?" I nodded before he grabbed my hand and pulled me into our tent that they sat up before I started shifting.

Once we got in the tent, I heard Violet in my head again, "Artemis, you need to complete the bond. If either of you gets hurt while the mate bond is not complete, it could mean death for the both of you."

"Violet, I am scared. I have never slept with anyone before; I don't even know what to do."

"It's okay, Artemis. Let him lead you, it will be easier, but you have to complete it because what Genius told you earlier is true; you can have two mates. But you know him. You guys are meant to be, so complete the mating bond."

"What do you mean I have two mates, Violet? What if I am meant to be with the other one?"

"Artemis, please trust me like your mother trusted her wolf. Waiting around for your other mate whom you don't know could mean the end of us all." Now I was trying to figure out what to do. *I have known Genius my whole life, but what if I am meant to be with this other guy?*

Then Violet appeared in my head again, "Artemis, I didn't tell you this to make you second guess your decision. I am telling you because I know Genius is who we were meant to be with. I have known the whole time, but I couldn't speak to you. Please, I am begging you to complete the mate bond with Genius. If, for some reason, you and Genius don't work out or if something happens to him, then and only then will I allow you to meet our other mate." I didn't respond for a while; that's when Genius shook me a little bit.

"Princess, are you okay? You haven't said anything since we got in here." I noticed I hadn't said anything because I was holding a conversation with Violet.

"Yes, Gen, I am just talking to Violet."

Genius smiled. "It's nice that you finally got to meet your wolf." I reached up and placed my hand on Genius's face; he leaned into my hand.

"Genius, do you love me?"

He was shocked at the question. "Princess, I have loved you for a very long time. I was just scared to say anything to you."

Genius looked sad; I didn't mean to make him frown. I reached up on my tippy toes and started to kiss him. He was shocked at first, before he started kissing me back. The more we kissed, the more excited Violet and I got. Finally, Genius laid us gently on the ground before breaking the kiss. "Princess, if we don't stop, I don't know if I will be able to stop myself."

I smiled. "Did I say stop?" That earned a smile from him.

"Art, are you sure? I don't want you doing this just because you think we have to."

I thought for a second before responding, "Genius, I have loved you for a very long time. I couldn't imagine spending another day without you. I want to grow with you. I want to have children with you. This is what I want." The moment those words left my lips, Genius was kissing me again. He slowly started to unbutton my shirt before kissing my neck. When he hit the spot right about my shoulder blade, I started grinding into him. But before we got too far into it, he stopped.

"Hold on, Princess. We can't do this here for your first time." With that, Genius picked me up, carrying me upstairs and into our bedroom. Once we entered the room, he placed me down so I could look. The bed was aligned with rose petals, the lights were dimmed, and he had candles.

I turned toward him. "Genius, when did you have time to set this up?"

He just smiled. "I had some help." He started kissing me, lifting me up and carrying me to the bed. He placed me gently on the bed, kissing me before slowly kissing his way down from my lips. He kissed my neck, then he worked his way down to my breast where he slid his hand behind me and released my bra. He slid my nipples into his mouth before he gently started sucking and nibbling on them.

By the moon goddess, I was starting to become increasingly wet. Then he released my nipple and started kissing his way down. He used his hand to gently slide my skirt down and off my body. Then he kissed his way down until his mouth was at my clit. He gently started licking it. I immediately moaned. *This feels amazing.* But Genius didn't stop there. He started licking me up like I was a dessert he couldn't get enough of. Right before I climaxed, he stopped and kissed his way back up to me.

"Artemis, I love you. Are you sure that this is what you want?" I looked into those big eyes, and, in that moment, I was sure that that was what I wanted.

"Yes, Baby, I want you. I want my first everything to be with you." That was all he needed to hear because he stripped his pants off, but he didn't immediately try to rush into my pussy. He let his penis sit just on the outside of my pussy. I could feel him pulsing.

"Princess, I want to take this slow. I don't want to hurt you." I knew he wouldn't hurt me on purpose. He slowly started sliding himself inside of me, but I was so tight, he couldn't quite get it in there even with me being as wet as I was.

"Princess, you are so tight. I am sorry, but this might hurt." He wasn't lying. I was so tight, but his member was so large, I didn't think it would fit inside me, but Genius got it in. The moment it was in, I screamed so loud, but after he went in and out a few times, it started to feel good. Violet started to shine through because the next thing I knew, I was grinding every time he went inside of me. He would throw his head back and moan each time he came back and started kissing on that spot again. That's when I noticed my canine teeth were out, so I gently slid them across the same place on him, and the moment I did, he went farther inside of me. But that's when I felt his teeth nick the spot on me. I almost lost control. That's when I bit him. The moment I did that, Genius bit my spot too, and we both climaxed at the same time.

Genius collapsed on top of me. "O, my princess, I never thought that our first time would be this good." I was so out of breath, I couldn't speak. He just smiled at me before cuddling up to me and holding me. "Princess, I love you." I smiled the moment he said that.

"I love you too, Genius." As soon as the 'I love you' was out, Genius fell asleep, and I felt that I soon would be too. *Today was amazing, and I am glad I got to share this moment, with my brother, Daniel, and my mate. I wish my mom could be here to see it too.* That made me sad, but I had to remember; she was there with me in spirit.

# Training

The next morning, I woke up to find Genius was not in bed. When I fully woke up, I began to panic. It was like somehow he knew, because the next second, I heard Genius in my head, "Princess, it is okay. I am in the house. Why don't you get dressed and come meet everyone inside?" That made me feel better, so I got my lazy butt up, got dressed, but the moment I stepped out of my tent, I smelled something strange.

The moment I smelled it, I heard Violet, "Artemis, get inside now. There is someone near, and you do not have the training to protect yourself yet." But I had a better idea.

I spoke inside my head, "Genius, I need you, Daniel, and Zeus out here now." The moment I quit thinking, out ran Genius, Daniel, and Zeus. They all looked at me. "I need you guys to smell. Do you guys smell that? Violet is concerned."

Zeus just cocked his head. "Who is Violet?"

I just shook my head. "My wolf. Now, smell." For some reason, when I said that, I had more power in my voice; it was enough to make Zeus whine. I was confused by what had happened, but they all did what I told them to.

Soon, they were all surrounding me, growling, and I was confused. I smelled the same scent, but they must've known the scent personally. Immediately, my brother, Daniel, Genius, and both my brother and Daniel's mates came outside, surrounding me, and, now, I was curious about what was going on. I soon heard a rustling in the woods straight ahead. I don't know what took over me, but I bee-lined it to where the sound was. Everyone was yelling, but I did not care. Someone was here, and they meant my family harm. I reached the edge of the forest when I heard a deep growl. I immediately got on all fours and let out the meanest growl I could. Soon, as the growl left my throat, I felt this power arise from the tip of my toes to my head; then I started shaking. Violet was helping me. I turned back to the forest and growled, but whatever they saw on my face made the intruder slowly back away with their head down. I turned back toward my pack and started walking toward them, but when I got near, they all had their mouths open. I was confused about why they were so shocked, but that's when Genius walked up to me.

"Princess, your eyes are purple."

Then Zeus walked up. "Art, I need you to calm yourself so your eyes will go back to normal. Nobody knows the extent of your power yet."

I was still confused, but Violet knew what they meant. "Artemis, I will change them back for now, but, eventually, they will stay purple. They will just change shades of purple."

I wasn't sure what she meant by that, but Daniel snapped me back to reality. "Artemis, come inside; we all need to talk for a moment." I agreed because I was still new and unsure of our ways. Once inside, my brother, Daniel, Genius, and I went into this big office that had my name on it. Once we were entirely in the office, Zeus closed the door.

"Okay, Art, now comes the important part before we talk about anything else. You have to choose your beta and your delta."

I was confused as to what he meant. "What do you mean, Zeus?"

That's when Daniel stepped up. "Your beta is second in command to you, and, Genius, your delta, is third in command. This is to help guide you when you are lost, to make decisions if you or Genius cannot." I looked to Genius, and he nodded.

"Well, that is a no brainer, guys. Zeus's my beta, and, Daniel, you are my delta." That earned smiles from both of them, but then Genius came up behind me, wrapping his arms around me.

"My queen, now we need to discuss who will help our beta and delta to train our pack."

I was confused because I hadn't met the rest of the pack yet to see who a better fit would be to help train our pack to protect ourselves. "Zeus, Daniel, and Genius, before we go on any further about what needs to be decided, I have a few things to say. First one, who was that in the woods? Two, I need training before I select anyone else to protect this pack. I need to be able to protect you guys first before I leave it in anyone else's hands." All three boys looked to one another like they were shocked that I had even said anything.

Zeus was the first one that came toward me. "Sis, you will be trained; we have one of our eldest warriors coming to train you how to fight tomorrow."

Then Genius stepped forward. "Princess, but as for your powers that we are all still not sure of, you will have to listen to Violet because she is the only one other than your mother that knows what those powers are, how to control them, and what to do with them." That was confusing to me. *How am I going to listen to her and train at the same time?* I didn't know what happened in the next few moments, but I gained a confidence that I never felt before. I looked to Genius, thinking it was coming from him, but he shook his head no.

I spoke forcefully, assertive, and firmly, "Okay, this is what I want everyone to do. First, there needs to be a perimeter built around our forest. It needs to be fortified. Second, I want surveillance over every nook and cranny of our home."

"Third, I need to know how many people are in our pack as of now." They all turned toward me, shocked at how quickly I spoke. I suddenly felt great pride, and that was coming from Genius.

Zeus was the first to walk closer to me. "Well, Sister, we don't have a big pack at the moment. Most of our pack got separated after the war. We have been searching, trying to find them." Daniel and Genius both nodded in agreement.

That's when I heard Violet again. She seemed to speak up at the most critical times. "Artemis, you can locate the members of the pack with our powers."

"What do you mean, Violet? I don't know how to use any of my powers yet."

"Well, Artemis, time for a crash course in using your locating powers."

I turned toward the boys. "I need you guys to step back. Violet knows a way to locate the other members of the pack."

Zeus was shocked at this point. "What do you mean?"

I just looked at my brother. "I am not sure, Zeus, I don't know how any of this works at this point."

I heard Violet again, "Okay, Artemis, I need you to sit down, take a big deep breath in. Now, I need you to clear your mind. Once you have done that, focus on the feeling you get from your brother and Daniel. That feeling of needing to protect them, do you feel that bond, not the bond of a mate but the bond of a pack?"

"Violet, I feel a strong pull, like the need to protect, but not of anyone in this area. I am being pulled in so many different directions that I am not sure how to decide which way."

I heard silence in my head for a moment before my wolf spoke again, "Artemis, if you're being pulled in different directions, that means you can locate them all at once. I want you to focus not on the directions that you're being pulled but the locations of them all."

"I can try, Violet, but I am not sure I can."

So I did what Violet suggested. I concentrated not on the pulling I was feeling but on the location of where my pack was. I found that about six of the pulls I was feeling were in Alabama, then there were two in Mississippi, and then there were ten in Tennessee. "Violet, I found the locations of the pulls I was feeling."

"Good, Artemis, now I want you to focus on sending a large mental message to all of those pulls you are feeling; it will be like a large telephone." I was nervous. I didn't want to mess this up. We needed the rest of our pack to come home, but I did what Violet instructed.

I sent the message, "To all that can hear me, this is your alpha, your queen. I am with Zeus, Daniel, and Genius. I am here. I am home. Please return home to our pack, we are waiting." I got the message out, but I wasn't sure if they heard me or not. "Violet, I sent the message down the pull lines, but I don't know if they heard it or not."

I heard a giggle in my head; it was Violet again, "Artemis, you did it. Just give everyone a moment, and you will start hearing a lot of voices in your head for a while."

I opened my eyes to look at the boys. "I found most of our pack. I am waiting to see if they got my message."

Zeus was shocked. "What message, Squirt?"

I looked at him, puzzled. "I sent a mental message to everyone to come home."

Genius was confused. "Princess, you haven't had the training to hear the whole pack. How do you know how to do that?"

I smiled at him. "Well, you told me to listen to Violet, so that is what I did." All three boys just smiled at me in unison.

"Artemis, you are amazing. That took us a week or two to learn how to communicate with other members of the pack."

I started to smile, but I got a whole swarm of voices in my head: "My queen, is it you, have you finally come, can we come home?" I was amazed. I never thought in a million years I could pull something like this off, but I had to say something for them to come home.

"Yes, this is your queen, your alpha. You all need to return home. For those of you that are new or if you have children, come to Daniel's. We are waiting." The moment those words left me, I heard everyone cheering in my head. Some said it would be a few days before they arrived, but they were all on their way.

I looked at my mate, my brother, and my friend. "Our pack heard me. They are on their way. Some, it will take a few days, others will be here by tonight." The next thing I knew, my brother, Daniel, and my mate were all hugging me.

"Thank you, Art. You are going to be an amazing queen." They got me to blush, but they were all still avoiding my other question.

"Now that I have got our pack coming home, now you will answer my other question. Who was that in the wood, and why did all five of you surround me?"

They all looked to each other before Genius spoke, "Well, do you remember your brother telling you about the war? Well, there are still people looking for you that would kill you if given a chance. That was one of the people that could harm you; they are from Oliver's pack." I was taken aback by what came out of his mouth.

"Why would Oliver save me if his pack wants to harm me?"

Zeus and Daniel looked at each other before Daniel turned toward me. "What do you mean Oliver saved you?" Now, I was unsure of what to say because I never told anyone what had happened at school.

"Well, the last day I was at school before Mom passed, Genius found out that I was made to tutor Oliver, and, well, he got a little protective and started growling, saying, 'YOU'RE MINE.' So Oliver made me run away until we reached my house."

At first, you could tell Zeus was angry, but he soon calmed down. "Squirt, there are two things I can almost guarantee you. One is, Oliver was not trying to save you. Two, he did not know where we lived." Now I was confused because Oliver led me almost all the way home before we even spoke.

"Then why did he lead me almost all the way home before speaking?" This had all three boys surprised, but I could feel Genius's anger rising, so I focused on sending calming energy to him via a mental voice, "Baby, calm down. I am yours, no need to get angry." He smiled, but I could sense that he was battling with his anger. "Okay, for now, we will worry about what we do know. We can readdress the Oliver thing after our pack has made it home. Now I need some fight training.

"Now, out of all three of you, which is the best fighter?" Zeus and Daniel turned toward Genius. "Well, Babe, guess what? You get to train me to fight, and don't take it easy either."

He just looked at me. "Princess, would I ever take it easy on you?" We all laughed at that. We all walked out of the office and back outside so that Genius could start training me. The first few times, Genius kept knocking me on my butt, but after a few times, I finally got it, and he couldn't pin me at all. So, then, Genius had me wrestle my brother, Daniel, and both their mates before he would go any further into the training. I quickly got through all of them, not even breaking a sweat.

They all just looked at me. "Are you sure you have never fought before, because you're picking up on this quick." That's when Zeus stood up.

"No, she has never fought, but, remember, this is our queen. She is stronger than all of us and will pick things up easier than most of us did." I smiled at him. I wanted to continue, but Genius shook his head no and nodded in the direction of the others. I hadn't realized that I took wrestling with them a little too severe; the girls looked injured. Even Zeus and Daniel looked terrible; I noticed that it was starting to get a night out when I heard a voice in my head again.

"Queen, our alpha, we are here." I started looking around, trying to locate them, then I turned toward the others.

"Ten of our pack are here. You will stay seated until they all come out, do you understand me?" They all nodded in unison. Then, one by one, I saw my pack coming out of hiding in their wolf forms. Some were hesitant to go near me. "I am sorry, Alpha, but some don't believe that you are who you say you are."

So I started stripping my clothes. I turned and handed them to Genius who looked confused. I got down on all fours and began to shift. Once I was in my wolf form, the other wolfs started coming around me, watching me. Most of them lay on their back, showing their stomachs and neck. But there was one who did not. They started pacing around me, so I did the same. That is when he jumped on me.

The others went to get involved when I sent the message, "Everyone stays back; this is my fight." I got him off of me when I started smacking with my paws. Before I began to click my jaws, I finally got him by the back of the neck and tossed him on the ground before standing over him, growling. I pinned his throat with my mouth when he let out a whine. I released him, and once I did, he came crawling to me on all fours and his head down, showing that he admitted defeat and acknowledged that I was his alpha.

Once he and I were done, I shifted back, and Genius handed me my clothes. I looked at my pack. "Everyone shift back now." I looked at the direction of the wolf I just fought. "You, shift back now and tell me who you are." They all started shifting back to their human forms. The white wolf that I just made submit turned; he was colossal, standing 6'3".

"Why did you challenge me?"

He hung his head. "I am sorry, Alpha. I just did not believe you were here. I would not have even done anything, but you have to understand we have been on our own for a while now." I stood directly in front of him.

"I understand that, but now you need to understand something. I am your queen; I am your alpha. You will not step out of line again or I will kill you." Everyone looked at me with fear and admiration. Now, I had to introduce everyone. "This is my brother, Zeus, his mate, and this is Daniel, his mate, and this is my mate, Genius. Zeus is your beta, Daniel is your delta, and Genius is your alpha. You will obey them." Everyone waved at one another; I was worn out from today. "Okay, now everyone goes inside. Daniel and Zeus will show you your room. You are to shower and get some rest. We will all meet in the meeting room in the morning to discuss everything." One by one, they all started heading inside. That just left Genius and me alone.

Then Genius came up to me, wrapped me in his arms. "Princess, you were amazing. You are doing such a great job."

I smiled up at him. "You think so?" With that, he picked me up and carried me to our room. With a devilish smile on his face, he threw me on the bed.

"Now that I have you to myself, how about I show you how much I cherish you?"

I just laughed. "O, but maybe I want to go to bed." With that, he slowly approached me on the bed, then he gently started nibbling on my mark; it shot sparks throughout my entire body. Genius knew precisely what he was doing because he kept teasing me until, finally, I had enough.

"Genius, I really would like to go to sleep. I am exhausted, could we please?"

He hung his head. "I am sorry, Princess. Yes, we can." So he laid next to me, and, soon, he drifted off to sleep. I laid there for a while, trying to figure out what to say to everyone tomorrow.

Violet appeared in my head again, "Artemis, quit worrying about tomorrow. For now, get some rest. We will figure out everything tomorrow." There was no point in arguing; I was so tired. I laid down, and, soon after, I started to drift off to sleep.

# The Pack

I woke up, turned over on my side to find Genius completely asleep, so I lay there for a minute before getting up to shower. I turned up on the shower and let the steam fill the room. Once I got into the shower, I was in there for ten minutes before Genius joined me.

"Morning, Princess, how did you sleep?"

I turned around and smiled. "I slept great, how about you, Babe?" He gave me this devilish grin, but before he could start in, I immediately traced my finger down the middle of his chest. He shivered, then I reached up on my tippy toes and started nibbling on his mark. Genius picked me up and slammed me into the shower wall.

"Princess, do you know what you're doing to me?" I smiled, but then I looked down; his shaft was long and hard at this point. So I reached down and slid him inside me. He shuddered; I was still so tight even though we had done this before.

He kissed me deeply on my lips before he slowly slid further inside me. I tilted my hips up and started to grind against him. He released the kiss. "Princess, I love you."

I smiled. "I love you too." The next thing I knew, he thrust inside of me. That's when my canine teeth came out. I bit into his mark, and, at that point, he reciprocated the same thing. By the time we were done, we looked like prunes; we had been in the shower so long. We both got out and went dressed. I turned to look at Genius. "Do you think I will be able to bring our pack together?"

He approached me and placed his hands on my shoulder and looked me straight in my eyes. "Babe, you got this, you brought them back. Now you just have to lead them." I smiled. Hand in hand, we walked down the stairs where everyone was waiting. I stood at the balcony.

"Hi, everyone, I want to thank Daniel for opening up his home to become our pack house."

Daniel nodded. "Now, before we begin, I would like to thank those of you that showed up last night. I hope you will accept Genius and me as your leader. Now, if you guys could, we would like you guys to introduce yourself."

The first one that stepped up was a young girl. She had blonde hair with the prettiest white eyes I had ever seen. "Hi, my name is Nina. I am eight years old."

Then the next one up was her mother and father. "Hi, my name is David, and Juanita is Nina's mother."

The next one that stood up was the one that tried to test my dominance. "Hi, my name is James. May I take the time out to apologize to our queen, I meant no disrespect to you last night. We just have not heard from anyone in our pack in a long, long time." One by one, the rest of the group that showed up last night introduced themselves.

By this time, Genius and I had already walked down the stairs and were standing in front of everyone. "I want to thank you all for introducing yourselves. James, I understand that this is all new to everyone, but I will repeat it: if you ever try to re-challenge me, I will not hesitate to kill you." I began hearing voices in my head again, so I tuned everyone out to listen, and it was the rest of the pack. "My queen, we are here."

I turned toward Genius, Daniel, and Zeus. "The rest of them are here. You three, follow me outside. The rest of you, stay inside till I say otherwise, understand? I want the children in the backroom; that's the safest room right now." Everyone looked at me, confused.

That is when Zeus spoke up, "You heard her; get to it."

Genius, Daniel, Zeus, and I walked to the back. Some of the pack had already changed to their human forms, and when I came up, they all got down on one knee before approaching. I had them stand with the boys while I approached the five that had not transformed yet.

"Okay, so are we going to do this the easy way, guys, or do you want to test the waters today?" Three of them flopped over on their backs, showing their neck and bellies; a sign of submitting to me. But the other two were not going to go down that easy, and I told the three of them to join the others, then I dropped down onto all fours and started my transformation. Once my change was complete, one of them immediately dropped to her back, submitting. I nodded toward the rest, and that is where she headed. I immediately started growling at the other one, but he was not backing down. I could see where this one was going to go. So I wasted no time this time. I jumped immediately on his back, biting on the back of his neck and kicking him with my hind legs, but he flipped me over and got me on my stomach. I saw Genius trying to step forward, and I growled at him, warning him not to do it, so he stepped back.

All right, now I was angry. I rolled over onto my back and pushed with all four legs, sending him flying back. Once I did that, I could feel my eyes changing to that deep purple. Then I let out the loudest howl I could. He came charging back toward me, and as soon as he did, he began floating in the air as I slowly approached him. I released him onto the ground where I immediately grabbed his throat. I would have killed him if he would not have surrendered, but he did, so I released his throat and began to transform back to my human form. I turned and looked at him.

"Transform now, or you will not make it another day." By this time, I was pissed. Who was he to challenge me and try to make me submit to him? He transformed into his human form, and man was he tall. He had to be at least 6'4" and 250lbs. I heard Zeus saying something from behind, but I was too pissed to care, and Violet was just as angry. "Who the hell do you think you are, trying to get me, YOUR QUEEN, to submit to you?"

He just smiled. "Well, Artemis, I see you have your mother's anger." That confused me. He put his hand up, stopping Zeus in his tracks. "You may not remember me, Artemis, but I am your uncle. I am your mother's brother, and I am the one that has come to train you.

"You have the gist of it, and, yes, you can defend yourself, but there is so much more I need to show you before you can become our greatest alpha."

That did not make me calm down in the least, and it didn't make Violet calm down either. "If you're my uncle, then where the hell were you while my mother was being killed? You're her brother, you're supposed to protect her, you're supposed to protect me." Suddenly, I saw him starting to back away from me, and my body had begun having a dark-purple aura admitting from me. My uncle's eyes went wide.

"OMG. Artemis, you truly are our queen. I need you to calm down. Please, I will explain everything, just calm down first." I couldn't calm down; I was shaking. That's when I noticed two distinct people standing behind me: one was Genius, the other was Zeus. Immediately, Zeus tried to grab me.

"Squirt, please calm down before you lose control; you haven't learned to control this part of you." I turned toward him, and you could tell he was nervous.

"Zeus, don't you tell me to calm down. How the hell could you not tell me that he was the one that was training me? He abandoned us when we needed him." Zeus started backing away slowly. That's when Genius walked up to me, not caring what would happen to him. He wrapped his arms around me and pulled me close to him. He was using our bond to try and help calm my anger.

"Princess, you have every right to be angry with him, but this is not going to solve anything. Can you please calm down?" No sooner than he said that, he placed a kiss on my lips, and I started calming down almost immediately.

I looked up at Genius and smiled. "Babe, I need to go lie down." When those words left my lips, he swooped me up in his arms and turned to Zeus and Daniel.

"Get these pack members settled in. We will meet with them later." Then, he turned directly toward Zeus. "You better handle your uncle, and you better have an explanation for your sister later."

Zeus hung his head low. "I am sorry, Artemis." With that, Genius carried me to our bedroom, not saying a word. He lay down with me on his chest.

"Princess, get some rest. You're exhausted; we can deal with all this later." He kissed my forehead. "I love you, Princess, don't forget that." And with those words, I slowly drifted into a deep sleep.

# Explanation

The next day came quickly. I awoke to me being on top of Genius, and he looked so peaceful when he slept. I couldn't move because he had his arms wrapped around me. So I tried prying his arms off of me so that I could go to the restroom, but I failed, so I shook him.

"Baby, I need to pee." I saw that beautiful smile of his.

"Princess, how are you feeling today?"

I shrugged my shoulders. "I'll be okay, but not if you don't allow me to go pee." He chuckled before releasing me, and I ran to the bathroom. I had never had to pee so hard before in my life. Once I was done, I came out of the toilet, and Genius was already out of bed and starting to change clothes; I whistled.

"Sexy man, sexy man."

He just smiled at me. "Princess, you need to get ready. We still have a lot to deal with today before we can even have you properly trained so that you can help protect our pack."

I immediately remembered yesterday. *Why would Zeus allow our uncle back after all of this time? What could he want? He walked out on us a long time ago.* I must have been frowning because when I looked back up, Genius was standing right in front of me. He lifted my chin so that I would look him straight in the eyes.

"Babe, I know that this is hard for you to accept or deal with, but no matter who he is, he is still part of our pack." I looked away from him.

"I know that, Genius, but that does not mean that I can forgive him for everything he has done." My uncle (Alcide) walked out on my mother and us when I was still young. We needed him, and he did not care. He just walked away and never returned. How could I forgive him? He was not the one that watched my mother stay up at night, crying. Genius wrapped his big arms around my tiny body.

"Princess, I know this is difficult, but at least let Zeus explain his side of things before we talk to your uncle. I know you do not want to, but this is part of being the queen and the alpha." I knew he was right, but it didn't change the fact that I was still angry at both Zeus and Alcide.

But, finally, I sucked up my pride. I looked at Genius. "Fine, I will do it, but I am not happy about it."

Genius smiled before kissing me on my forehead. "Thank you, Princess. Now get ready and meet us in your office." Then he turned around and walked out the door, and I went to the closet to pick something out. I wanted something that said I meant business but was sexy at the same time. I found the perfect dress; it was red and black. It complimented my eyes very well. Then I found a pair of black high heels. I slipped this outfit on before walking out of my room; I walked down the stairs until I came to the office. I stood there and let out a big breath of air before opening the door. When I opened the door, there stood Zeus, Daniel, and Genius; I walked in the room, closing the door behind me. I walked behind the desk and sat down because I was unsure of how I would react to Zeus telling me his side of things.

Once I sat down, Genius walked around and stood next to me, placing his hand on my shoulder, trying to comfort me. I knew he felt how angry I was still. I turned and looked at Zeus. "So, you wanted to explain your side of things. Get to explaining."

Zeus hung his head. "Look, Squirt, I am sorry that I didn't tell you Alcide was the one training you, but that was because I knew how you would react." I just stared at him, encouraging him to continue. I needed to understand why he did this. "Artemis, look, our uncle is the only one that can train you. He trained our mother to become the alpha. Yes, you and Mom have similar powers, but you are stronger than even her.

"So I asked him to come to see, to prove that you were truly our queen. He did not want to believe me, but he came when you called, and, no, I haven't even got an explanation for why he left all those years ago. I am truly sorry, but I had no choice." I sat there quietly for a moment, trying to figure out what to say to him. I was still hurt that he didn't even talk to me before deciding that this was the right course of action.

That was when Daniel stepped up. "Artemis, I need to apologize as well because I knew who Zeus was calling. I didn't know the extent, but I knew Alcide was coming to train you."

I just looked at Daniel. "Daniel, this is not your fault. Zeus knew how I felt about our uncle; this is all on him." Then I turned toward Zeus. I remained seated because I was still angry and upset all at the same time. "Zeus, some of your reasons are very valid, but you should have given me a heads up. You knew my feelings toward Alcide." I just shook my head. "You weren't the one that was a comforting Mother after our uncle left us, I was. You didn't see how bad it hurt her; you weren't there comforting me; you knew how close me and Alcide were. Then he just got up and left without any explanation as to why." My eyes began to water; I was really trying not to cry. That is when Genius squatted down and just hugged me.

Zeus walked closer to the desk. He never liked when he upset me; this time was no different. I knew that he wanted to comfort me, but, at the same time, he knew that not touching me was what was best. "Squirt, I am truly sorry, and you have every right to hate him, but let him explain everything before you just turn him away, please." I turned toward Genius, and he just nodded, acknowledging what my brother said was true.

"Fine, Zeus, but you can bring him to the office. The pack does not need to see this, and the only reason you and Daniel are allowed here is that you two deserve an answer too." I got a smirk from Zeus and Daniel.

"Okay, Squirt, I will go grab him." He left the room, along with Daniel.

Genius turned toward me. "Princess, I know this is hard, but you are doing the right thing, and who knows, maybe there is a reasonable explanation as to why he left." I hugged Genius.

"Babe, thank you for being here; I wouldn't be able to handle all of this without you."

He squeezed me back. "Princess, there is no need to thank me. I wouldn't be anywhere else. I love you and would not allow you to do this by yourself." That is when I heard a slight knock on the door. I knew who it was, but I was nervous now to listen to the explanation.

"Come in." In walked Zeus, Daniel, and Alcide. Alcide made sure he stayed by the door, but Daniel and Zeus walked over by me and sat on the extra chairs. Genius squeezed my hand to give me some encouragement.

"Okay, Alcide, you should be thanking these three men right here for convincing me to hear you out. Now, would you like to explain why you abandoned us?"

Alcide hung his head before taking a deep breath. "Artemis, I am sorry that I walked out on all of you, but I didn't have a choice. Your mother wouldn't allow me to be around you two."

That confused both Zeus and I. "What do you mean? You, Alcide, and I were inseparable."

He took a moment before responding, "Yes, I know me and you were inseparable, but, Artemis, let me explain everything before you interrupt me, okay?" I nodded, acknowledging that I would try not to interrupt. "Now, do you guys remember the day before I left, your mother and I went for a very long walk?" Zeus and I nodded in agreement. "Now, Artemis, on that walk, your mother thought me being so close to you would start to remind you of your powers, but I assured her that would not happen.

"Now, on the walk, we ran into someone that was looking for you. They wanted to do you harm, so your mother and I fought them side by side to protect you.

"After we defeated them, your mother wanted to move again because she feared they knew where you were, and we could not allow that to happen, so I offered to leave and continue to fight."

I held my hand up for a minute, stopping him from continuing. "So you are telling me that you left to try and protect Zeus and me." He nodded. "Okay, if that is so, why wouldn't you contact us at all ever? Why is it when Mother died, you did not come back? You weren't there to protect us when it went down, yet that's why you left." By this time, I had already started crying, and you could tell it was upsetting everyone in the room because they knew how close I was to him.

"Artemis, I am sorry, but I couldn't have told you because you would have tried coming with me. You were like my daughter, Art. I did what I thought was best to make sure you were safe.

"I didn't return for your mother's funeral because, at the time, I was being held prisoner. They were torturing me to learn of your whereabouts, but I see that someone already found out where you were."

I was crying at this point. "How do I know you're not lying about that? If you loved me, you wouldn't have left no matter what the situation was."

He shook his head back and forth. "No, Artemis, that wasn't an option at the time. Your life was more important, and as for the proof." Alcide lifted his shirt, showing his chest and stomach, and it were lined with scars. When he turned around, the same thing. This only made me cry harder. Genius stood up and motioned for Zeus and Daniel to follow him.

"Genius, where are you going?"

He blew me a kiss. "Sorry, Princess, but this is something that you need to finish yourself." With that, all three of them left me alone with Alcide.

Alcide turned back toward me, slowly approaching the desk. "Artemis, I am sorry I left to protect you. I never meant to cause you this much pain. I would not have left if I didn't have to." I just kept crying. That's when Alcide walked around the desk, wrapping me in his arms. "Art, please forgive me. I promise I would have come back if I could, but at the time, if I had come back, it would have put you in more danger; you hadn't come into your powers yet or realized who you were." I just sobbed into his chest for what seemed like hours before I finally fell asleep. I don't know how long I was sleeping, but when I woke up, he was still holding me, but Genius, Daniel, and Zeus were back in the office.

I sat up, rubbing my eyes, and said, "I am sorry. I didn't mean to fall asleep."

Genius just smiled. "Princess, it's okay. You were exhausted from crying. Your uncle luckily was able to hold you for so long in that position or you would have fallen out of the chair."

I just chuckled; I turned toward my uncle. "Alcide, so are you telling me you stayed gone this long to protect me from our enemies?" He nodded in agreement. "Okay, so do you have any intel on who has been searching for me all these years?"

He smiled. "See, you already have the alpha mental thing going on, but, in short, it's a mixed answer. Yes and no."

That confused me, but Genius was the one that spoke first, "What do you mean that is a mixed answer?"

Alcide just stared at us. "Well, I know what pack it is, but not all of the members want to cause you harm. Some would like to join you, but they can't tell me who the Alpha is. He forced them not to." That seemed to make sense to all three boys, but I was still completely lost.

"How could the alpha make them not say something?"

Alcide was the first to speak, "When you are alpha, you have power over your pack. If you swear them to an oath, then they have to abide by that oath or else one of two things can happen. One, they can have their tongues cut out, or, two, they could be killed for disobeying their alpha."

I was still confused, but that went to prove I had a lot to learn about being an alpha. We all sat there and talked for a while before I had to attend to the other members of the pack. Genius and I walked out of the office and down the stairs where the rest of the pack was sitting. I looked at Genius, and he smiled, then we turned toward the pack.

"I want to thank all of you for coming back home. Now, as a way for us to bond, I would like us all to go outside and transform into our wolves and run as a pack. It will increase our bond and allow us to become one under the moon." I smiled at Genius. That was a great idea. We walked outside, and the whole pack followed Genius, and I transformed first before the pack did. We all ran for hours before finding an open field where we all could lay down for a while.

I turned to look at my pack. *These are my people, this is who I am supposed to protect, and I will defend them with my life, if it comes to that.* We all laid under the moon, laying in a group with one another. This was my family, and I may not know all of them that well, but I love every one of them. The whole pack started dozing off one by one. Well, this was where we would rest until morning when we could all run home.

# Return to School

Genius and I woke up at the same time. We lay there for a while before I spoke, "Babe, you know we have to go back to school today, right?"

He just frowned. "I know we also have to enroll the rest of the pack that is under 18 in school as well. Luckily, Alcide knows a school that is nearby that he can get the rest of them into, but, unfortunately, we have to go back to the old school." I sat up on my elbow, staring at the man I was going to marry.

"It's okay, Babe. You know why we get to graduate this year since we have all our other credits." We got up out of the bed and started getting ready for school. "Babe, you know Zeus is taking us, right? He also volunteered for assisting the football coach. That way, he is close just in case something happens." I turned toward Genius and nodded.

Once we were dressed, we walked downstairs to meet the pack. Everyone was waiting at the bottom of the stairs in the living room. "Good morning, everyone. So today's plan is Alcide will take all members under age 18 to a school nearby to enroll, the warriors chosen in yesterday's selection will start their training till about noon, then the warriors will remain here while Daniel takes the rest of you to his ID guy for IDs so you can get jobs. That way, nobody is too bored sitting at home."

I finished walking into the living room. "Genius and I have to return to our old school so we can finish out this year; we graduate with the rest of the senior class. If you have any questions or feel something is off, please mind link one of your leaders."

That is when Genius stepped forward. "Nobody is to know where you live or what you are. Also, if you hear Artemis's name at all, you're to immediately contact one of us and inform us." With the morning meeting over, Alcide rounded up the pack members that needed to be registered in school. Daniel made everyone else go outside for training, then Zeus came over to us.

"You ready, Squirt?"

I just rolled my eyes. "Ready as I ever will." This was the first time I or Genius had been back to school since my mother passed. Luckily, our school gave me time to grieve and, well, Genius's mom just said he was sick.

Genius and I walked outside and got into Zeus's car. The drive was a while away from Daniel's house, which was fine because I just kept watching the scenery; it was soothing to me, allowed me to clear my head. *So much has changed for me since I turned 16.* I found out I had this whole other life that I wasn't aware of. *Granted I love this, but I wish my mother would have told me about this sooner, so I would have been more prepared for my role as alpha.* But nonetheless, I had a responsibility now no matter how difficult that it may be; it was my duty, and they were my family. I would protect them with my last breath, just to make sure that they got to live another day. Suddenly, the car came to a stop. I just realized that Zeus had made it to school in record time.

"Geez, Zeus, did you speed the whole way here?"

He just laughed. "Well, Squirt, you guys were going to be late on your first day back." I just shook my head. Genius got out the car, came around to my door before opening mine.

"Princess, are you ready for this? You know everyone is going to stare. Also, Oliver is here, so don't say anything to him unless necessary."

I nodded. "I know, Genius, this isn't my first go around, you know." He smiled, grabbing my hand. We walked into the school, hand in hand, all the way to my locker. Soon, as we got there, Genius was right. Everyone was watching me or staring. But that is when I smelled something; it smelled like smoked cedar chips, coffee, and cologne.

Then I heard Violet, "Artemis, you remember when I said you had two mates. Well, unfortunately, we go to school with both of them." I just kept shaking my head. No way was my other mate here, but around the corner, there came Oliver. The moment he came around the corner, he titled his head up, taking a deep breath. *O no, he figured it out too.* I immediately turned around, burying my head into Genius's shirt, trying to hide. Luckily, Oliver went the opposite way. Genius looked down at me.

"Babe, what's wrong?" I didn't know if I should tell him or hide it, but with the mate bond, it was damn near impossible to hide anything. So, I pulled him into the utility closet.

"Babe, do you remember when you said I could possibly have two mates?"

He nodded. "Well, you were right. I do have two mates. You are one, but Oliver is the second, and, no, I didn't know before returning to school, but I want you to remember I bonded to you; I am marrying you." He just stood there, clearly in shock from what I just told him. He just stood there, not saying anything for a while.

Until he finally looked at me. "Princess, I am not going to lie to you. I am not happy about this at all, but you are mine and nobody will take you from me, not even Oliver. I will kill him if he tries." I couldn't say anything. All I did was hug him; he hugged me back. "Princess, we have to get to chemistry before we get into trouble." He opened the door for me, and we headed to our chemistry class which, unfortunately, we shared with Oliver, so, needless to say, that was going to be one weird class.

We walked into the class; everyone began to stare except Oliver; he was trying his hardest not to look at us. Which I was grateful for, because I didn't want Genius getting angry again, not here. We took our seats in the front where Mr. Green welcomed us back to class. Once we sat down, Mr. Green began his speech, but I was having trouble concentrating. *Why did this have to happen to me? I wish my mother was here; she would know what to do.* I started zoning out.

That is when I heard my uncle, "Artemis, I know you're in class and I apologize, but I wanted to let you know the other members are enrolled. I signed up to teach history class. That way, I could remain close to them just in case."

I instantly responded, "Thank you, Uncle. That was a good idea. Keep Genius or I updated on anything that happens." I hadn't realized that I zoned out for so long. Luckily, Genius heard everything between my uncle and me. The bell rang shortly after that. Genius and I walked back to my locker.

Once we got there, we switched out our books for our next class, then Genius looked a little uncertain and I could feel it too.

"Babe, what's wrong?"

He just looked at me. "Princess, we don't have our next classes together, but you do have a class with Oliver next. I am nervous, to say the least."

I moved closer to him. "Babe, you have nothing to worry about. I am yours, nobody else's." We both knew that was a lie no matter how hard we tried to convince each other otherwise. Genius walked me to English before kissing me goodbye. I walked into a class where Mrs. Evans was waiting. This time,

Oliver was staring at me and wouldn't take his eyes off me. Unfortunately, my old seat was given away, and the only seat that was open was the one next to Oliver's. Boy, was this class going to be interesting. I walked over to my seat, trying not to stare at Oliver or say anything to him.

But he had other ideas now that Genius wasn't around. He leaned in. "Artemis, I know who you are, just like you know who I am. You are my mate, and you will be mine one day." That shook me. I didn't want Oliver. If anything, I wanted to avoid him, but I didn't know what else to do.

Genius felt what I was feeling, because I immediately heard him in my head, "Princess, is everything okay? You seem nervous. Did something happen?"

I didn't know what to tell him. "Babe, have Zeus come pull me out of English now." I waited around for 20 minutes before there was a knock on the door; the front desk lady was talking to the teacher. After she left, Mrs. Evan called me up front. I could feel Oliver's eyes on me.

"Artemis, your brother said that you needed to leave for an appointment, so grab your things and head to the office so that he can pick you up."

I walked back to my desk to grab my things. That is when I felt a hand on my arm. I turned around to see Oliver right there next to me.

"Why are you leaving, Artemis? You know what I said was true, you will be mine." That is when he noticed the mark on my neck and shoulder, mine and Genius's mark. He started to grab my arm tighter. "How can you be mated already if you're my mate?"

I yanked my arm free from him. "That is none of your business. Now leave me alone." I turned, walking toward the door. Genius and Zeus were waiting for me outside my class. I just kept walking; I didn't even say anything because it would only be a fight that nobody needed now. Once we reached the car, that is when Genius stopped me.

"Babe, what happen to your arm?" I just shook my head.

"I am fine, Babe. Let's just go. I don't want to be here anymore."

He wanted to ask more but decided against it. He opened up my door for me before getting in himself. I didn't have much time to think before Daniel was mind-linking me.

"Artemis, we did our training, but now the guards and I smell something around the property. We need you home now." I looked at the boys.

"Zeus, move the car out of the parking lot. We can make it there quicker if we shift." Zeus drove the car to our old storage unit. We all jumped out and immediately started to transform. Once we were all done, we took off toward the house. The closer we got, the more we could smell it: there were wolves, an enchantress, a necromancer, and something I wasn't quite sure of. We got closer to the house and that is when Genius and I noticed someone was watching our pack.

We took off toward them. Genius got there first; he immediately jumped on him, pinning him to the ground, but Genius couldn't stay on him long. That is when I came in. I bit down on the man's left leg, ripping a piece of flesh from the bone. The man kicked me with his right leg, sending me back a little bit. Genius and I went in for a counterattack, but he just disappeared. *Where could he have gone?* I lifted my snout up in the air, but I couldn't smell any blood; he was gone.

Genius and I ran back to the pack house. We shifted as soon as we got on to our territory. Zeus was the first to walk up to us.

"Well, did you see who it was?" I looked at Genius before turning back to Zeus.

"Yes, we engaged them. I bit his leg, but when we went to counter, he escaped. I can't smell him anywhere."

That was concerning to all of us, because people just don't vanish, so I mind-linked us with Alcide, "Alcide, we have an emergency at home. Round up the pack members and everyone comes home." I waited a second.

"Okay, is everyone all right?" I was shocked he even asked that question.

"Yes, we are fine. Just come home now." Then I closed the mind link. "We want everyone inside. Daniel, did you get the fences up and the camera going?" He nodded. "Okay, now do we have any strong enchantresses that will help us fortify our territory and home?" I looked at everyone, but Genius was the only one that stepped forward.

"No, Princess, we don't, but mind-link Violet because your mom and her wolf were able to protect the property, and you're stronger than your mom was."

I was confused, but I did what he asked: "Violet, how can we put up a protective barrier around the property to protect the pack, meaning only pack members are able to get through the wall?"

It took a moment before she responded: "Artemis, yes, there is a way for us to do it, but I can't help you do it till tomorrow on the full red moon. The moon's magic will make the barrier stronger, so, until then, everyone needs to stay inside." *Well, that's disappointing.*

I turned toward the boys. "Okay, we will do it tomorrow, only time I can, but in the meantime, do we have a safe room that the pack could sleep in comfortably?"

Daniel looked at Zeus, and Zeus nodded. "Ya, we have one."

I was excited at that. "Okay, so as soon as Alcide gets here with the others, everyone that is not a leader or warrior is to go to the safe room until tomorrow night."

Genius, Zeus, Daniel, the warriors, and I stood our ground out back, waiting on Alcide and the others to get back. It took them a few hours, but when they arrived, we explained everything, then Daniel took the others to the safe room before returning to us.

I turned to Alcide. "Uncle, do you know what that was that did that?"

He looked at me. "Yes, but I haven't seen one in almost a century; they are what you would call a Quil. They are half-wolf half-enchantress. Some have special abilities like the one you guys meet today, others are just deformed, some are just a half breeds." That confused all of us. Apparently, the boys hadn't heard of this either.

"Uncle, how do we defeat it?"

He sat there and thought for a minute. "Well, the only way I know to kill it and it not come back alive is to dismember it, then burn each body part separately."

That was weird, but if that was the only way to kill it, that's what we would do to protect the pack. "Okay, everyone, so this is what is going to happen. We will stand guard for the night two off. That way, they can rotate with the other members when they start getting tired. Tomorrow, I will set the barrier and, after, we will try to track this Quil." They all started cheering, so we all got to our posts while two of us went inside to rest. *We will stand here all night until tomorrow comes.*

# Warrior Selection

The next morning, we all awoke in the forest, surrounded by the beautiful trees. I mind-linked, "Everyone, time to go home. I have some training to complete, then, after that, there will be warrior selections. Those of you who think that they are the best and will battle Alcide, or one of the leaders the ones that fight the best will be the bodyguards and help train the rest of the pack alongside us." With that said, we all started running home. Once home, we all transformed back into our human form before going inside. Genius and I went upstairs to change, but it seemed Genius had different ideas because soon as our door closed, he picked me up and carried me to our bed. Once there, he started nibbling on my mark, causing me to grind against his already-hard shaft; my intimate began to soak my pants. That is when Genius tore them off my body after tearing his own off. He slid inside me. I was always tight no matter what. *He is very large which makes it hurt at first.*

Genius looked at me before sliding in me hard again. "Baby, I love you with all my heart. I will show you how much." At that moment, I felt every emotion coming from him while he went in and out of my intimate area. We finally both reached and climaxed at the same time. I just smiled at him.

"Babe, I didn't know you missed me that much, but we have to start my training." He just smiled before getting up and changing his clothes. He tossed me my training outfit he picked out. I mind-linked Alcide while I changed, "Alcide, I will be down in a moment. Had some personal things to deal with."

After I got my top on, he responded: "Ya, I know. The whole pack heard you two, but I am glad that you're happy." I had to be blushing; I felt like I was blushing, but Genius didn't say anything about me blushing. *O well, time to meet Alcide out back.* So Genius and I walked down the stairs and into the backyard where Alcide, Zeus, and Daniel, all waited for me.

Once I met up with them, my brother and Daniel were giggling like little schoolboys, so I knew a smartass remark was coming. "Squirt, you know I am glad you found your mate, but you're going to have to soundproof your room. I am your brother; I don't want to hear you." Now, I knew I was blushing because Zeus fell on the ground, laughing.

"Shut up, Zeus, at least he can make me scream. I have heard your mate yell not once. Are we coming up short in that area, is that why you're upset?" As soon as I finished my sentence, Genius, Alcide, and Daniel all fell on the ground, laughing. Zeus, however, was not, and he was not blushing. Finally, Alcide was able to stand up without laughing. He turned toward me.

"Now I remember why you were my favorite, Artemis, but enough games. Now, we start your training."

I had no clue why, but that terrified me. I hadn't trained with my uncle since before he left us all those years ago. But I accepted the challenge because now I had a whole pack to protect, not just myself. Alcide stepped closer to me.

"Now, Art, I need you to come at me with everything you have. Don't hold back. Let your instinct take over. Allow you and your wolf to become one. That is the only way you will beat me."

I just smiled, and that is when I heard Violet, "Ha-ha, we shall show him. Artemis, close your eyes and imagine us becoming one completely. I am you, and you are me." I did as Violet told me. I never knew that we could become one of our thoughts, our emotions were one; we were a complete team. When I opened my eyes, I went after Alcide with everything that I had. I jumped in the air, came down, and punched him dead in his nose. He started leaking blood immediately. Alcide looked shocked, but I didn't let up. I swept down low and hit his knee, then I came up behind him and put him in a chokehold until he tapped.

When we stopped Genius, Zeus, Daniel, and Alcide, all had their mouth's wide open. I didn't understand what was wrong. "Why are you guys looking at me like that?"

Alcide was the first to speak, "Artemis, you do not need training for fighting. You are unbelievable. I guess a lot of the training from when you were little stuck."

Then Zeus, "But on another note, you do know that you have wolf ears and a wolf tail. I have never seen anything like it before, Squirt."

Genius walked up to me. "Baby, you were impressive, but Zeus is right. Why is only part of your wolf showing?" I just stared at them for a moment before reaching on top of my head to find that my wolf ears were out.

Then I heard Violet, "Artemis, this is what happens when we become wolf. You are human with wolf features; it is one of the amazing powers we possess."

I was able to answer all the boy's questions at once now, "Violet says this is what happens when she and I become one; it's one of our many powers."

Alcide thought for a moment. "O ya. I remember your mother saying something about you would be able to do that before. I don't know why it didn't come to me before, but you are in no need of fight training. The training you need, only Violet can provide now."

I smiled. "Well, then, everyone, we have another task to complete. Are we ready?" Everyone nodded, so I mind-linked the pack members, "Everyone, it is time children stay inside. If you are 16 and up, you are required to come outside and meet me in the field." Shortly after that, everyone came out. I already knew that James was going to be on the bodyguard team because we had already fought, but I wanted him to fight Alcide before deciding one-hundred percent.

Once everyone was outside, I nodded for Alcide to proceed for the first part of the session. Alcide walked in front of everyone. "Hi, everyone, those of you that don't know who I am, my name is Alcide. I am Artemis's uncle. Now, we will proceed with the fights. Those of you worthy enough will be chosen for the pack's bodyguard team. The rest you will train hard just in case we ever have to defend our domain or protect our queen." Everyone cheered before forming a circle for the warrior selections to begin.

Like I thought, James was the first one up. He didn't waste any time; he immediately rushed Alcide. Honestly, he almost got him on the ground, but Alcide knew all the tricks, but Alcide did end up with a black eye at the end of the battle. I nodded for Zeus to go in and replace Alcide. That way, he could rest in between fights.

The next one that stepped up was David. He tried a different approach instead of jumping straight on Zeus. He slid between his legs, then did a spin kick, knocking Zeus on his front half. David thought that would be the end of it, but Zeus heel kicked him, dropping him down as well. That's when David decided to punch Zeus hard enough to make his lip bleed. I could tell Zeus was not expecting that and so could David. He immediately put Zeus in a chokehold, but that wasn't enough to stop Zeus. Zeus head-butted him, making his nose bleed before kicking his knee out and locking his ankle up in a hold, causing David to tap out.

I nodded for Zeus to go over by Alcide. Then Daniel went in. The next one that entered the circle was Juanita, David's wife. She went straight in toward Daniel, kicking Daniel straight in the stomach before spinning around and kicking him in the face. She was good, she might get Daniel out, but Daniel immediately spun around, punching Juanita directly in her eye, causing her eye to swell up. Juanita stumbled back for a second before sliding and kicking Daniel's knee out from under him. When she got him in a chokehold, she then wrapped her legs around him until Daniel tapped.

I nodded for Daniel to leave the circle, then I entered. That's when I noticed that Zeus's mate, Dream, had entered the circle. *Well, this should be interesting.* We circled each other for a second before she came running after me. She went to punch me, but I moved to the side, grabbing her arm, spinning into her, catching her eye with my elbow. Her eye immediately started bleeding, which made her angry, because the next thing I knew, she was on my back, trying to choke me out. But I was not going. I fell back on top of her before rotating my body so that I was facing her, then I started landing elbows. That's when Dream wrapped her legs around my head and grabbed her foot; she was trying to choke me out. So, I picked her up, slamming her on the ground until she released. The moment she released, I started punching her repeatedly until she tapped on the ground.

She walked out of the circle and I stayed because I knew that Daniel's mate was going to be the next to try. I was correct because she didn't just walk into the circle, she came running directly toward me before jumping behind me, kicking me in the back of my knee, making me buckle. Then she went to elbow me on top of my head, but I was prepared. I spun around with my leg, knocking her on the ground. That's when I put her leg into a leg lock, causing her to tap immediately. I had her leg so tight, if she wouldn't have tapped, I would have broken it. The warrior fights went on for a while before I called it quits.

At the end, that's when I spoke, "Okay, so the ones that made the cut are James, David, Juanita, Dream, Jade, and Prometheus. These are our elite warriors. They will train the rest of you as well as the children." Everyone cheered. I had made Daniel and Zeus get a bonfire going. That way, the pack could relax around the fire, so we all sat around the fire. Genius and I were cuddled up next to each other, listening to our pack members tell their stories.

I stood up. "I want to thank you all for coming home and being so supportive. Now enjoy the festivities. My mate and I are going for a swim in the pool before going to bed." I looked at Genius, but that is when he stood up.

"Well, Princess, not quite yet. I wanted to do this in front of the whole pack."

I was confused. "Do what?"

He just smiled at me. "Artemis Cage, I have loved you from the first time I saw you. We became best friends, but somewhere along the way, I fell in love with you. I always knew that we would be mates even though I could not tell you about who I was truly." Then Genius got down on one knee. I was shocked. "Artemis, will you do me the honor of becoming Mrs. Genius Light?" I was completely shocked; I never thought he would do this, but I knew that I couldn't spend another moment without him in it.

"Yes, Baby, yes." He placed the ring on my finger before standing up to kiss me. The whole pack began to ooh and ah before congratulating us.

Soon after he proposed, he carried me to our room. He kept smiling like this was the best moment of his life. "Princess, you do not know how happy you just made me."

I smiled before kissing him on his lips. "Babe, you don't understand how much this means to me. I honestly thought I would always be alone, then you came along." Genius kissed me so passionately that I forgot everything for a moment. He carried me to the bed before laying me down. This time was different though. He was undressing me but not himself. I was completely naked, laying on our bed. He was just staring at me.

"Princess, do you know how beautiful you are?" Then he started nibbling my mark before kissing his way down to my breasts where he suckled my nipples, causing me to let out a small moan. He kissed his way down toward my intimate area. He spread my legs open, slowly licking my clitoris, then he slid two fingers in hitting a spot inside that I never knew existed. He kept going for what seemed like hours. Before I was about to climax, all I could scream was, "OMG, Genius, don't stop. Please, I am about to climax." He didn't stop either. He waited till he had every part of me inside his mouth before coming up to kiss me.

"Now, Princess, get some sleep. I love you." I cuddled up next to him, passing out soon after that.

# Red Moon

As dawn approached, Genius and I had been out all night, guarding the property while we let the others take turns getting some rest. I knew I needed to rest for what I was going to do tonight, but I wanted to make sure that the rest of them were able to get some rest to help guard me while I performed the protective barrier. Daniel and Zeus came to relieve us so that we could go inside to rest. Before leaving, I wanted them to understand something. "If you guys see or hear anything at all, no matter what it is, you are to wake us immediately. Do you understand?" My beta and delta both nodded their heads to confirm that they understood what I meant. There was one more person I needed to see before heading to bed, so I sent Genius in before me.

I went to visit Alcide; he was in the kitchen, making breakfast like he used to. "Uncle Alcide, I have a question. Tonight, while I perform the spell to put up the barrier, will you make sure you are outside with the rest to help guard?"

He looked at me, confused. "Artemis, I wouldn't allow you to go through that without being there protecting you. I may have not been there to save your mother, but I will not allow a thing to happen to you now that I am home."

I gave him a hug before making my way up the stairs. Once I reached our room, I opened the door to find Genius completely asleep. So, I curled up next to him and drifted into a deep sleep. While sleeping, I had a dream about my mother. She was standing next to her favorite tree at the top of the hill, so I walked to her, then she turned around. She started talking, but, at first, I couldn't make out what she was saying. But I stood there a moment before I could hear her voice, "Artemis, can you hear me now?" I was shocked.

"Yes, Mother, I can hear you, but how? You're dead, how is this possible?"

She just smiled. "Baby girl, I have been trying to reach you since I passed, but I couldn't get through to you or Violet." I was still in disbelief that this was happening.

"Mom, there is so much I want to ask you. I have so many questions." She touched my cheek, and I started crying immediately.

She embraced me before saying anything, "I know you do, Baby, but we don't have that much time. You are about to perform the protection barrier, correct?" I nodded; I couldn't speak. "Okay, Baby. I want you to understand that in order to perform this barrier, to make it the strongest you can during the red moon, you are going to have to have sex with Genius in front of the whole pack."

I was taken aback by what she said. *How could she expect me to have sex with Genius in front of everyone?* She shook her head.

"Artemis Cage, you have always been stubborn, but on this, there is no choice." I started crying again. How could my mother ask me to do something like that?

"Mom, please tell me there is another way."

With tears in her eyes, "Hunny, I wish there was. I wish I could be there to protect you, but I can't. It is now your responsibility to protect yourself and the pack. I know that you do not want to do this, but it is the only way." I was scared; I didn't know if I could do this part.

"Mom, what else don't I know? I need answers."

She caressed my cheek. "I know, but I cannot stay here much longer. You and Violet will figure out how to reach me again. Until then, my child, I love you, and I know that you will do the right thing. Remember to trust your instincts and Violet's above all else." With those last words, she was gone, then I woke up. I woke up at a loss for words. *Was that real, or was it just a dream?*

I must have been rolling around or talking in my sleep because when I turned over, Genius was just staring at me.

"Princess, did you have a nightmare? You were tossing and turning."

I gulped before responding, "No, Genius. I spoke to my mom." His eyes became wide and his mouth dropped wide open.

It took him a moment before he could respond. "How?"

I just shrugged my shoulder. "I honestly don't know. I thought it was a dream, but it wasn't. It was my mom."

He scooted closer to me, holding me. "Well, Babe, what did she say?"

I just looked down at the blanket. "She knew of me performing the protection barrier today, and she told me that the only way to make the barrier unbreakable is I had to have sex with you in front of the pack under the red moon." He was shocked. He knew that my mother would have never asked me to do that.

"Princess, how could she ask you to do that? She always said sex was intimate between you and your partner."

I just looked away. "I know that, Genius."

He scooted closer to me, hugging me. "We will do what is needed of us, but are we supposed to be in wolf form or human form?"

Now, I was confused because Mother never said. "I don't know. I have to ask Violet. Mother didn't say." He looked at me, urging me on. So I closed my eyes.

"Violet, are you there?"

"Yes, Artemis. I am always here. What's wrong?"

I sighed. "Well, Mother just informed me that I had to have sex with Genius in front of the pack under the red moon, but she never told me if I had to be in human form or wolf form."

That earned a big laugh from her before she spoke, "Well, Artemis, I am sorry you didn't hear it from me, but you have to be in wolf form in order for it to work, and be strong, because when you have sex in wolf form, you both will end up spilling a little blood; it is only natural." I kind of figured that was what she was going to say. So I came back to Genius.

"Well, we have to be in wolf form. She said something about when you have sex in wolf form, you're bound to spill some blood." That earned a laugh from him.

"Well, she is right about that, but you might want to include the other three, since they're family, because, if not, they are going to be mad."

I agreed with him. So we got out of bed and I mind-linked the three of them, "Meet in the office in five minutes. Please, nobody be late. This is urgent."

They all replied back, "Okay, be there in a sec." I looked at Genius. He came over and kissed the top of my head.

"Everything will be okay, Princess. Just remember that no matter what, I will be here for you."

I just smiled. "I know. Thank you. I love you." We finished getting dressed, then we meet the other three in the office. Closing the door behind us, Genius and I took our seats by the desk.

Alcide was the first one to say anything, "Okay, Artemis, what is going on?"

Zeus stood up. "Ya, Squirt, what was so important that it couldn't wait?" I looked at Genius, and he urged me to speak up. He knew I didn't want to have to say this out loud let alone do it.

I took a deep breath in before speaking, "Well, last night, I had a dream, but not an ordinary dream, I spoke to Mother." They stopped dead in their tracks, just staring at me like I was crazy or making that up.

Alcide just looked at me for a moment. "Artemis, there is no way you communicated with your mother. She is dead." I just shook my head. He of all people didn't want to believe me.

"Alcide, have I ever lied?" He shook his head no.

Finally, Zeus said something, "Well, what did she say, Squirt?"

I took another big breath in. "Well, she knew that I was doing the protection barrier tonight when the red moon was high, then she informed me that in order to make this barrier unbreakable, I had to have sex with Genius in the middle of the pack under the red moon in our wolf forms." They all looked at me and started laughing. They thought I was joking around.

Genius stepped forward. "Guys, she is not joking. She is being dead serious. You know she would not be doing this if she didn't need to protect the pack."

They all looked at me, then Zeus was the first to speak, "Well, I can say I don't want to see my little sister having sex, but, unfortunately, my wolf side is not going to mind." The other two boys shook their heads in agreement with what Zeus said. I finally stood up, holding my head held high.

"Well, it is decided. Tonight at the red moon's fullest, everyone will shift to their wolf forms while Genius and I have sex under the red moon." They all agreed, then left Genius and me alone. He grabbed my hands, kissing them.

"Princess, I know this will be uncomfortable, but I assure you that our wolves will surely enjoy this part. Mine has practically been begging me since our mating."

That earned him a laugh. "I am sure Violet has been dying to." We kissed each other goodbye, then went into separate bathrooms to get ready for the ritual. I stripped down and put a robe on.

I heard Violet, "Artemis, I will not lie. I am going to enjoy every minute of this, but when the moon is at the highest, you will have to repeat the words

I say before you shift. Once you shift, you are to let Genius mount you from behind, not moving. Once he is inside of us, he is not allowed to cum until the barrier is up. The moment he cums is the moment the barrier fails. This is based on both of your powers, energy, and life force." I didn't respond for a moment. I had mind-linked Genius so that he could hear Violet too. "Well, just make sure you say the words on cue. That way, we don't have to wait." I heard her laugh in my head. "Well, it is about time. You need to head outside into the center of our property."

I mind-linked the pack to let everyone know that the ceremony was about to start. They were to meet us outside with their robes on, including children. I walked outside, and Genius was already waiting in the middle of our pack. I reached him, and he held his hand up to silence our pack.

"Okay, so everyone knows that Artemis is performing the protection barrier tonight, right?" They all nodded in agreement, then I stepped forward.

"This is what will happen, so there is not to be any confusion. I will speak the enchantment before I shift, then once I shift, everyone is to shift. Once Genius and I are fully shifted, he is going to have sex with me. Now, for the adults here, if you are not married, you need to find a female because you will be following suit. As for the children, when you see each male draw the female's blood, you are to dip your fingers in it and draw the symbol on your heads. No male is allowed to cum before the barrier is up. You will know the barrier is up once I arch my back further against Genius."

They all seemed okay with it, but Genius looked at me and whispered, "I didn't hear Violet say that."

I just shook my head. "Ya, she decided to tell me that part on the walk over here."

He just chuckled. "Well, it is about time. Are you ready?"

I just looked at him. "Ready as I will ever be."

With that said, I took my robe off. Everyone followed me, then I heard Violet in my head starting the words I needed to repeat. It first was to be said in English, then in Latin. "Goddess of the moon, mother of all wolves, we call upon you to help protect our pack. We ask that you allow me your queen to put up our mighty protection barrier to ward of any evil, any threats to our pack. I ask you humbly to grant me this wish in order to protect my pack." Everyone repeated what I had said word for word. Now it was time for the Latin part. *"Dea lunae, Lupi matrem omnium, invocaverimus te ad auxilium praesidio*

68

*sarcinis, nos quaerere quod liceat mihi regina vestra aggere magno praesidio posuere si ad arcendum malum, nec minis ad fasciculum, Ut det mihi velle quod a te supplex in praesidio maxime ordee."* Everyone repeated the words exactly as I did, then I stripped my robe off and started to transform. Soon, my purple-tinted fur appeared. I looked around; all the females were following my lead, so I stepped forward a little bit and allowed Violet to take over after Genius mounted me.

Violet and Genius's wolf had been waiting for this, I was not about to ruin this for them. Violet told me to just watch around the perimeter. That way, I could tell Genius when the barrier was up so he could tell his wolf to cum as well as other pack members. I sat there for a moment before I felt a sharp pain in my neck. That is when I realized Genius's wolf bit Violet's neck; this is what they meant. I noticed the children doing what I told them. That made me proud. Now I sat there and watched the barrier go up through Violet's eyes this time. The barrier started off really slow, but it started to pick up speed as the boys started picking up speed. Once I saw the barrier was completely sealed at the top, I mind-linked everyone, "All right, guys, you have been waiting this whole time. Now, everyone, cum at once." That is when Violet informed me that we would all be stuck together for a few seconds after they released. *Well, that's nice to know.*

Everyone sat there for a moment before separating. I thanked Violet before transforming back to my human form and putting on my robe once again. Once Genius and I were back in human form, we turned toward our pack members.

"I know this was awkward for some and others enjoyed themselves, but the barrier is up. It is now time for everyone to rest easy for the night. Nobody will be getting through anymore.

"Everyone head inside and go get some rest. I know you are all exhausted from tonight's festivities." Everyone turned to go inside. Then Genius and I stood outside, watching the red moon.

"Well, Princess, we did it. The barrier is up, so that is one problem down. Now we have another one to address tomorrow." I just stared at him for a moment.

"What do you mean?"

He just shook his head before chuckling. "Princess, did you forget, we have to start tracking that Quil-thing Alcide was telling us about."

I just shook my head. "I might have forgotten."

He just laughed at me. "You know, the wolves were happy tonight."

Now I laughed. "I know. That is why I completely blanked out. That way, she could enjoy herself tonight."

Then I heard Violet, "Well, thank you, because I did enjoy myself. Now just wait till you're 18 and we have our first heat. You will want to participate in that, but if you fight it, boy will we be in pain." Wait, what was she talking about? Genius must have heard her because he started laughing his ass off. I smacked him.

"Well, Princess, she is not lying. I've seen my sisters and mother go through it. That is also a good fertility day for us."

I just pushed him. "Well, I guess we will have to see where that day comes, huh." He just laughed at me, then we sat down under the moon for hours...

# Investigation

The next day, following the red moon, everyone was in better spirits; you could tell. They all knew that they were safe because of the barrier, but not only that. Since the ceremony, there were a lot of new couples here too. But, now, it came time to start investigating the whereabouts of the Quil that tried to harm Genius and me. So, I sat up in bed. Genius had already gotten out of bed and headed outside to train with the boys about an hour or so ago. So I got out of the bed, got dressed, and mind-linked the boys.

"Meet me in the office."

They all responded with, "Yes, Alpha." I headed downstairs and greeted everyone on my way through to the office. Once there, I sat down and started going through the books that were there, seeing if I could find any information on the Quils. But I couldn't find anything, which was only frustrating me, but, finally, in walked Alcide, Daniel, Zeus, and Genius.

Daniel looked at me. "What's up, Boss, why did you call a meeting?"

I just shook my head; *it's like they all forgot.* "Do you not remember that we needed to find out who this Quil was that was trying to harm us?"

They all dropped their mouths to the floor. Well, except Genius, because he was the one who reminded me. All three boys said in unison, "Fuck, we totally spaced that out." I couldn't even be mad at them because I had forgotten also.

"We need to gather more information about them. Also, are any of our pack member good at tracking?"

All three boys looked at one another before Zeus spoke: "Well, ya. James is the best tracker we have in the pack."

I turned toward Alcide. "Are there any books that we could read up on, or is there an elder still alive that we could speak to that would know about the Quils?"

He sat there for a moment, thinking. "The only person that was alive and knew about the Quils was your mother, so unless you can speak to her again, I can't think of anyone else that would know about them. As for literature about the Quils, your parents used to have some back at their old castle in Romania, but I don't see how we are going to get there without someone noticing who you are."

*Well, I can try contacting my mother again here soon and see if she has any ideas on how to get into our old castle, because we need that to learn and teach the other pack members. Even if she explains everything to me, I don't want to get anything messed up in translation.* I turned back toward Alcide. "Uncle, do you remember anything else about these Quils. Like, why they would attack us? We haven't done anything to them for them to attack." He sat there, staring at me like he was shocked I didn't know that answer.

"Well, Artemis, Quils usually only attack when they feel threatened or if someone is ordering them. See, Quils lost most of their free will after your mother and father lost the crown. The other wolves started treating them like property instead of another race. I understood to an extent because some of them had lost their minds completely, but the ones that were sane, I never understood why people would treat them that way."

Genius and I looked at each other before speaking, "Well, maybe we can fix that once we find the one that attacked us.

"But in the meantime, Genius and I are going to head back to school. The other pack members need to as well; we don't need the school sniffing around. The other pack members will be safe here. The ones that need to go to work can go, they just need to be a little extra cautious. Also, I want to speak to James before I leave to school." After I finished that sentence, everyone left except Genius, which I was fine with. He was my mate and my fiancé after all, so I mind-linked James, "Hey, James, could you meet me and Genius in the office really quick? It is important." I waited for a moment for him to respond.

"Yes, Boss, give me a sec to finish feeding the kids."

Well, that was sweet of him. While we waited, I turned toward Genius. "Babe, are you okay going to school? Because you know we don't have to. I can have Zeus sign paperwork stating I'm being homeschooled or dropping out, and you know your mom never wanted you attending school anyway."

He cocked his head to the side. "Princess, I am fine going to school. No, I am not happy about the situation, but it is not your fault, so why would I punish you for something that is out of your control? I know you're not going anywhere even if I do get jealous sometimes; I can't help it." I gave him a hug, and right when I was about to kiss him, in walked James. He covered his eyes.

"O, I am sorry. I can come back."

I just laughed. "James, it is okay. You act like you haven't seen us do much worse." That earned a smile from him; he started laughing.

"Ya that is true. Okay, what did you guys need to see me for?"

Well, Genius and I looked at one another before speaking in unison, "Do you remember that Quil that attacked me and Genius?" He nodded. "Well, do you remember the scent it left behind?" He nodded again. "Well, okay then, we have your first mission; this is purely scouting. You are to avoid any conflict at all and take at least one other pack member with you that you trust, but we want you to track that scent and immediately report it back to us. Once you know where it is at, come home."

James got excited the moment we said we had his first mission; you could tell he was getting restless in the house all the time. "James, we need to know you understand your mission." He stopped jumping around for a minute.

"O, yes, sorry, I do. You want me to track the Quil, avoid conflict, report anything I find, and once the location has been discovered, come home. O, also, I can bring one person I trust with me."

I nodded. "Yes, that is correct. Now I want you to grab some things and your partner, whoever it is, and head out. We will be going to school, so just mind-link one of us or Zeus."

With that, James left the office, then in came Zeus. "Squirt, you guys ready? We got to go or we are going to be late than we already are." I waved at him. I looked at Genius. He grabbed my hand, and off to school we went. Once we got there, I could already tell that Oliver was there. I could smell him a mile away. That started to make me uncomfortable with how everything happened between us the last time. Genius could see that I was becoming uncomfortable the closer we got to school.

"Princess, why are you nervous? Are you ever going to tell us what happen the last time or not?"

I just looked at him. "I am fine, Genius. Just nervous about my English test today." Luckily, he seemed to buy it because he didn't ask about it again. Zeus pulled into the employee-parking lot. He waved us goodbye before going in the employee entrance. Genius and I went into the office because we were late.

We had to get a tardy slip from the office. We walked to my locker to gather our things. Before Genius walked me to English, he gave me a kiss on my forehead.

"Good luck, Princess. You know you will ace this test. You always do."

As soon as I walked into the classroom, there sat Oliver just staring at me. Luckily my old desk was available, so that is where I sat. I didn't want to be anywhere near Oliver right now.

The English teacher passed out the tests. "You guys have the class to finish the test. Remember, this counts for half of your grade. Once you are done, bring the test up to me, then you are free to leave the classroom." Well, that was good. We had never been able to do that before, so I got started on the test. After about 15 minutes, I was already done. Genius was right; it was easy, so I got up and took the test up to the teacher before walking out of the classroom. I wasn't sure what to do because I had never been able to leave class early before without a good reason, so I walked to my locker and put my English stuff up. I grabbed my reading book from inside the locker. I sat down in front of my locker and started reading my book. That is when I noticed a familiar scent and a familiar, uneasy feeling. I was scared to look up because I knew who it was; it was Oliver. Why was he here? He knows I want nothing to do with him.

That is when Violet decided to pop up. "You know you can reject him, right? But I wouldn't advise doing it alone; I would wait for either Zeus or Genius because the way he is acting, it will get ugly."

"Well, Violet, should I do that or not?"

"Sweety, that is a decision that you need to make, but just because you reject him now doesn't mean it will work. It didn't work for Mother. She rejected her other mate, and he just waited around for Father to die, then came back into her life. You remember that man she was dating? That was her other mate."

I wasn't sure what the right thing was. I wanted to be with Genius; I have loved him forever, but here Oliver was, trying to get my attention, but how do I know that he doesn't want it for the wrong reasons? I didn't, and that is why I must do this.

I peered up to notice him just smiling away at me. "What do you want, Oliver? I told you to leave me alone."

He just started laughing. "Do you really think that I would stay away from my mate?"

I just shook my head. "Genius is my mate and my fiancé." I pulled my shirt down just enough to show him the mark, then I showed him my engagement ring. That pissed him off, because the next thing I knew, he grabbed my wrist really hard.

"I will remove his mark. You are mine."

I just stared at him. "Oliver, let go. That hurts." But he started squeezing my arm harder. Now, I was starting to get pissed. I reached behind his head and grabbed his neck, forcing him to the ground. "You will remove your fucking hands from my damn wrist before I snap your neck."

He just started squeezing harder. "Do you really think you scare me, Bitch?" Zeus and Genius must have felt how angry I was becoming because both came rounding the corner. I held up my hand, signaling them both to stop, but Genius did not want to. I let out the deepest growl I could, send him a warning that this was my fight.

I flipped Oliver over onto his back before straddling him, pinning his arms above his head. I could tell Genius was getting pissed, so I sent him a message, "Babe, trust me, I have this handled. If he continues after this, you can do your thing, Baby, okay? But I have to do this, just trust me." He gave me those puppy-dog eyes.

I turned back toward Oliver. "I want you to understand something. Just because I am your mate does not mean I have to be with you. If you think treating me like that would ever make me love you—you are sorely mistaken, and just because of that, Oliver, I reject you as my mate. I reject our mate bind. I reject you." The moment those words left my mouth, everything that I felt for Oliver went away. I didn't notice his scent anymore. But that is also when Oliver became enraged. He started to shift underneath me, but he didn't know who I was. So I remained on top of him. That is when my eyes turned dark purple and I forced him to stay human. "Oliver, if you keep playing with me, you see my wonderful mate sitting behind you? He is just waiting to kill you, and be grateful that it is him and not me; I could do it slowly and painfully."

Once he saw my eyes, he became frightened, like he knew what I was and that was not allowed, so I held him a minute before asking Violet something, "Hey, Violet, can we erase other wolf's memories?"

She laughed at me. "Yes, you can, but you're not a vampire, it doesn't work the same way. You have to place both hands on the sides of his head and manually erase whatever it is you need to erase."

So I did just that. I erased the image he saw of me, with my eyes changing colors before getting up. Once I got up, I heard James in my head, "Alpha, I followed the smell 30 miles from the last place you guys saw him. Should I continue?"

"Yes, James, follow the smell and find the location. Once that is done, contact us. Let us know, then meet back at the pack house." I walked over to Genius. Zeus stood guard in front of us. Oliver slowly started to back away.

"Artemis, this is not over. I do not care if you rejected me; you will be mine." Genius let out this loud and mean-sounding growl, and that is when Oliver turned around and left.

Genius turned toward me. "Princess, did you really just reject him?"

I just looked at him like he was stupid. "Babe, you literally just watched me do it."

He smiled. "Thank you, but I don't understand why you didn't tell me he wouldn't leave you alone."

I just shook my head. "Because, Babe, this was my fight. I had to deal with it my own way. I love you, and he will not ruin that no matter what." He picked me up, pressing me against the lockers, kissing me long and deep before Zeus cleared his throat to get our attention.

"Well, Love Birds, I think that I am going to pull Artemis out of school; Oliver just saw your eyes." I started cracking up, laughing. Both the boys just looked at me.

"You guys don't have to worry about that; I wiped his memory of that." That shocked them.

"Wait, for what? How?"

I just started walking away. "Don't worry your head about that. Now come to the office with me. I am going to talk to the principal really quick."

So they followed me to the principal's office. I walked into Mr. Vios's office. "Hi, Mrs. Cage, to what do I owe this pleasure?"

I shook his hand. "Well, Mr. Vios, as you know, Genius and I are graduating early due to us having our credit that is needed, so I was wondering if we could just get our diplomas without attending the graduation ceremony this weekend."

That seemed to confuse him. "Well, Artemis, I thought you wanted to walk across the stage like everyone else."

I hung my head. "Well, I did, but that was when my mother was alive. I really would just like to get my diploma now and go home. If not, Zeus here will be pulling me out today."

That shocked him; he turned toward Zeus. "Is this true?" Zeus nodded in agreement; Zeus knew what I was doing. Mr. Vios got up from his desk and went over to the filing cabinet that he kept locked. He grabbed two envelopes out of the filing cabinet. "Well, I can't say that this isn't upsetting news, but I do understand why, so here are your diplomas. You are free to go."

I smiled. "Thank you, Mr. Vios. I appreciate it, and you were a wonderful principal to have."

With that, we left his office. Genius grabbed my hand. "Well, that was smooth." I just smiled, brushing air off my shoulder.

"I know I am just good like that." Zeus and Genius fell on the floor, laughing. "Okay, guys, let's head home. Don't forget, I still have to get a hold of Mom tonight." They were able to finally stand. We got to Zeus's car, but we noticed that the tires had been slashed. This had to be Oliver's doing.

"Well, Squirt, what do you want to do?"

I just chuckled. "How about you just post a free-car sign on it? I will buy you another one."

Now, he was truly confused. "How are you going to do that, Squirt?"

I just looked at him like he was stupid. "Did you forget that Dad had left me money in the bank for when I graduated?" He made that 'O ya face.' "Now let's get to the woods so we can shift and get home. I am tired." Zeus made the free-car sign and signed the title, leaving that and the keys in the glove compartment. We jogged until we were deep in the forest, then we shifted into our wolf forms.

Once we shifted, we took off toward the house, just running like we never had. Finally, we reached the barrier and came running in at the same time. That is when we ran into each other, tripping over one another. Once shifted back, all we could do is laugh. Alcide came over to us.

"What is so funny, and why are you two not at school?" I got up, putting the robe on that Alcide brought with him, and I held up Genius's and my diploma. Alcide just stood there with his eyes wide open. "I thought the graduation was this weekend?"

I nodded. "It was, but I didn't want to attend. It wouldn't be the same without Mom there, so I just asked the principal and he gave them to us."

He just shook his head. "Artemis, you know that your mother would have wanted you to walk across that stage."

I just started walking away. "Well, she isn't here now, is she?" With that, I went inside the house. I went into the kitchen where food had already been put on plates for Genius, Zeus, and I, with juice in a glass next to each one of them.

I grabbed my plate and drink and went upstairs to my room. I sat there and quickly ate my food. I wanted to be asleep before Genius came upstairs. I didn't want to talk about what I said because I knew it was wrong, plus I still needed to try and contact my mother. Once I finished my food, I sat the plate and cup on the stand next to my bed. I lay back and started humming the song my mother would sing to me when I couldn't sleep, and, soon, I drifted into sleep. I couldn't hear or see anything, not yet. It was all black and static. The vision started to clear a little bit, but I could hear my mother's voice. I kept trying, but nothing yet...

# A Mother's Wish

As I drifted further and further into my dream, my mother's favorite tree appeared; I walked closer to the tree. The closer I got, the more peaceful I became. I hollered out for my mother, trying to connect with her spirit again, but she didn't answer. So, I sat down by the tree, trying to figure out how I connected with her the last time, but I honestly had no clue how I did it.

I sat there for what seemed an eternity before I heard her voice, "Artemis, can you hear me?"

I was shocked; I had been trying to see or hear her for a while. "Yes, Mother, I can hear you. Please come out." There was silence again, then a figure started to appear by the tree. I stood up, moving closer to it.

"Artemis, why have you come back to this place?" I looked at my mother, confused.

"Mom, I need the truth about some things."

She just sighed. "What do you need?" My mother was acting weird and I could not understand why.

"Who are the Quils?"

She stood there with shock on her face. "Why are you asking about them?"

I just shook my head. "Because, Mother, one of them attacked Genius and me." She turned toward me with fear in her eyes.

"What do you mean one attacked you guys?" I didn't understand why she was being so short about everything.

"He attacked us. He bit Genius. I was trying to locate him now, but I need information about it, Mom, and Alcide said you were the only other one that could tell me anything about them."

She let out a deep breath. "Well, that means they're back and being controlled by someone. Artemis, if you do not get them on your side, they will be a big problem." I nodded, acknowledging that I knew that. "Okay, so the Quils used to be werewolves, but they had betrayed their alpha, and since they

79

were half werewolf, their alpha had their mother, one of the strongest enchantresses at the time, cast a spell on them." I was mortified. How could a mother do that to their child? But like my mother knew what I was thinking, she immediately continued, "So, no, some of them are stuck in their werewolf forms, others have special abilities. Some are deformed, some are just simple half-breeds, nothing special about them. But what nobody knew is the spell the enchantress cast on them made it so they were easily controlled. I broke that spell while you were young; the Quils were free.

"But they chose to stay beside me to help protect the pack, so, in return, I made them a part of the pack, but when I fled the castle, I had to leave them behind, so I am assuming that is when they ran into someone else that redid the spell and, now, they are slaves."

I was shocked. "Mother, how could a mom do that to her own children?"

She held up her hand to stop me. "Artemis, the person that cast that spell was your aunt, those are your cousins. I did not tell anyone that because your aunt had abandoned us for the alpha of the black-jade pack. He was her mate, but he was not a great person.

"Artemis, how do you think you're able to cast spells? You are the most powerful wolf, but you are the most powerful enchantress alive today. You are half-werewolf half-enchantress." I was shocked. Why didn't my uncle tell me this? Why did Mom keep this from me?

"Mooommm, why didn't I know this? Why didn't Alcide tell me?"

She lowered her head. "Because, Baby, nobody knew. I kept it hidden from everyone because you were already endangered. I just wanted to protect you, but, now, you must know who you are, because if your cousins are under someone's control again, there will be a great war coming."

Now I was confused. "What do you mean that there will be a great war?"

"Artemis, my sweet girl, I had to bind your powers at a young age because they started showing earlier than they were meant to. Nobody wanted a half-wolf half-enchantress child running the kingdom. You were our future, our queen. This was your path. I had to protect you from everything and anyone that tried to do you harm.

"During the last war, I had to kill you aunt to protect you. That was one of the most horrible things I have ever had to do, but I had to in order to protect you."

My mother had tears welling in her eyes. "Artemis, I was not always a wolf. I was born an enchantress, but the Great Spirit that created wolves saw your future before you were even born. She made me who I was. Your father was one of the most powerful alpha wolves around, then I was the strong enchantress, but the great moon-spirit made me the most powerful wolf with the power of the enchantress to go with it. It gave me special abilities, but none of them could amount to you. You are born this way, not made; the moon god cannot change you."

I was in utter shock by this. My mother hid a lot from us. I never even knew that I had an aunt. I wasn't sure what to say to my mother. Finally, I found the words, "Mom, I understand for the most part why you kept this all a secret, but because of you doing this, now I am forced into a world I know nothing about. I have no clue what I am doing, I have no clue what I am supposed to do half the time, and, now, I don't even know who I am."

My mother completely lost it. "Artemis, I am so sorry. I never meant for any of this to happen. I was going to tell you everything the next morning, but I never got the chance to. I am so sorry I am not there to guide you the way I was meant to." I just walked closer to my mother and hugged her; there was nothing else that I could have done.

"Mom, I am sorry too, but there is another question I need to ask you. How do I get into our old castle undetected?"

She pushed me away. "No, Artemis, you can never go back there, it isn't safe there."

"Mother, I have to. Everything we need is there. Why are you acting this way now?" I was again confused by my mother's behavior. *This is not like her at all.*

"I am sorry, Artemis. I will not tell you how to go back there. I will not allow it at all, it is too dangerous for you."

I kept shaking my head. "Mother, I must. I have to for the pack and myself. I have to go back, and if you won't help me, I will figure out another way." I went to turn my back to my mother, but she grabbed my arm and spun me around.

"Artemis, please don't go back there. Promise me you won't."

I just shook my head some more. "Mother, I cannot promise that. I have a responsibility that you left me unprepared for, so I will do what I must."

She lowered her head down and started weeping into her hands. "Artemis, my baby, I am so sorry for everything. my wish for you is to understand why I did everything I did." I just stood there, staring at her, not knowing what else to say. "Baby girl, I know you and Genius have mated as well as are engaged. My biggest wish for you is that you grow happy, have children, and never know the heartache that I have felt." With that, my mother disappeared. She just left with nothing else to say. Nothing. She left me by myself. I walked away back toward the darkness of my mind.

When I woke up, Genius was staring at me. I wiped my face; I could feel the tears on my face. Genius gently laid my head on his chest. "Princess, what happened, why are you crying?"

I just took a deep breath. "I saw my mother. I just found a lot out, and, now, I am questioning who I am."

He just stared at me, confused. "Well, what did she say, Princess, that has you this upset?"

I sat up on my elbow, turning toward him. "The Quils are my cousins. My aunt is the one that cursed them. My mother freed them, but after she left, she doesn't know what happened, but if they are under someone else's control, that means another war is upon us."

Genius was shocked. "Wait, I didn't even know you had an aunt." I just stared at him for a moment, trying to decide if I should tell him the rest. *But he is my fiancé, my mate I can't hide anything from him.*

"Genius, there is more. Apparently, my mother wasn't always a wolf. She was born an enchantress, but the moon goddess saw my future before I was born and gave my mom the wolf with the strength of the gods. She will also not give me a way in the castle." Genius couldn't even speak; he was in such shock. "Babe, she said it was dangerous for me to go back to that castle." He finally came back to his senses.

"What do you mean it is still dangerous for you to go back to the castle? It should be safe after all these years, right?"

I just shrugged my shoulders. "I don't know, Genius. I honestly don't know what the hell to think anymore. My mother lied about so many things. Yes, I understand it was because she needed to protect me, but she should have told me before she died, not after her death." Genius didn't say anything else. He just pulled me into his arms before kissing me on my forehead.

He just sat there and held me for a while before he spoke, "Babe, you know we have to tell your uncle and brother what your mother said, right? They both deserve to know the truth as well."

I sat quietly for a minute. "Yes, I know, but not tonight. Can you just hold me until I fall asleep again? In the morning, we can tell them, but, tonight, I just need your comfort." Genius did exactly that; he held me till I fell asleep...

# Truth

The next morning, I woke up to find Genius was not in bed. He must have gone outside for training. I sat in bed, still in shock from the things that my mother told me the previous night. *How could she keep all this from Zeus and me? These are things that we needed to know for the future.* I got out the bed so that I could get dressed and headed down to the office. That way, I could inform Genius of what happened when I contacted my mother.

"Genius, Daniel, Alcide, and Zeus, meet me in the office. We need to talk," I mind-linked them, but I also had to mind-link James to see if he found the Quil's location.

"James, have you found the Quil's location yet?" It took a moment before I heard anything back from anyone.

The first one was from the boys. "Okay, be there in a moment." Then the next was from James. "Yes, Queen, I have, but you will not believe where the Quil is at. They are at the castle in Scotland." I hung my head on how did I know that was what was going to happen.

"Okay, James, good work. Now head back home." I walked into my office, waiting for the boys. I stared off into space for what seemed like forever before the boys came into the office. I turned around. They all looked concerned. I assumed because of the look on my face.

Zeus was the first to speak, "Squirt, what is going on?" I just hung my head. I was unsure how to explain everything, then I felt a familiar warmth behind me. I looked up to see Genius. He placed his hand on my shoulder. I knew he was trying to comfort me because this was not an easy thing for me to tell them, but I had to. I stood up, walked around the desk to stand in front of the boys.

"So, you know how I contacted Mother last night even though we still don't know how I am doing it?" They all nodded their heads. "Well, Mother informed me that the Quils, they are cousins."

They all spoke at once, "How is that possible? Are you sure that it wasn't just a dream?"

I took a long, deep breath before speaking again. "Apparently, there is a lot that Mother kept from us both. Do we have anything that needs to be done today? Because, if not, we will be here awhile." They all turned toward one another before turning back toward me, and they all just said no.

I figured as much: I didn't want to explain it. *But, now, I guess I have no choice.* "All of you, sit down. This is going to take a while to explain, and no interruptions till I finish, okay?" So I went on to explain what Mother had told me. The boys' faces said it all; I didn't have to ask them. After a few hours of explaining, Zeus stood up and punched the wall behind him, leaving a hole in the wall. I walked to him in tears, wrapping my arms around him, trying to comfort him because I knew exactly how he felt.

"Squirt, how could Mother lie to us about this stuff?" Before I could open my mouth to speak, my uncle spoke first, "Your mother lied to me; she told me our sister had drowned. She never told me that she killed our sister. Why would she hide that from me of all people after everything I did?" I felt bad because I could not offer them any type of comfort, because I felt the same thing.

Daniel was still standing there with his mouth open. He was not sure what to say or how to help either. We stood in silence for a while before Genius decided to speak, "Look, guys, I know that this is hard, but you have to get it together. We have plenty of work to do. Not only that, but we have to help Artemis figure out more about herself." We had all forgotten about the fact that I wasn't a full werewolf.

Zeus spoke, "Wait, but doesn't that make me half enchantress too because Mom was?" I was confused, because my mother never told me that part, so I couldn't answer his question honestly.

"Zeus I am not sure. Mother didn't tell me, but it would make sense that, if I am, you are."

My uncle stood there with this guilty look on his face like he knew something, but before I could speak, Genius did, "Alcide, you're hiding something, so you need to tell us while we're all here."

My uncle just hung his head, and, at that moment, I knew what he was about to say would be something that neither Zeus nor I would want to hear. "Artemis and Zeus, I want to apologize because I should have told you sooner, but I didn't think it was important until now. Zeus, you don't have the same mother as Artemis. Yes, she raised you both, but your biological mom died giving birth to you. Your dad was with someone prior to meeting your mom." I stood there with my mouth open for a second before turning to Zeus; the look on his face broke my heart.

"Alcide, why didn't Mom tell us this?"

He just shook his head. "Because, in her eyes, he was her son. Nobody could have changed her mind on that. Your dad thought that she wouldn't say, but your mother did more than that. She stayed, she married him, and raised Zeus just like he was her own son." Zeus still didn't say anything; he looked defeated, like something broke inside him.

"Zeus, look at me, just because we do not share the same mother does not mean anything. You are still the son of a powerful alpha. We have to understand why Mom never told us to some extent."

He turned toward me, and that is when I noticed the tears in my brother's eyes. "Artemis, why would she not tell me? I should have been told. Someone should have said something to me. I deserved to know that much."

Before I could speak, he turned around and left the room. I went to chase after him, but Daniel stopped me.

"Artemis, give him some time. That was a lot to take in for everyone, especially Zeus. I will keep an eye on him. I will give you three sometime. You have some things to discuss and figure out." With that sentence, Daniel turned around and walked out, closing the door behind him.

I turned to look at Genius and Alcide. "Well, I think that, today, everyone needs to go sort through what was just shared. We will meet here again in the morning to discuss plans."

My uncle turned toward me. "Artemis, I am so sorry. I hope you can forgive me."

I looked confused, because there was nothing for him to apologize for. "Alcide, you have nothing to apologize for. Our mom should have told us this information soon, not withheld it no matter the reason."

I gave him a hug, then he left the room. I turned toward Genius; I just broke. I fell to the ground, crying. He knelt down on the floor beside me, grabbing me up and holding me. "Princess, it will be okay. You guys are stronger than you think. Just breathe, okay? Everything will be okay." I couldn't speak. All I could do was cry. My mate just sat there and held me, not saying anything. All I wanted was him to comfort me. I felt defeated. What kind of Alpha was I? I couldn't protect my own brother from being hurt, how was I going to protect the whole pack?

Almost instantly, Genius pulled me to face him. "Artemis, I never want you to think that again. This is not your fault. You are an amazing leader. You can't protect him from something that you never knew yourself." I just pushed him away and started running. I shifted into my wolf and just started running through the forest. I heard Zeus, Daniel, Alcide, and Genius all yelling for me to stop, but I couldn't; I needed to run.

Before I knew it, I was in the middle of the forest, not realizing I had traveled much further than our protection barrier. I heard something behind me, so I immediately got on the defensive. The next thing I knew, this man appeared from behind the tree. He was about 6'2", and he was built.

"Well, we finally meet the princess." I was confused. The only one that called me that was my mate. I let out a growl that shook the ground we stood on so that he knew I wasn't playing. He just laughed at me. "O, come on. Is that any way to speak to your father?" I stood there, frozen. *My father is dead, so who is he?* So I shifted back into my human form so I could speak to him.

"My father died. Who are you?" He just stood there, staring at me.

"You truly do look like your mother. Speaking of which, where is she? We have much to discuss, she and me."

I just looked at those eyes. *I have seen them before, but I can't remember where.* "She is dead."

That man literally just started laughing. "Your mother can't die. Her body can, but not her spirit. I see she kept you in the dark about a lot of things, but it is okay; I know why."

I was confused, but before I could speak, Genius jumped from behind the tree, but when I looked back, he was gone; the man was gone. I just stood there, confused. Genius, at some point, shifted back.

"Princess, you can't take off like that by yourself with everything going on. You had us all worried." He just looked at my face. "Artemis, what is wrong? What happened? Are you okay?"

I just turned toward him. "This man just appeared, claiming to be my father." His eyes grew big.

"That is impossible; it has to be a lie. Let's get you home." With that statement, I agreed things were getting way too weird for one day, so I shifted back and began running home. Once I got closer to the house, I could see Zeus, Alcide, and Daniel all standing there, looking around, but I honestly didn't want to see anyone then. I just wanted to be alone.

So I mind-linked all the boys, "Please just leave me alone tonight. I will talk with you more tomorrow. Some more information just came to light." I ran straight to my room and closed the door. I got into my bed and wanted to fall asleep straight away. I needed to see my mother again. She needed to tell me everything, but I knew she wasn't going to come tonight. Something inside my body and soul knew it, so I just lay there, staring at the ceiling. *Today has been exhausting. All I wanted to do was sleep, but I don't know if I will be able to, but one thing that I do know is my mother will tell me the truth, and she will speak it all.*

# Spirit World

I sat in my room for a while, trying to relax, but I couldn't. Everything that had happened today had me stressed out. I honestly didn't think that Genius would leave me alone. *He never does, even when I ask.* But he must have known that I needed to be alone for a while because he didn't follow me into the room. So I did the only thing that I knew that would relax me. I went out onto our balcony and looked up at the moon. It looked so beautiful; the one thing that always calmed me was the moon. I never understood why, but it was my safe zone. Anytime something bad would happen, this was what I would do to clear my head. I didn't know if it would help this time, but it was worth a shot, so I went to sit down. But before I could, I heard a knock at my bedroom door. I just rolled my eyes; I knew the quiet wouldn't last forever. "Who is it?" I waited a few moments, waiting for a reply, but it took a few minutes before I received one.

"Squirt, is it okay if I come in? I know that you wanted to be alone, but I really need to talk to you."

I knew that I needed to let him in, because I could hear it in his voice. "Come in." My brother walked in, and you could tell that he had been crying because his eyes were red and puffy. He refused to look at me.

"Squirt, is there a way that you can take me to see Mom? I really need some answers, and I don't want to wait." I just looked at him in shock, because not once had my brother expressed an interest in trying to go with me. I stepped closer to Zeus and picked his chin up with my hand.

"I don't know if I can, but, for you, I will try, because you need closure too." He finally looked at me, and I could see the tears begin to form in his eyes again. *I have never seen my brother like this before.* He looked so defeated. The man that had always protected me now looked like a small child. I knew I had to try for him. I didn't know if I could, because I had never tried to do it with anyone else before.

I hugged my brother to try and comfort him; I didn't know if it would help, but I felt that was the only thing I could do at the moment. "Zeus, I need you to understand that I can't promise that it works. But if it does, you have to hang onto me at all times, because I don't know what will happen if you let go." He just looked at me with those same tears in his eyes. I could tell he didn't care; he just wanted an answer to his questions. "Okay, well, I have to mind-link Genius because I don't want us to do this alone. I am pretty sure our bodies won't be able to defend ourselves while we're there." Zeus just nodded. "Genius, could you bring Alcide and Daniel to our room please? It is important." Zeus and I walked out onto the balcony to stare at the moon while we waited for them to get here. I didn't know where they were, but I knew they weren't close to my room. I could feel it.

After what seemed like hours, finally, Genius, Alcide, and Daniel walked into the room. At first, they just stood by the door till I and Zeus walked into the room. They all stared at me.

Genius was the first to speak, "Princess, what is wrong?" I just held my hand up to let him know to stop.

"I am going to try and take Zeus to see Mother, but I don't know if I will be able to, because I am not even sure how I am doing it. But, Genius, when I have done it, what happens to my body while I am doing it?"

He seemed concerned by the question. "Well, Princess, you look dead. That is why I try to be with you while you're doing it, because I don't want anything to happen to you, but you have a bad habit of doing it without me in the room. But I am glad you called us this time. That way, we can protect you guys while you're doing whatever it is you do."

That seemed to shock Alcide and Daniel because their mouths fell open. "What do you mean my niece looks dead when she does this?"

Genius turned toward my uncle. "What do you think it means? She goes pale, she barely breathes, her heart slows down; it's like she isn't alive, but she always returns just fine." That part seemed to concern Daniel a little bit because he scrunched his nose. "But if you look like that when you're doing this, why would you keep doing it? Doesn't it seem kind of risky?"

Before I could speak, Zeus looked up at everyone. "She does it because she has to. There are things that only our mother knows that can help us raise the pack in the future and to protect our family." I nodded in agreement with Zeus. *No use in trying to explain it better than that.*

"Okay, so this is the game plan. Zeus and I will go lay on the bed. You guys are to watch over us no matter what. Genius, if you notice anything different about me compared to when I have done this before, you are to immediately grab my hand and use our mate bond to help pull me back, and while you're doing that, I will use my bond with Zeus to pull him back with me."

You could tell that none of them were comfortable with what I just said, but none of them argued because they all knew it was useless. I turned toward my bed and walked to it with my brother right behind me. Once we were laying on the bed together, I turned toward Zeus.

"Are you sure that you want to do this? You don't have to go with me."

My brother just looked at me with such sorrow on his face. "Squirt, I have to or I will regret it." That was all I needed to hear before I knew this was something we had to do together.

"Okay, Zeus, I need you to relax. Close your eyes and clear your mind, focus on my touch, and I will do the rest, okay? If this is going to work, this is the only way that I can think it will work." So he followed my instruction and closed his eyes. I followed suit; it seemed like it wouldn't work. But just as I was about to stop, our mother's tree appeared. I looked beside me to see if Zeus was with me, and there he stood, looking around.

"Artemis, is this Mom's tree?" I just nodded, then I slowly started walking forward, holding Zeus's hand just like when I was little.

Something was different about this visit, something felt weird, like we were being watched. "Mom, it's Artemis. I brought Zeus with me." There was just silence; she didn't respond. Zeus turned toward me, and I just shook my head because I didn't know why she wasn't appearing. Suddenly, we started hearing voices. I had never heard voices there before other than my mother's, so that started to worry me. Zeus must have felt the same way because he tightened his grip on my hand.

"Squirt, what is going on?"

I just looked at him. "I honestly don't know; this has never happened." Which began to worry me more. Zeus and I looked around until we saw a dark figure walking toward us. They had a hood of some kind on, concealing their face; it wasn't my mother because she would never hide her face from us.

"Well, well, well. What do we have here? If it isn't Artemis and Zeus, I would say it is a pleasure to meet you, but I am sure you don't even know who I am."

I was so confused; who was this person and how did they know us? "Who are you, and what do you want?" The figure just let out this laugh that made my ears hurt. It was so menacing and deep, I started to grow concerned.

"I see that your mother left out a lot about her history and yours." Zeus and I looked at one another.

"I will ask you again. Who are you and what do you want?" Again, the figure just laughed; it was becoming alarmingly concerning.

"I would tell you, but that means you're going to leave this place alive, and I don't think that is part of the plan." Soon as that last word left the figure's mouth, it charged toward us, but before it reached us, out popped our mother from the dark.

"Stop right there. Leave my children alone now or you know what I will do to you. Back off."

The figure stopped and turned toward my mother and let out this most awful growl I had ever heard while backing into the dark. Who the hell was that and why were they trying to hurt Zeus and me? But I didn't have time to think about that that second; my mother had finally appeared.

She turned toward us. "I am sorry, but, Artemis, you shouldn't have come back, and you shouldn't have brought your brother along either. It is dangerous for you to keep coming here." I was immediately angry with her. *No, she never told me it was dangerous because she never told me anything.*

But before I could speak, Zeus started pulling me forward with him, making sure not to let go of my hand. He got right in front of my mother's face. "You lied to us our whole life, and you want to give us orders. We're not little kids anymore, and you have to right to speak to us that way." That seemed to shock my mother because she stepped back from Zeus and she looked a little worried.

"Zeus, what is wrong with you? Why are you so angry with me? You have never talked to me that way."

I tried to stop Zeus, but it was too late. "Why am I angry? Are you really asking me that when you know exactly why you lied to me my whole life? You're not my real mom." That seemed to make my mom worry a little bit because her facial expression changed completely.

"Zeus, who told you that?" By this time, my brother was crying all over again.

"Our uncle told us. He thought you had told us, but you didn't. You lied to me, and you lied to Artemis. How can you call yourself our mother but continuously lie to us about everything?" That seemed to hit a nerve with my mother because you could see the tears begin to form in her eyes.

As she began to speak, you could tell she was having a hard time trying to get out the right words, "Zeus, I never meant to lie to you, but in my eyes, you were my son. I never thought you needed to know because I had raised you your whole life." I could tell that Zeus was becoming angry because he started squeezing my hand harder and harder.

"You didn't think that it was important to inform me that you weren't my biological mother? You didn't think that telling me that Artemis and I had different mothers? You were so concerned about protecting her that you forgot to be honest with me and tell me the truth."

My mother just put her head down. You could see the tears hitting the grass. At this point, I finally stepped forward. "Mom, you have to understand why this hurt him so much. Not only did you lie to him, but he had to hear it from our uncle." She looked up at me with tears in her eyes. It broke my heart, seeing the two of them like this; they never fought or yelled at each other until now.

"I am so sorry, Zeus. I never meant to hurt you by keeping this from you. I honestly felt that you were my son, and I never thought how it would affect you hearing it from someone else."

Zeus just turned his head away from her. "Who is my biological mom, do you know?"

My mother just started crying more. "Zeus, I honestly never knew her. Your father never spoke of her. When I came into the picture, you were just a baby. I asked your father, but all he would say is she died giving birth to you." Zeus just became silent; he didn't ask anything else. The silence became deafening. I waited a moment to see if he would say something, but he never did. Which made what I was about to ask so much harder because I never told Zeus that I ran into someone in the forest that was claiming to be our father.

My mother went to turn away, but before she could, I said, "Mom, wait, I have to ask you something." She turned to face me; her eyes were red from crying.

"What is it, Artemis?" I looked down at my feet, not sure how to ask the question. They were both upset, and I knew that was going to make it worse. Zeus squeezed my hand.

"Well, when I went for a run in the forest today, I wasn't paying attention and ran past our barrier." Zeus turned toward me; I could tell he was concerned. *I guess Genius never told him that part.* "Well, when I stopped and I heard a noise, then a man appeared. He knew me, he asked about you, and he claimed to be our father." As soon as I finished, I looked up, and my mother's eyes were huge. I looked at Zeus, and his eyes were the same. I looked back to my mother.

"That cannot be, Artemis. Your father died when you were young."

I held my head up. "But, Mom, he knew you. He said there was a lot that you keep us in the dark about. He also said that your body is the only thing that can die."

I wanted to ask more, but my mom held her hand up. "Artemis, there is a lot I have hidden from you, but your father being dead wasn't one of the things I have lied about."

I was confused. "Can it be him though? Did you see his body before you left?" My mother put her head down.

I knew the answer before she spoke it, "No, I didn't, but I felt him die through our mark." I was trying to get her to elaborate, but she wouldn't. She just stopped with that sentence. I was becoming frustrated; what was she hiding?

"Is there a way to manipulate the mate mark to make one think that their mate is dead?"

My mom just started crying again. "Yes, there is, but I would have been able to tell the difference. It didn't feel like the mark was being manipulated."

Before I could speak again, her eyes became wide, like she just thought of something, but Zeus was the first to say something, "Mom, you just thought of something, what is it?"

She just stared at us for a moment, not speaking. She was just crying. The longer she stood there, the harder she cried. Then, she began to fade into the darkness. Zeus and I looked at one another, then looked back.

"MOM, WAIT, THERE IS MORE WE NEED TO ASK YOU." But she didn't respond. The next thing I knew, the darkness grew around us. We could no longer see our mother's tree; it was just darkness, then we heard the screaming. Zeus looked at me with this worried face.

"Artemis, what is going on?" I honestly didn't know. *This was new to me.* Normally when my mom disappeared, I just woke back up in my room.

"I don't know, Zeus. This has never happened before." I was becoming worried because I didn't have an answer, but before I could speak again, I woke up in my room, with Genius standing over me, shaking me and yelling. I sat up, quickly turning toward Zeus; he was sitting on the edge of the bed, shaking and crying. I went to touch his shoulder, but he got up and ran out of the room.

I went to get up and chase after him, but Genius wouldn't allow me to get up. He turned toward Alcide and Daniel. They must have known what he wanted them to do, because they immediately ran out of the room after Zeus. I turned back to Genius. I was about to ask him what happened, but I collapsed.

# The Plan

I woke up later the next day. I had woken up to find Genius laying next to me, squeezing me. I couldn't help but smile; my mate was so concerned for me. But I couldn't remember much of what happened after we left the spirit realm. Wait a minute. I can't remember if Zeus made it out with me. I started shaking Genius. He looked at me, then sat straight up.

"Princess, what is wrong?"

I started to cry. "Did Zeus make it back with me?"

Genius seemed to take a deep breath. "Yes, he did. He is okay. But what happened, Princess?"

I just shook my head. "I can't remember anything after everything went dark." I could tell that my mate was concerned. "I am fine now; don't look so worried." He just shook his head.

"You don't understand, Princess. Your heart stopped beating for a moment. We were all worried that we were going to lose you, but then you came out, then collapsed. We need to know what happens in there."

I just smiled. "Genius, you are so cute when you're concerned." I had just realized we hadn't been alone a lot lately with everything going on. What was going on with me? I know we needed to figure out what happened, but all I wanted was Genius inside of me.

I slowly started kissing my mate's neck until I reached our mark. Once I got to the mark, I immediately bit him as hard as I could, drawing blood.

He moaned, "Princess, what has gotten into you? We have more important stuff to do right now." I just ignored him. I slowly pushed him back so that he was laying on his back before I started to kiss my way down. His penis was harder than I had seen it in a while. I slowly slid him inside of my mouth until I couldn't go any further. Genius moaned which just sent me into some sort of frenzy. I started going up and down, sliding his member in and out of my mouth, but before he could even reach his climax, I climbed on top of him. I slid him inside my hot, wet vagina. I immediately moaned; it felt so good to have him inside of me. But I couldn't think for long before Genius rolled me over till I was on all fours which just made me start dripping more. Genius thrusted inside of me with such force, all I could do was scream out his name. He slammed all the way into me until he couldn't go in any further, then he would slowly slide out, causing me to throw my head back, moaning. My wolf couldn't hold in her excitement anymore; she started growling. Genius's wolf growled back in return. Genius's penis seemed to grow even larger inside of me. I yelled out but not in pain; it felt absolutely amazing to have him inside of me.

Genius grabbed my hair and started slamming inside of me faster and faster until I reached my climax. Just as I started to release, I could feel him release inside of me, which made me cum so hard, I started crying. *Sex with Genius has always been amazing, but today was on a whole different level.* We both fell back on the bed. I just smiled at Genius.

"Well, Princess, I think I figured out why you are so excited out of nowhere."

I just looked at him. "What do you mean?"

Genius just laughed. "Babe, do you realized what month it is?" I still didn't understand what he was talking about; he just looked at me, shocked.

"OMG, Princess, I forgot your mom never told you."

"What are you talking about, Genius?"

He just started laughing uncontrollably. "Princess, you're in heat. After you shift for the first time, shortly after, the female goes in heat which makes them want to have sex uncontrollably."

Well, in a way, that made sense because there was no rhyme or reason for me to be this fucking horny out of nowhere. "Well, we have another issue then, because our wolves want to play too and I don't know how we can do that with everything going on?"

He just smiled at me. "You do realize that if you're in heat, that means that every she-wolf here is in heat right, which means we will have a fertility ritual." Now I was very confused. I had never heard of that before. "Well, wait. Does that mean to try for a baby thing?" Genius just stood up and started walking to the bathroom. *God, I loved the way his ass looked while he walked.* He must have noticed me looking, because he smiled.

"We will finish this conversation later. Would you like to join me in the shower? That way, we can call a meeting and come up with a plan of action for everything." I didn't even respond; I just got up and went into the bathroom. Now it was his turn to watch me.

Genius just licked his lips while he watched me get into the shower, after I got the water running. I guess this meant that there was going to be round two. My guess was right, because Genius slammed me against the shower wall, picking me up so my vagina was right by his mouth. I knew what he wanted to do which made me get wet instantly. The next thing I knew, he licked me right between my lip until he reached the spot he was going for. Once he hit my clitoris, I lost all sense of reality. I started moaning and screaming his name. At one point, I tried to climb away, but Genius just held my thighs harder. I started grinding up and down; I started screaming again, "I'm coming, I'm coming." But Genius just swallowed all of me before lowering me down, but not where I could touch the floor. He lowered me down just to where his penis was; at the entrance of my vagina. Then he just smiled, slamming inside of me. He threw his head back, letting this howl out that I had never heard before.

He started slamming inside of me harder and harder, and just as he was about to release, he bit me right on my mark, causing me to instantly cum again, screaming his name. I felt him fill me up completely this time. Once he finished, he smiled and kissed me before putting me down.

"All right, Princess, that should hold you over for a little bit. Let's wash up so that we can call a meeting." I just smiled, but I couldn't move quite yet; my legs were still shaking. Once he noticed, he just smiled even harder.

"I told you I was holding back before." But what he didn't know was so was I, but he would figure that out later. I was finally able to stand without shaking and washed my hair and body before getting out. Once I was out, I wrapped the towel around me. I mind-linked the boys, "Meet us in the office in ten minutes." Then I headed to the bedroom. Genius already had an outfit out for me; it was this beautiful red dress. I just smiled; he always knew what I liked to wear. I got my dress on with the heels that he had out too. Genius walked out the bathroom, fully dressed. He leaned against the door, just smiling at me. "Princess, you look beautiful."

I just smiled. "All right, Sexy, we need to get downstairs before were not able to leave the room for the whole day." He just laughed, but we walked out hand in hand. We reached the bottom of the stairs when I realized the whole downstairs was empty.

Genius just chuckled. "See, I told you the girls are in heat. We probably won't see much of anyone for a while, but that also means that Daniel and Zeus's mates are going to be moody if we keep their mates away for too long." Genius was right about that; I would be pissed if the situation was reversed, so I grabbed Genius's hand and ran into the office.

When we entered, the boys were all sitting on the couch in my office with their hands crossed over their chests. Daniel was the first to speak, "You know, you guys are not quiet at all; the whole house heard you."

I just laughed. "Sorry, I couldn't exactly help it, but I bet your mate wasn't quiet either with all of us females being in heat at the same time." They all turned toward me with shock on their faces, like they weren't expecting me to know that or something. Honestly, I wouldn't have known if Genius didn't tell me. "Okay, quit staring at me like I am weird or something."

I turned toward Zeus. "Are you okay? Do you remember what happened after we talked to Mom in the spirit world?"

He just turned toward me. "The last thing I remember is we were surrounded by darkness, then we woke up." I just shook my head. How could neither of us remember what happened? Well, I would have to figure that out later; we needed to make a plan.

I held my head high before speaking, "Okay, so I haven't told Daniel and Alcide what happened on my run." They both turned toward me. "When I went for the run yesterday, a man jumped out from behind a tree. He claimed to be my father." They were both shocked which would be expected.

Alcide turned toward Zeus and Genius. "Is what she says the truth?" They both nodded in agreement. "But it can't be. Your mother said he was dead."

Zeus and I just looked at one another before I spoke, "That is the thing. When I brought it up to our mom, she was so sure about him being dead until I asked if there was a way to manipulate the mate mark to make her think he was dead. She just started crying, then faded into the dark."

Alcide's eyes were wide. "What do you mean?"

I didn't know how to explain it, so I turned toward Zeus, so he spoke up, "When Artemis asked her that, she thought of something, but she faded into the dark before we could ask her any more questions. She was hiding something from us."

I turned toward my uncle. "Do you know of anything that could make someone think that their mate is dead when they're not?" My uncle didn't respond for a few minutes; you could tell he was thinking.

"I have never heard of anything, but, then again, your mother hide things from me too. Well, I don't know what else I could have expected; we would have to figure this out later."

"Okay, well, we will come back to this later, but we need to figure a way to get into the castle. We have to figure out who is controlling the Quils, maybe then we can get some more answers." I turned toward Alcide. "I know you have been in the castle before, so I need you to find a blueprint or draw some up that would allow us to go into the castle undetected." He nodded. "Alcide, you need to find James and talk to him. He knows where the Quils go in at."

After I said that, he left the room. I turned toward Zeus and Daniel. "I need you two to do research. See if you can find any information on if there is a way for the mate mark to be manipulated." They both nodded, then turned to leave the room. "Wait, before you leave, let everyone know that tonight is the fertility ritual, so everyone needs to be present."

Zeus just looked shocked. "Squirt, do you think that it is a good idea with everything going on?"

I just looked at him, confused. "Zeus, right now is the perfect time. With everything going on, the pack needs to know that we are still one. We can't have anyone second-guessing us as their leaders." He didn't question me any further; he just left the room.

I turned toward Genius. "Now, I need your help. We need to find someone that knows more about being an enchantress. I am going to need more training both with my magic and with my wolf side."

Genius just walked up to me and wrapped his arms around me. "We will find someone to help, but the wolf training, I can help you with that, and so can the pack."

I just kissed him. "Yes, I know, but now I need you to sit down and tell me about this fertility ritual we have to do tonight." He just laughed, but we both sat down.

"Princess, the fertility ritual is one of the most sacred things a pack can share with one another." I just shook my head so he knew I wanted him to continue. "On the night of the ritual, the alpha and his luna are to have sex, surrounded by their pack, then the pack follows suit." That shocked me.

"Wait what?"

He held his hand up. "But it is not just in our human form; we have to do it in our wolf forms as well as the pack too." Now, I was nervous as hell. I never had sex in front of anyone before. Hell, Genius was my first, but I knew we had to for the pack. "Okay, well, if we have to do it, we will. I just need to know that nobody will judge me for this." He started laughing. He was laughing so hard, he fell out of the chair. When he finally stopped, he sat up and looked at me.

"Princess, do you honestly think anyone will care? We see each other naked anytime we shift as a pack."

Well, that was true. "Okay, so I need you to get everything ready for the ritual tonight. I know nothing about how it is to be prepared, so can you do this for me please?" He stood up and kissed me on my forehead before leaving the office. *Now, I just need to convince myself that I can do it.* I just wanted to meditate and relax until tonight. *So that is exactly what will happen until then. The next time I will leave this office will be for the fertility ritual tonight.*

# Fertility Ritual

As nighttime approached, I became increasingly nervous. *I don't know if I can do this. How can I have sex not only in my human form but in my wolf form in front of everyone? I don't know how I am going to make it through tonight. I am way too self-conscious about this.* So I closed my eyes, trying to relax, catch my breath, but just as I was starting to completely relax, I found myself drifting further and further into the darkness that was surrounding me. *No, no, no, I can't drift into the spirit world alone until I know what happen the last time.* But there was no stopping it. I drifted further and further into the dark till there was a white light. I walked closer to the light. Once my eyes had adjusted, I noticed that there were a group of wolves sitting there, looking at me. *I don't know who they are; could they be part of our pack.* "Who are you? Why am I here?"

Nobody answered at first, but then the black wolf with the crystal-blue eyes was the one to step forward.

That is when I heard a woman's voice in my head: "Hello, Artemis, it is finally good to see you, dear." I was slightly concerned because I didn't know this wolf.

"Who are you?" Her wolf seemed to smile.

"Sweetheart, we are your ancestors. We felt your concern about the fertility ritual tonight, so we felt that it would be best to bring you here to try and quiet your fear." Wait how did they know that I was uneasy about the ritual?

"How did you know that I was uneasy about the ritual tonight?"

The wolf just shook its head back and forth. "My, my, someone doesn't know a lot about her history, does she?" I lowered my head to look at the floor. That is when the smaller wolf with red fur and pink eyes stepped forward.

The next voice I heard was deep; that little wolf was a man. I would have never guessed. "Please, tell me you know of your history as a wolf?"

I just kept looking at my feet. "Well, I didn't find out till recently that I was even part wolf. My mother hid it from me and I didn't find out until after she passed." The black wolf shifted back to her human form; she was beautiful. She had long, black, wavy hair and her eyes were stunning. They were as blue as the ocean when the sun hit it. She placed her hand on my shoulder.

"My dear child, you have no idea of your past. We will talk more about that later, but for now, let us discuss the fertility ritual tonight." I nodded in agreement. I couldn't speak; I was speechless.

After she shifted, she took a step back. "Well, Artemis, the fertility ritual is an important part of any pack, but with ours it is essential, because not only does it strengthen the pack, it allows our pack to grow by creating offspring." I knew that it most likely meant that pregnancy chances were higher, but I was still unsure if I was ready to have a pup yet.

"But what if I haven't decided that I was ready to have a pup yet?" The red-haired wolf was the next to shift. He was this short, stocky man; he had red hair with the pink eyes to match, just like his wolf.

"Artemis, it is essential that all pack members rear a pup, but at the same time, not all she-wolves will become pregnant on this night."

I was confused. "But how? If all she-wolves participate in it, wouldn't we all fall pregnant during the ritual?"

The lady just chuckled. "No, sweet girl, the moon goddess is the one that makes that decision during the ritual. If you fall pregnant outside of the ritual, then it was your body's way of saying that its time." Why was this whole thing so confusing? She must have seen my face. "During the fertility ritual, the moon goddess selects who will bear the first pups of the season. This prevents all she-wolves from becoming pregnant at the same time. As you could imagine, having a whole bunch of pups around the same time could be dangerous, because that is fewer people to help protect you and the pregnant she-wolves."

Okay, that made a little more sense; the male stepped forward. "It also brings the pack closer together because we are bonding through more than just a pack. We are bonding through intimacy. Your job as alpha is to show the pack that you're willing to open yourself up to them, not just as their leader but to show them the most intimate and sensitive part of you." I was slowly understanding why it was so important for the pack, but I was still so insecure with myself that I didn't know if I could do it. But there was still one wolf that

103

had not spoken that kept staring at me. This wolf had straight, black fur with a hint of blue to it, and red eyes. It was actually kind of scary; this wolf finally stepped forward.

"Why are you still so unsure of yourself?" This took me by surprise. His voice was so deep but so sexy, I could linger on his voice forever. I just stood, frozen. That is when he shifted. This man stood at least six feet tall, and he was solid muscle. He stood in front of me, naked; he was built, and I couldn't keep my eyes off of him.

"Artemis, look at me when I speak to you. You have no reason to be shy about your body or the fact that you will sleep with your mate in front of others." All three of them stepped forward completely naked and in unison. "Artemis, strip down in front of us now."

That caught my attention. "Um, why do I need to do that?"

They just shook their heads. "We are your ancestors, and the only way for you to get over this fear is to stand naked in front of us." I didn't want to anger them because I knew that it could have bad consequences, so I complied. I stood there completely naked which wasn't the issue I was having. I had never had sex in front of anyone before.

"I don't have a problem standing naked in front of my pack. I am feeling self-conscious about having sex in front of them. What if they judge me or don't like how I have sex with my mate?"

The woman stepped forward, placing her hand on my stomach and stepping behind me. She whispered in my ear, "The key is to not think of who is watching, but focus on your mate, his scent, his sex, what he is doing to you, allow him to consume you, and the rest will not matter." My heart started beating rapidly. *Why did I feel this way when she was touching me? Was she doing this on purpose?* The next thing I knew, she was kissing my neck right where Genius had marked me. That set a fire inside of me and warmed all the way through my pussy; I was throbbing not only there, but my nipples were hard as rocks. I closed my eyes, trying to calm myself down, but when I opened them, I was leaving the light.

All three ancestors spoke at the same time, "Now, Artemis, I think you're ready. Go to your mate and complete the ritual." When I opened my eyes, I was back inside my office. My pussy and my breasts were still on fire. *I need Genius now.*

When I looked outside, the moon was high and I knew that it was time for the ritual to happen. I turned to walk toward the door. When I opened it, Genius was waiting for me at the door. "Well, Princess, everything is ready. Are you sure you want to do this?"

I just shook my head. "Lead the way, Babe." Genius grabbed my hand, which just made me wetter. What was happening? Genius led me outside where the whole pack turned to stare at us. It was absolutely beautiful; the moon was shining down on a small section that had roses all around it. I turned toward Genius. "Are the roses part of the ritual?"

He just smiled. "No, I did that especially for you. Are you ready to bring our pack closer together?" I just nodded and allowed him to lead me to the pile of roses that he had laid out for us. Once we reached the pile, I turned toward our pack.

"I want to thank everyone for being patient. I realize I am slightly late, but, tonight, we will do our first fertility ritual of the season. I will be honest. At first, I didn't think that I could do this, but, no, I am surer than ever that I can. Tonight, we shall be one."

As soon as I finished my speech, Genius slowly started kissing on my neck as he unzipped the back of my dress, allowing it to fall to the ground. He slowly kissed his way down to my breast, slowly sucking and nibbling on them before working his way further down. He was slowly lowering me down to the ground on top of the rose petals. He kissed his way down till just before my clit. Then, he looked up at me before slowly licking at my clit. He started sucking, nibbling, and licking until I was completely soaked. Once he realized how ready I was for him, he climbed on top of me, sliding his member inside of me. My eyes instantly rolled back in ecstasy; he was so large, but it felt amazing. He would slide out of me, then slam right back into me, sending a ripple of pleasure through my body. I looked around and the pack had followed suit. I turned my focus back toward my mate. He slid his hand behind my back and lifted my hips up, then he started slamming into me harder and faster.

I was screaming his name by the time I had to release my orgasm; we both climaxed at the same time. Genius laid his head down on my chest before looking at me. "Now, it's our wolves' turn, and mine will not hold out any longer." I just smiled at him because, little did he know, my wolf was riding on my orgasm the whole time. I shifted right underneath him, allowing Violet to come out. Genius followed suit, allowing his wolf out, and they wasted no time. Violet had turned so her ass was facing her mate. Once he mounted us, he bit our neck, which seemed to turn Violet on more. He was sliding in and out of us continuously. I could feel every part of him entering Violet, and it felt more amazing than I could have imagined. Finally, I could feel him release inside of us. We stayed stuck for a moment before he was got off of us. I turned toward the pack and lifted my head to the moon and howled. Everyone followed suit; the ritual was over. I shifted back into my human form, and so did Genius. He walked up to me, grabbed my hand, and just kissed me.

"Princess, I love you. I am happy that you chose to do this because now the pack will look more toward you not as only a leader but as their hero." I didn't want to talk with anyone tonight; I was exhausted. It seemed everyone had the same idea because everyone started walking away. Genius carried me to the room and laid me on the bed, then he crawled in behind me, wrapping his big arms around me.

"Goodnight, Princess, get some rest. We have a lot to do tomorrow."

# Panic

I woke up the next morning. I went to roll over to cuddle up with Genius, but he was not there. Where could he have gone at this time? We didn't have any training this morning. I was hoping to speak with him a little more, but it will have to wait a while longer. I got out of the bed and went into the bathroom. I turned the shower on as hot as I could. The bathroom was very steamy before I got in the shower; a nice, hot shower is what I needed after last night. I still can't believe that I went through with it, but that lady was right. Once I focused on Genius, nothing else seemed to matter. I started getting wet just thinking about it. Where could he have gone to? I wanted to fuck the hell out of him and he was nowhere to be found. So I got out the shower, wrapped a towel around me, and went into the bedroom. I opened my closet to find something to wear. I wanted to torment Genius since he wasn't there when I woke up. I knew just the thing. I put on these tight jeans with these nice, thigh-high heels, then I put on a crop top showing the top part of my body. He was going to regret leaving me in this bed by myself this morning.

Once I finished getting ready, I went down to the kitchen to grab something to eat. The house was oddly quiet this morning. Maybe everyone was exhausted from the ritual last night; I wouldn't blame them. I made a bowl of coco puffs; *mmm, this tasted amazing*. Once I was finished, I went to the office. I needed to start researching more about enchantresses. Once I got into the office, I went to the side with all the books to see if there was any about enchantresses on the shelf, but surprise, surprise. Nothing there. I went and sat down at my desk, opening my laptop. I would have to hope that maybe the internet had the information today. I went on the internet and typed in 'ancient enchantresses' information,' but still nothing popped up. I shouldn't have expected anything less. They're an old race, of course. We don't have anything on them. But if I could get to that castle, I know the information I would need would be there, but I can't go there without a plan.

I sat back down, frustrated because I had no idea where to look for more information, and the only way I was going to learn more was by studying upon them. Which I couldn't do because there was no information. I had sat there for a moment, just then realizing I had not heard from any of the boys today, which began to frighten me because normally they checked in with me by then.

So I decided it was time to use our mind-linking: "Daniel, Zeus, Alcide, Genius, where are you guys? I haven't heard from you all morning." I waited for a few minutes, but I still wasn't hearing back from them. No, this was not okay, so I got a hold of James. "James, have you seen any of the boys this morning? They aren't responding, and I haven't seen them."

It only took a few seconds for him to respond, "No, Queen, I haven't. Could they still be sleeping?"

I shook my head. "Well, I know Genius was gone before I woke up, but the other ones, I don't know. Could you check and then come tell me in the office please?"

What the hell was going on? None of them have ever done anything like this before. Usually one of them is around just in case I need them, but it seems none of them are here. I started pacing back and forth, waiting on James to come to the office. I seemed to be pacing for hours when I heard a knock on the door. "Come in."

James walked in. "Queen, I went and checked their rooms, but none of them seem to be in their rooms. What do you want me to do?" Now I was becoming panicked.

"James, go find Daniel and Zeus's mate and see if they know where they are. I am gonna see if I can find a way to use my mark to sense Genius." James didn't say anything else; he just turned and walked out of the room. I had no clue if I could use our mate mark for sensing, but I damn sure was going to try. Why would Genius take off without letting me know?

I sat down on the floor, crossing my legs. I closed my eyes, trying to find our connection. But I wasn't sure if I could do it and, if I could, I didn't know how. That's when I heard a voice in my head, "Just focus on your bond, the rest will flow on its own." Who the hell was that? I couldn't figure that out now; I had to find Genius. I just sat there trying and trying, but I wasn't having any luck. I opened my eyes and stood up. I turned and punched a hole in the wall behind me. This was beginning to frustrate me and worry me, and I didn't like it. I turned toward the clock. *It has been six hours and I still haven't heard anything from them. Fuck this.* I went to turn toward the door to walk out, but that's when I heard a knock. *Please, Moon Goddess, let it be one of them.*

"Come in!" Alcide was the one to walk in. He turned toward the wall. "Artemis, what happened, are you okay?"

I just started bawling my eyes out. Alcide ran to me and hugged me. "Artemis, what happened?"

I can't find the boys, you took off. I tried to get a hold of you guys, and nobody is responding. I still haven't heard from Genius, Daniel, and Zeus. What if they are in trouble?"

Alcide just hugged me. "It will be okay. I am sure they are fine. I am sorry that I didn't respond. I was busy with research, like you asked me to." I couldn't help but giggle. I should have known that was what he was doing. *He never responds to me when he is studying, just like when I was younger.* But the other three, they would have never left without telling me. They know me too well for that.

"I should have known that you always do that when you're studying, but what about the other three? Have you heard anything, did they come to you?" I just stared at him; I needed answers.

"Artemis, I honestly don't know. I haven't seen them since last night." I couldn't take this anymore; I had to do something. I shoved Alcide out the way and took off on a dead run to the backyard. I started shifting immediately, not caring about my clothes.

I heard Alcide hollering at me that it wasn't safe for me out there at night, but I didn't care. I needed to find them. Something had to happen for them not to answer. I started running through the forest. I would stop every so often to see if I could pick up their scents. But I couldn't find them, but I did find a scent that was slightly familiar. I howled, letting the man claiming to be my father know that I knew he was there, but he wouldn't show himself. Why wasn't he showing himself tonight? I didn't care, I needed to find them. I closed my eyes, trying to sense Genius, but I still couldn't pick up on anything. I let out a howl, maybe they could hear me this way if nothing else. I heard a howl back, but it wasn't their howl; it was Alcide. He must have shifted after I ran off, but I didn't care. I heard the leaves rustle behind me, so I turned to find a large, gray wolf clicking its teeth at me and growling. I held my head high, letting the most ferocious growl out that I could to let this wolf know who exactly I was. But this wolf was either stupid or didn't know who I was, because he charged at me. I stood on my hind legs, swatting him to the ground. He just got up again and tried the same thing. This time, when he charged in, I was able to grab his neck with my teeth. I tasted the metallic taste of blood.

The wolf started growling harder, so I released. Now it was time to let my Alpha shine. I towered over him, sending the alpha vibe to him. But this damn wolf just wouldn't submit, so I shifted back to my human form, standing there naked as could be. The wolf just stared at me; he didn't move, didn't growl, just stared at me, then took off. What the hell was that about? So I shifted once more, trying to follow the blood smell, but I only tracked it so far, then it just disappeared. By this time, Alcide had got up with me.

"Artemis, we need to get back to the house. What if they show up and you're not there, then they will freak out." He was right and I knew it, so we started racing back to the pack house. When we reached the backyard, I looked up to see Daniel and Zeus looking around. *O, thank the moon goddess.* I shifted as soon as I reached the patio. I didn't care that I was naked. I ran straight in the house and up to my office. I ran right up to them both and hugged them.

"Squirt, why are you naked?"

Did he really just ask me that? After being gone all day and not responding, that was his first question? I released them both from the hug, then I punched both of them in the face as hard as I could. They landed on the asses and started bleeding immediately from their noses. They looked up at me with shock on their faces. I turned around and grabbed the robe that was hanging up. I put it on, then turned back toward them. "You have been gone all day, with no response, and the first thing you do is ask me why I am naked? How about a reason for where you have been all day?" I was pissed off. I went to charge at them again when they didn't respond, but Alcide grabbed me.

"Artemis, I know you're angry, but give them time to stand and speak please." I just stood there and crossed my arms.

"Well, do you two want to explain, or am I gonna have to bounce you around the office?"

Zeus stepped forward. "Squirt, I am sorry. I didn't mean to scare you, but we were really busy today on patrol." Really, is that his excuse? But before I said anything, I turned toward Daniel.

"Well, is that true?"

Daniel looked at Zeus. "I am sorry, Bro, but I am not getting my ass kicked." He stepped closer toward me. "No, that isn't true. We went to

Scotland to get a closer look at the castle." He couldn't have just said what I thought he said.

"YOU DID WHAT? HOW STUPID ARE YOU TWO? I TOLD YOU TO WAIT FOR ALCIDE TO GET THE DAMN BLUEPRINTS, AND YOU GO BEHIND MY BACK?" Both the boys dropped down to one knee, grabbing their head, and I knew what it was, but I didn't care; I was their queen and sister, they have pissed me off.

"GET OUT OF MY FUCKING OFFICE. I DON'T WANT TO SEE YOU THE REST OF THE NIGHT, AND DON'T LEAVE THE GROUND UNTIL FURTHER NOTICE. THAT'S AN ORDER." The queen's orders could be painful, and I could tell it was because they started crawling out of the office.

I turned toward Alcide; he was just staring at me with large eyes. "WHAT?"

He started stuttering, "Artteemmiiss, yooooouuuurrr eeeyyyyeeesss."

I didn't care about that. "I DON'T CARE. GO FIND GENIUS NOW OR EVERYONE WILL NOT LIKE WHAT HAPPENS NEXT. I SUGGEST YOU ASK THE TWO DUMBASSES DOWNSTAIRS." Alcide didn't say anything else. He couldn't; I gave him a direct order. I knew I shouldn't be angry with him, but at this point, my anger was reaching a new height. I started pacing back and forth. I needed Genius. I couldn't calm myself down this time, but I was angry with him, so I didn't know if it was a good idea for him to see me either. I paced and paced when I heard a knock on the door.

"WHAT?" Alcide came in slowly.

"Artemis, the boys said he went to Scotland too and would be back in a few minutes." O, that was the last straw.

"HE DID WHATTTTT? WHAT THE FUCK IS WRONG WITH EVERYONE? DO YOU NOT KNOW HOW TO FUCKING LISTEN WHEN I GIVE AN ORDER?" I heard howls coming from downstairs and Alcide hit the floor, and I didn't care. None of them listened to me. I kept pacing for a few minutes and that is when my door flung open and in walked Genius, but he stopped as soon as he saw my eyes.

"Princess, I need you to calm down. Let me explain please." Let him explain, really, like there was a good explanation for this.

"REALLY? YOU LIED TO ME, IGNORED ME, WENT AGAINST MY DIRECT ORDERS THAT YOU AGREED TO, AND YOU WANT ME TO

CALM DOWN?" Genius grabbed his head, but he didn't drop; he was alpha now, so I figured it wouldn't affect him as badly as the others.

"Princess, please calm down. You are hurting us."

I started laughing. "YOU WANT ME TO STOP BECAUSE YOU GUYS ARE HURTING. WELL, GUESS WHAT, I COULDN'T GIVE A FUCK LESS. I HAVE BEEN SEARCHING FOR YOU GUYS ALL FUCKING DAY. I MIND-LINKED YOU AND NONE OF YOU FUCKING ANSWERED ME, BUT YOU WANT ME TO CALM DOWN." I was yelling so much, I hadn't noticed that he moved closer to me. I knew what he was about to do, but I didn't want him touching me right now. But, unfortunately, I didn't get that option, because as soon as his hand touched me, I felt our bond reaching out, trying to help calm me. I felt his wolf trying to calm Violet too. *God damn him, why did he do that?* "Genius, I really don't want you touching me right now."

I could see that it hurt his feeling, but he didn't move. The longer he touched me, the calmer I became. With the calmness came the tears. I just broke down, crying. I dropped to the floor, bawling my eyes out, and Genius just held me.

"Princess, I am so sorry. I never meant to cause you to panic." I just didn't want to hear it tonight. I pushed him away and walked out the room. I went to my room, closed the door, and sat in front of it. *I can't believe that none of them listened to me. Do they have that little respect for my words?* I just kept crying until I slowly drifted to sleep.

# Talk

I had woken to the sun being in my face the next morning. I was still sitting in front of the door. I stood up and walked to the bathroom. I needed a bath after everything that happened last night. *How could they make me worry like that? Why would they not listen to me? Did none of them think I could do this? Did they think I wasn't strong enough to handle the pack and responsibilities?* Once I had the tub completely filled with water, I slowly slid in, resting my head on the back of the tub. I heard a small knock on the door. "Who is it?" I couldn't hear anything at first.

"Artemis, it is Dream. Can I come in?" Of course, my brother's mate would come.

"Come in, Dream." She slowly opened the door. Dream was beautiful. She had long, blonde hair with pink eyes. I could see why my brother loved her so much aside from being mates. I just turned my head toward her. "Let me guess, the boys sent you in here to see if I was still angry?"

She picked her head up, looking me in my eyes. "Honestly, no. I came up here to see if you were still angry. All the boys are still upset about everything that happened. I just thought you would need family to talk to that wasn't the boys." I just looked up at her with tears in my eyes.

"Dream, they didn't listen to me, they didn't answer me, and all that shows me is that they believe I am not ready to handle this. Maybe I am not. This was all just thrown on me. I never knew this life before, but now that I know it, all I want to do is protect them." Dream walked closer to the tub and kneeled down beside it, wiping my tears away with her hand.

"Artemis, I don't think that they meant to do this to hurt you or because they think you're not ready but to help protect you." I knew that was partly true, but none of them seemed to think what would have happened if I lost them.

"Dream, that may be true, but did any of them stop to think what would happen to me if I lost any of them?" Again, she lowered her head. I felt bad. I wasn't trying to upset her, but then she looked up with a smile.

"Well, why don't you tell them that and let them explain before you go all queen she-wolf on them again?"

I let out this loud laugh. She really thought I went she-wolf on them. "Thank you, Dream. I needed that laugh, but go ahead and head downstairs. Let the boys know to meet me in the office in ten minutes and tell them not to be late." She stood up and started walking toward the door before turning back to me.

"Sis, I don't think you will have to worry about them being late ever again." Then, she turned and opened the door, closing it behind her. I was grateful that she treated me like her little sister, especially with everything going on. It was nice to have someone that listened to me and didn't judge me for my thoughts or emotions. I soaked in the tub a little longer before getting out and wrapping a towel around me. I walked into my room and over to my closet. I grabbed a pair of blue jeans and a t-shirt with my steel-toe boots. I just didn't feel like getting all dressed up today, not after yesterday. I turned to look at myself in the mirror. You could tell I had been crying; my eyes were red and puffy. But I didn't care right now. I was still upset by everything that had happened last night.

I walked out my room and down the stairs, passing some members of the pack. When they saw me, they all knelt down to one knee. I guess they were scared from everything that happened last night, and I couldn't blame them either. I walked past the kitchen. I wasn't really hungry either. I walked to my office and stopped in front of the door. Taking a deep breath before I walked in there, *I hope they don't hate me after last night.*

I opened the door. I walked in, closing it behind me. When I turned around, I saw them all sitting there with their heads down. Obviously, they were still upset too. I walked to my desk and sat down on top of it. Genius was the first to raise his head. He went to speak, but I held my hand up. I could see the hurt in his eyes, it was killing me. But they all needed to know what they did was wrong on many different levels. I looked at Zeus, Daniel, Alcide, and Genius. They all looked like they didn't get any sleep.

"Do you guys understand how worried you had me yesterday? None of you told me anything, none of you answered me, and none of you listened. Do you know how it feels to have four people who I love not listen? It makes me feel like you don't trust me or think that I can run this pack." Tears started welling up in my eyes again, but I refused to cry in front of them right now. They needed to know that they were wrong, not me.

Zeus stood up and came closer to me. "Squirt, I am sorry that we didn't inform you what was going on, and that we ignored you."

Daniel stood up behind Zeus. "Artemis, we never meant to make you worry. That wasn't our intention."

Alcide just stayed seated. "I should have kept better track of all of them."

Then I turned toward my mate who walked till our faces were touching. "Princess, don't blame them. I am the one that asked them to come with me. I just wanted to see the castle and see if we could find a way in without the blueprint, but none of us thought about how you would feel or your opinion about it either." I just scooted further back on the desk so that I could see his eyes better.

"Genius, the fact is you lied to me, you ignored me, and, worst of all, you brought Daniel and Zeus in on this instead of just coming to me and talking. But none of you took the time to stop and think what would happen to me if I lost any of you.

"We all agreed to wait for Alcide to find the blueprint or a way into the castle, but none of you cared to listen." I hung my head. I wasn't sure whether to get angry or cry. I decided that I couldn't do either at the moment. "But putting that aside, what did you find?"

They all turned toward each other before turning back toward me. "Well, we found a way in, but it is heavily guarded, and unless we have some advantage or another way in, we can't go in that way without risking lives."

I turned toward Alcide. "Have you found any blueprints, or have you remembered a secret way into the castle yet?" Alcide just hung his head and I knew that answer before he even spoke.

"Artemis, I can't recall the time at the castle, and the castle is so old, I don't know if there are any blueprints for it." I just let out a deep breath. I turned toward Genius.

"Well, did you even do what I asked and try and locate another enchantress that could help train me?" His eyes became wide.

"Fuck, Princess, no, I forgot all about that. I am so sorry." I just shook my head. How the hell were we supposed to breach the castle when nobody would listen to me?

I just sat there in silence for a minute before speaking, "Okay, well, this is how this is going to go. None of you are to go to that castle again until we have a better plan. Next, Daniel, Zeus, and Genius, please try to locate an enchantress if you can, as well as see if there is a way the mate bond can be manipulated. I have to train with this power I have or I won't be able to control it."

Then I turned toward Alcide. "Since you can't remember the secret path to get into the castle, I guess we will have to try and unravel your memories together."

They all turned toward me with worry on their faces, but Genius was the first to speak, "What do you mean you guys are going to have to unravel it together?" I just shook my head. Surely, they knew by now that I could do stuff others couldn't.

"Exactly what I said. You guys know I can do stuff that others can't. While I am not one-hundred percent sure that I can, this is our only chance for me to try entering his memories."

I waited for someone to say something, and, again, Genius spoke while the others sat in silence, "Okay, Princess, we all agree to the terms that you have set. When do you want to do the memory thing with Alcide?" I thought for a moment. My powers were stronger during a full moon and a red moon, but a red moon wouldn't happen again for a little bit.

I turned toward Daniel because he was always the moon nut. "Daniel, when is the next full moon supposed to happen?"

He just turned toward me and smiled. "Tomorrow night will be our next full moon, why?"

I couldn't help but laugh at him. He was such a dork when it came to stars, moons, and stuff like that. "Okay, well, tomorrow night, we will do the memory thing for Alcide. Until then, everyone just relax and do as much research on enchantresses as possible, please." Daniel, Zeus, and Alcide all got up and left the room. I kind of expect Genius to go too, but he did not. Instead, he sat down in the chair. Genius looked up at me with such sadness in his eyes.

"Princess, I really am sorry. I never meant to cause you to panic, and I didn't do it because I thought you couldn't take care of our pack." I looked down at my feet.

"Then why, Genius? I was scared. I thought I had lost you guys. You ignored me. You never ignore me." He got up from the chair, walked over to me, lifting my head with his hand.

"Babe, I was trying to protect you, and so were the boys, but I see that I hurt you more than protect you." I couldn't fight the tears back any longer; I let them go in front of my mate.

"Genius, I was so scared I had lost you."

"Princess, I will never leave you. I never meant to hurt you. I am sorry, and, no, none of us stopped to think what would happen to you if we didn't come back." I just kept crying, letting it all out. Genius just held me tight, not saying anything else. I started getting sleepy again; I assumed from crying. Genius could tell because he picked me up and laid me down on the couch in our office. He kissed me on my forehead.

"Get some rest, Princess. I am going to get the boys, and we will do some research while you rest, okay?" But I didn't want him to leave me.

"Please stay until I fall asleep." I didn't have to say anything else. Genius sat down on the couch, and I rested my head on his lap; he started playing with my hair.

"Babe, I love you. I promise I won't do anything like that again." I just smiled because my eyes were getting heavy. I started to drift in and out of sleep before I finally succumbed to it.

# Alcide's Training Has Begun

The next morning, I rolled over and Genius was still asleep, so I slid from under his arms and sat on the edge of the bed. I went to my closet and picked out a sports bra, jogging pants, and my tennis shoes. I mind-linked Alcide, "Meet me in the office in five." Then, I went to the mirror. Realizing I needed to fix my hair, I decided to put it up in a nice bun. After I checked one more time in the mirror, I quietly left the room, not wanting to wake Genius up; he needed to rest.

I walked down the stairs. To my surprise, everyone else was still asleep. I stopped in the kitchen to grab a bottle of water before heading to the office. I walked in the office. Alcide was sitting in the chair across from my desk, so I walked over to him. "Alcide, I need to train some today while the boys are asleep. Both in my human form and in wolf form. That way, Violet and I can start working together more." Much to my surprise, he just looked at me blankly for a moment.

"Artemis, are you sure that you want me to train you? I thought you wanted Genius to train you?"

I just hung my head for a moment. "I want to train with him too, but, right now, he needs his rest after the last couple of days, don't you think?" My uncle just stood up. He was smiling, then he embraced me in his arms for a hug.

"I love you, Art, you know I would love to train you today, but I won't go easy on you."

I just laughed. "I am counting on it." With that, we walked out of the office into the backyard. We walked to the middle of the field. I took my place across from him.

"So what do you want to start with, Uncle?" To my surprise, my uncle walked over behind the rock that was out there and came out with sticks, large sticks. I was confused. "Why do you have big sticks, I thought we were going to train?"

He just laughed at me. "You have to learn how to fight with many different things, Artemis. A stick can become a deadly weapon if you are properly trained with it." He tossed one of them to me and I caught it. "Now, Artemis, take your stance and try to stop the hits if you can." I spread my feet apart and crouched down a little bit, preparing for him to start swinging at me, but, instead, he started circling me. So I did the same. I couldn't let him get behind me or he would have the upper hand.

Then, he charged at me and swung the stick at my head. I dodged it but not by much. Then he swung the stick at my feet, causing me to jump back. Then what he did next, I wasn't expecting, because I didn't think we were using anything but the sticks. But he swung the stick at my head, and when I dodged that, he kicked me in the ribs, causing me to grimace in pain, but he was not there. He hit me with the stick straight in my stomach, causing me to hunch over, and once I didn't, he uppercut me, caused me to fly back onto the ground. I lay there for a moment. My uncle just literally kicked my ass in less than five minutes; he wasn't playing when he said that could be deadly. When I looked up, Alcide was standing over me.

"Are you okay, Artemis?" I just stared at him.

"I told you I wasn't holding back this time." I sat up slowly. Sitting on the ground for a moment, I really did need to train more. Alcide brought me the water bottle I brought out with me to allow me to get a drink. Then, he looked at me. "On your feet. This time, try to do better." *O, I planned on it now that I know we're not just using the sticks.* We got into our stances, but I didn't let him charge first. I swung the stick at his feet, and when he jumped back, I attempted to roundhouse kick him in his head, but he dodged that.

Then it was his turn. He swung the stick out, trying to hit me in my stomach, but I managed to dodge that hit. Then he came at me, punching me in my face. I swung my fist at his face, and when he brought up his hand to block, I kicked him in his ribs, causing him to show a sign of pain. Once he hunched to the side I hit, I kicked him in the side of the head, sending him to the ground. He sat up with a smile.

"I see you still learn as quickly as you did when you were a kid."

I laughed. "Well, I haven't trained since we were a kid either, so I never knew that I could do any of this."

He stood up. "Well, I think we did enough stick training today, but, Artemis, we will come back to this at a later date. Now follow me." I did as he asked. He led me deeper into the forest and behind a large rock, then he did something to the rock, causing a door to appear. My mouth fell open. How had I not known about this the whole time?

"Alcide, where are you taking me?"

He just looked at me. "I am taking you to do some more training, but this won't be as easy." I didn't like the sound of that at all, but I followed him down the stairs, descending further and further down till we came to a room where there was a table with straps, a big basin of water, and a tray filled with sharp tools.

I was shocked. I had never seen anything like this before besides in horror movies. I turned toward my uncle. "What is this room, Alcide?"

He just lowered his head for a second. "Artemis, this is where we bring people that we need to get information out of, which leads me to our next section of training." Now I was concerned.

"What do you mean the next part of our training?"

He just shook his head. "Artemis, you need to understand that you are our queen which means you will always have a target on your back, but do you know what to do if you're ever captured and tortured? Do you know how to stay calm and not freak out?"

I just stared at him. "Of course I don't know any of that. I've never been kidnapped before and tortured." Now I was beginning to worry because I didn't like where this was heading. "Alcide, where are you going with all this?" He just stood there with this sad expression on his face like he didn't like what he was about to do either.

"Artemis, I want to train your mind and body to stay calm in the event that you are ever taken, because staying calm and strong is the only way you would ever be able to get out of the situation and come home." I just stared at him. I knew he was right, but the thought of anything like that happening utterly terrified me, and maybe that was the point. Because he is right; if I was ever taken right now, I would be screwed. I would give because I have never had pain purposely inflicted on me. I let out a long breath before looking at him. "Okay, Alcide, what do you want me to do?" He looked shocked; I don't think he thought I would actually be okay with doing this, and I wasn't by a long shot, but I knew I had to do it just to be safe. That way, I knew I was okay if it ever happened. He stepped forward, looking me in my eyes.

"Well, we will start with something easy today, okay? Go over to the table and lay down. I will strap you in." I did what he asked of me. Alcide came over and strapped me in, then went over to the water basin and filled a large bottle up as well as grabbed a rag. Now that was concerning. Why did he need those things?

But like he read my mind, "Artemis, did you know that when you drown, your brain only registers one thing: that you are going to die." I just looked at him. I knew what was about to happen. I had seen it in movies before and I also knew that this was going to be a changing point for me.

He walked closer to me. "The key to surviving this is to remain calm and to be able to hold your breath for as long as possible." Then he walked over to me, placing the rag over my mouth and my nose, and started pouring water continuously over the rag. I immediately started panicking, throwing my head back and forth. I must have freaked out a little too much because I passed out and didn't even know it. I woke up to my uncle looking at me.

"Artemis, are you okay?" I just shook my head, unsure of what to say. I knew he was doing this for a reason, but I was still scared. I think he could tell too because he just stared at me for a second. "I think that is enough for today. You did a little better than I expected. You lasted five minutes before actually passing out, but we will continue this tomorrow, okay?" He walked over, unstrapping me from the table and helping me up to a sitting position. I just stared at the ground. "Alcide, did you ever have this happen to you?"

He seemed shocked by the question. He hung his head. "It never happened to me, but it did happen to your mother." That shocked me even though I knew that it shouldn't, because she had lied to us about so much that I wasn't quite sure what all she had hidden from us. I heard Genius in my head, so I tuned out my uncle for a second.

"Princess, where are you?"

"I am in the torture room with Alcide." He didn't respond, so I turned back to my uncle.

"Did you train Mom too?"

He had such sadness on his face. "No, I didn't, and she wasn't prepared for it when it did happen. When we got your mother back, she was never quite the same." We heard footsteps coming down the stairs. We both looked at each other before grabbing a sharp tool off the small table. We were ready to pounce, but Genius was who walked in. He looked back and forth between us.

"What is she doing down here, Alcide?" He just looked at me.

"We were training, Genius."

His eyes narrowed at Alcide. "What do you mean you were training?"

I could hear the anger in Genius's voice when he spoke. I figured it was a good time to step in between them. "He was training me in the event I was ever taken, I would know what to do instead of panicking." Genius clenched his jaw. I could tell he was pissed off because he was giving Alcide the death stare.

I turned around, facing Alcide. "Go back to the house, get some rest. We don't have much longer before the full moon is upon us, and then you know what we have to do." I didn't have to say anything more because he was gently walking past Genius and me. Once Alcide was out of sight, I turned back toward Genius who was obviously still angry.

"Artemis, why the hell would you even agree to this? You weren't even supposed to know about this room." After Genius finished his sentence, you could immediately tell he regretted saying something.

"Genius, what do you mean I am not supposed to know about this room. I am your queen, am I not supposed to know what happens in my territory?

"As for agreeing to this type of training, I did it because he was right, Genius. If I was ever taken away against my will, I would never know what to do and I would cave immediately."

Genius started pacing for several minutes before responding to me, "Princess, I didn't mean that you shouldn't know. I just didn't want you to know because this is something you shouldn't ever have to do. As for your reasoning, I don't like it, but I won't disagree with you." I was shocked; it was so easy to convince him, but I had a feeling he had alternative motives because he kept staring at the table then back at me. I hadn't realized before that neither Genius nor I had touched each other sexually in a couple of days. So I did the one thing he never would have thought I would do. I walked back over to the table slowly, rubbing my hands back and forth on it.

"You know, Genius. I have this fantasy about being strapped down by you." His eyes became wide. I could see his pulse was picking up.

"Princess, I wouldn't want you doing that for me."

I walked over to him, stood on my tippy toes, and whispered in his ear, "I never said it was for you." Then I slowly sucked on his earlobe before playing with it with my tongue. That was all he needed, because he picked me up, carrying me to the table.

He laid me down, but before he went any further he looked at me. "Princess, are you sure that this is okay? I don't want you to feel weird or anything."

I sat up on my elbows, wrapping my legs around him, pulling him closer. "It is okay, Genius. I really have been having a dream very similar to this."

He let a smile come across his face, then he slowly slid my pants off, then he strapped my legs down but separated. Then he strapped my hands above my head, then he turned back around and stripped out of his shorts. He walked over to me but didn't immediately enter me. Instead, he lowered his head till he was near my pussy. He slowly started licking me before spreading my lips, exposing my clitoris. Then he started sucking and licking, causing me to moan and scream, then he slid two fingers inside of me while he was still licking my clit, causing my eyes to roll into the back of my head. I wanted to move, but I couldn't, and that seemed to turn me on more. Genius was in complete control, and I loved it. This had to be the heat cycle still in effect because I didn't know if I would have had the courage to do this otherwise. But Genius brought me back to reality because he sucked on my clit, slid his fingers in and out of me faster and faster, then he used the tip of his tongue on my clit. I was about to climax. He started flicking his tongue faster and faster, doing the same with his fingers.

My back arched, and I couldn't do anything but scream his name, "OMG, GENIUS, DON'T STOP, I'M CUMING." I felt my tense body release all my fluids into his mouth; he just drank them down like it was the only thing that he had drank all day.

But he stood up, stepping closer. I could feel him rubbing his penis on the outside of me up and down across my clit. I started shaking; God, it felt so good. He was teasing the hell out of me, but then he stuck the tip barely in me, causing me to gasp. I looked at him. *This man, my mate, was absolutely breathtaking.* Then I felt him slide further inside of me. My pussy wrapped around his enlarged shaft like a vacuum, sucking him in but not wanting to release him. I looked up, and his eyes rolled back into his head. I couldn't do anything else but smile. That is when he slammed in me, causing me to scream and my eyes to roll back into my head. This was pure, pleasure, and I was loving it. Genius started thrusting in and out of me faster and faster. He lowered himself down and started sucking on my breast. Once he had a mouth full, he started slamming inside of me harder and harder, causing my pussy to convulse around his enlarged shaft.

"GENIUS, I AM CUMING AGAIN. OMG, BABY, PLEASE DON'T STOP." Then he reached up by my neck where our marks were and bit me, causing a surge of electricity through my body. I could feel him starting to pulse inside of me, and I knew he was close to climaxing himself. Then he started slamming inside me harder and faster till I felt his shaft convulsing. I looked up at him and his head was thrown back.

We sat like that for a few moments before he got off of me; he had the largest smile on his face. "Princess, that was absolutely amazing."

I just smiled. "Yes, Babe, it was, but could you unstrap me now please?" He just chuckled before unstrapping my legs and hands. He helped me up off the table, allowing me to get dressed before walking back over to me. He wrapped me into a hug and kissed the top of my head.

"Artemis, I love you."

I just smiled. "I love you too, Baby." Then I turned to look at him. "Babe, we have to head back to the house. We have to get the office ready for tonight. Remember, I have to go into Alcide's memories, if I can, so we can figure a way into the castle." He hung his head for a second. I knew he didn't like the idea, but he didn't say anything else. He just grabbed my hand, interlacing our fingers together, and we walked up the stairs, out the door, and back to the pack house.

Once we were inside, we headed straight to the office where all three of the boys were. They all turned toward us with big smiles on the faces, but Daniel was the first to speak, "I see you guys put the table to good use." I blushed. I know I did because I felt my face become warm.

"Well, that is for us to know and you not to find out about, huh." They all let out this obnoxious laugh, but then I got their attention. "Okay, so, tonight, we need to have guards at the door and around the property."

They all looked to me confused at first. I just shook my head. "Remember, tonight is the full moon, and do you guys remember what I have to do tonight?" They all looked at each other, then back at me and nodded. "Okay, so I want everyone back in my office by 11 p.m. No later, do you understand?" They all nodded before leaving the office. I walked around the desk, taking a seat in the chair. I don't know if I could do this, but I was sure going to try. We needed to figure a way into the castle. *So, tonight, I will be going into unknown waters. Hopefully, this all turns out okay.*

# A Trip Down Memory Lane

I was sitting in my office, staring at the sky. I could see the moon full as the day. I looked at the clock and noticed it was 10:30 p.m. It was getting close to time, and I was becoming more nervous by the second. I wasn't sure if I could do it, but I knew I had to try at all costs. I heard the door open. I turned around to see who it was; it was Genius. I figured he would be here first.

"Hey, Princess. How are you holding up?" That was a loaded question. I just looked at him.

"I am nervous, but I know that I have to do. It is the only way we can find a way in." He walked over to me, wrapping his large arms around me, doing the only thing that he knew he could do at the moment. He kissed me on top of my forehead.

"Princess, if anyone can do it, you can. Never doubt that, and we will be here watching over both of you while you do this." I knew he was right, but I was still very nervous because it could go very wrong.

The door to the office opened again. Genius and I both turned; Daniel and Zeus had walked in. "Hey, Squirt, you doing okay?" I just gave him a look that only Zeus would know. "It will be okay, Sis. You got this. Don't ever doubt that."

Daniel walked over, placing a hand on my shoulder. "Artemis, you got this, okay?" How could everyone else have more faith in me than I have in myself? I looked back at the clock; it was 10:55 p.m. *I hope Alcide gets here soon because I want to get this started as soon as possible.* I waited a few more minutes. I was beginning to think he wouldn't show up, but just as that thought crossed my mind, in walked Alcide. You could tell he was nervous, and I didn't blame him; I was about to go into his mind and see personal stuff. I looked at him. "Are you ready, Uncle?"

I knew the answer. I don't know why I even asked. Of course, he wasn't ready. His niece was about to be playing around in his head. "Come on, Alcide, lay down on the couch. That way, we can get started. I know you don't want to do this anymore than I do." He just lowered his head. I could tell he really didn't want to do this, but it had to be done. It was the only way that we were going to get into the castle. So Alcide walked over to the couch and lay down. I went over there and sat right beside him, having him lay his head onto my lap. I looked down at him.

"Okay, Alcide, I just need you to close your eyes and relax." He did as I asked him to do, then I placed my hands on his head before closing my eyes. I cleared my head, focusing on reaching out to Alcide's mind so that we could connect.

That's when it happened. I saw a flash, then I saw my uncle as a child. Only reason I could recognize him was because Mother showed us their child photos before she passed. He was running around in a forest with my mother right beside him. I could feel every emotion that he was feeling; he was happy and having fun. But then a white flash happened, and we were inside of a bedroom, but I wasn't sure of where because there wasn't much in his room for me to figure out what. When he got up and walked out of the room, that is when I noticed that we were in the castle.

So we found the memory of the castle. Now, we needed to see if this was the memory that told us how to get in and out of the castle undetected. But he was heading down the stairwell to a large dining hall. At the table, I could see my mother, grandma, and grandpa; they had all been talking but fell quiet when Alcide walked into the room. Why were they all staring at him?

That is when my grandmother spoke: "Alcide, come take a seat, Hunny. We need to discuss some things with you and your sister." So I saw my uncle walking over to his chair. He pulled it out and sat down, looking at my grandparents; my uncle was nervous, I could feel it. "So you know that there is a lot going on around us right now, right?"

My uncle nodded his head, so my grandfather spoke this time, "Well, we are going to have to make preparations just in case things go sideways at any point while we live here." I could feel Alcide's concern grow, then my mother turned toward him.

"Brother, you know that Artemis isn't safe here even with me concealing her powers, so we must have an exit strategy in play."

I finally heard my uncle speak, "Well, what do you propose we do, and where is your mate, Sister? Shouldn't he be here for this conversation too?"

My mother looked down, but before the memory could continue, I saw another white flash, and we were in the castle still, but there was what looked like a fight going on. I saw my mother kneeled down beside a man, crying. My uncle was holding me, with Zeus standing next to him, crying.

"Sister, we have to go now." My mother stood up, and then she grabbed me while Alcide grabbed Zeus; they ran into a library and pulled a book on the second shelf before entering into this large space. They started running through this corridor that seemed like it would go on forever till it came to a small room. My mother stopped.

"Alcide, we have to go the rest of the way, but the children are making too much noise. I will have to use my magic to put them to sleep till this is all over." My mother spoke words that I could not understand, but then I saw myself and my brother fall asleep in my mom's and uncle's arms.

They continued through the corridor for what seemed like hours till I saw a light at the end of the tunnel. When we exited, we were in a large, dense forest. My uncle turned toward my mom. "What now, where are we supposed to go?"

My mother turned toward my uncle and smiled. "It is okay, Little Brother, just relax. I will get us out of here." That was the last thing I saw before the memory faded and I was back inside of my office. I was panting heavily. I was exhausted, but I couldn't think of that now. I turned, and Alcide was sitting up, with tears running down his face. I went to say something to him, but he got up and stormed out the room before I could. Daniel looked at me.

"I'll go after him and make sure he is okay." I just nodded. I felt horrible. I didn't want to bring up any memories of his, but that was the only way that we could find the entrance to that tunnel. But even then, I was not sure if I could find it. Genius and Zeus came over to the couch and sat down beside me.

"Princess, what happened?" I just hung my head before Zeus grabbed my hand.

"Squirt, did you find the entrance we need?"

I took a breath before speaking, "Yes, and no. I know what it looks like but not entirely sure where. It is in a dense forest, but I am not sure if it is in Scotland or outside of Scotland."

They both looked at each other before turning to me. "What do you mean you don't know if it is in Scotland?"

I just shook my head. "Exactly what I said. They were in that tunnel for hours before they saw any light, so that means the entrance is anywhere. The only hope we have is maybe Alcide remembers." I looked down again, and Zeus placed his hand on my shoulder.

"Well, we are going to have to give him some time because I would assume that even the littlest memory was too much for him, especially if he blocked it out." Of course, I knew that, but I didn't want to wait.

"I know that, Zeus. We just really need to get there. Our cousins need us." That is when Genius gentle pulled my face toward him.

"Princess, we will, but give him some time. That was probably traumatic for him remembering that stuff. Plus, we still have to find a way to train with your magic or it will be useless." I knew he was right, but I just wished I could have stayed there longer to try and figure out where it was or how we got from there to where we were now. I stood up.

"Speaking of, have you two found anything yet, because I couldn't find anything either."

They both hung their heads. "Princess, we still haven't found anything. I don't know where else to search for the information." Zeus was being oddly quiet for once. Genius and I turned toward him at the same time.

"Zeus, did you find something?"

He looked up at me. "No, but the only person that knows is the one person that hid everything from us." I just looked down at the ground. I knew who he was referring to, but I wasn't sure if I wanted to contact Mom again with what happened the last time, because neither of us could remember what happened after she disappeared, which made me nervous. Genius seemed to know exactly what I was thinking because he looked at Zeus.

"Ya, you guys' mom may be the only one that knows, but I don't think that it is a great idea with neither of you remembering what happened after she disappeared." This was too much to think about right now. I was so tired after doing that. I didn't understand why. I didn't do anything. I turned toward the boys.

"Well, let's pick this up tomorrow. That way, Alcide has time to gather himself, and I need to sleep. I am exhausted." They didn't argue with me. Zeus left the room, and Genius followed me upstairs. All I wanted to do was sleep. I crawled into our bed and Genius did the same. I lay my head on his chest and fell asleep shortly after.

# The Body

I woke the next morning still feeling uneasy from the night before. My uncle had to still be upset by the memories. I hadn't spoken to him since last night. I rolled out of the bed, careful not to wake Genius. I went to the bathroom to take a shower, hoping that the water would help clear my head. *I need to train today, but I don't know if Alcide will be up for it today.* I got the water going, making sure the steam filled the bathroom before getting into the shower. I rinsed my hair while letting the water run down my body. It was relaxing. *I know that there is a lot to do today, but right now, I just want to stay in the shower. But I know that I can't.*

So I finished rinsing off before shutting the water off and getting out. I wrapped a towel around me. Stepping back into my room, I walked over to the closet, grabbing a sports bra and a pair of shorts. I dried myself off before getting dressed, then I put my hair into a bun and put my shoes on. I looked back at Genius. He was still sound asleep, so I quietly closed the door behind me, heading down to the kitchen. *I think it is time I cook everyone breakfast. Hopefully I can get everyone in a better mood today.*

I walked down the stairs, through the living room, and into the kitchen. I grabbed eggs, bacon, and pancake mix from the fridge. *I think pancakes, eggs, and bacon with freshly squeezed orange juice should cheer everyone up.* I got the eggs mixed into a bowl with some milk, the pancake mixed into another; the bacon was open. I heard two females coming into the kitchen, so I turned around to see Dream and Jade.

I never paid attention to how beautiful the two of them were. Dream was a little taller than me, with bright green eyes and brown hair. Jade was the same height as me, with brown eyes and brown hair; she was beautiful.

"Morning, girls. I was just making breakfast for everyone. I didn't think anyone would be up yet." They just looked at one another, then back at me. Dream stepped forward.

130

"Well, Artemis, would you like us to help you?" That made me happy because I hadn't got to get to know them that well. I turned to both of them.

"Yes, please, that would be great." They both smiled at me and came straight into the kitchen. I made the pancakes, Dream made the eggs and back, and Jade made the orange juice. We had to make enough to feed an entire army; the boys alone could eat five or more plates alone and we knew it.

I turned toward Jade because I got to spend a little time with Dream when she was comforting me in the bathroom after I freaked out on the boys. "So, Jade, tell me a little about yourself? We haven't had much time together."

She just smiled like she had been waiting for this for a while. "Well, I love reading, writing, and fashion."

I just laughed. "Well, I could need some fashion advice. Mine sucks." They seemed to be loosening up which was what I wanted; they were family, after all. It was nice getting to know them some. We started talking more, preceded by laughing. We were so busy talking and cooking, we hadn't noticed the boys standing there, watching all of us, so when we turned around, they scared the crap out of us and we all screamed. The boys fell on the ground, laughing at us, so we threw an orange at them.

"You could have said something instead of scaring the shit out of us."

Daniel stood up, wiping the tears that had been pouring down his face. "Sorry, Artemis, we didn't mean to scare you."

Then Zeus stood up, doing the same thing. "Seriously though, you should have seen your faces."

Then Genius stood up. "Sorry, Princess, we didn't mean to scare you. We were just watching how well you were getting along with one another."

Alcide was still on the ground, laughing. I thought he was going to puke from laughing so hard. He finally stood up, catching his breath. It was good to see him in better spirits today. Jade looked at the boys with her hands on her hips.

"Well, since you guys wanted to scare us, maybe we will let the rest of the pack eat all the food and not save you any."

Then Dream chipped in, "Ya, I mean, we just did cook all of this, so maybe we should not let you guys have any."

The boys' mouths fell open, and all at once. "No, please, we didn't mean to. It smells so good, don't do that." Then we fell on the ground, laughing. Their faces were priceless. They looked so sad when they said that.

After a few moments, I stood up. "Well, I guess you guys can have some, since you looked so sad." I mind-linked the rest of the pack, "Everyone, come into the kitchen. We made breakfast." The boys had all gotten a heaping pile of food and were eating when the rest of the pack came in. Their eyes were wide. I think it was because they had never seen us cook before or because their queen did. I couldn't tell, but it only took a few minutes before they all got their plates.

I just stood there, watching my pack, my brother, Dream, Jade, Daniel, Alcide, and my mate. I was completely happy here and now. I would do anything for these people; I truly do love them more then they will ever know. Genius noticed me watching and just smiled at me. His smile could melt me. He was happier than ever. I finally made my plate, then headed to the table to sit down with everyone to enjoy our meal. Everyone thanked Dream, Jade, and me for the meal before going about their day, then the girls got up and left.

When it was just me and the boys, I looked at them. "Well, before we do any more training or anything, I need to go back into the spirit world. We have to find out from Mom where I can train my magic more." They all just stared at me. Genius went to speak, but I held up my hand to stop him. "I know you don't want me to, with us not knowing what happened, but I won't go by myself this time. Alcide, you are going with me."

He just looked at me with shock on his face. "Artemis, I don't know if I should."

I just laid a comforting hand on his. "Alcide, you have things you need to hear from Mother, and I need someone to help keep me safe. Don't you think that is worth it?" He just hung his head; he was nervous, and I couldn't blame him, but I needed to do this, and so did he, but before we did that, I wanted to go for patrol. I hadn't been on one in a while.

I stood up and turned toward the boys. "But before any of that, let's go on a patrol, boys. Our wolves need to run." I started stripping my clothes off on the way to the backdoor. I turned and the boys were just staring at me.

"Well, come on, or I'll just go by myself!" Then I turned around and headed out the backdoor, into the yard leading to the forest; I started to shift. You could hear my bones breaking and shifting into my wolf. My skin started peeling off, my body showing Violet's purple-tinted fur. The shifting was so much easier now than it was when I first started. I looked to each side of me and there stood all four boys in their wolf forms; I couldn't help but smile at that.

I started running to the forest with them in tow. We went deeper into the forest before I saw Daniel lifting his nose up; he smelt something. I tilted my head toward him before lifting my nose in the air; I could smell it too. It smelled like rotting flesh. So we took off toward the smell. The closer we got to it, the worse it stank. We peered over the hill, and that is when I saw it.

There was a body just laying on the ground. I turned my head toward the boys, mind-linking them, "There is a body up ahead. Be careful." They were all on alert now. Genius's wolf walked closer to me, then we proceeded to get closer to the body so we could figure out who or what it was. When we got closer to the body, we could barely recognize if it was someone we knew. You could tell that other animals had fed on it because the eyes were missing, and so were most of the insides. The flesh was rotting, so it was obvious that the body had been there for a while.

I turned back toward the boys. "We need to carry it back to the chamber so we can have the doctor run some tests. We need to know if it was one of ours or not." I didn't have to say another word; Daniel shifted back to his human form, lifting the body like it was nothing, placing it on Genius's back before shifting back.

So we ran for another 20 minutes before reaching the entrance to the chamber. We all shifted back, and Alcide opened the door while Genius carried the body down the stairs and placed it on the table.

I turned toward Zeus. "Go, get the doctor. Tell no one else about this until we know more." Then I turned toward Daniel. "Go to the pack and see if anyone has come up missing within the last few weeks, please." Both boys nodded before heading back up the stairs. We heard the door close behind us. Once the doors were closed, I turned toward Genius and Alcide. "Can either of you make out what happened?"

Alcide was the first to speak, "I can't tell anything; the body is so decomposed. I can't see if there is a mark for our pack or not."

I turned toward Genius who hadn't said anything since we got there. "Babe, can you figure out what happened?"

He just stood there, staring for a moment before speaking, "No, but I need to know what happened and why the body was left for us to find."

Alcide and I looked at him. "Why do you think the body was left for us?"

He just looked at us. "Why else would it be on our territory if it wasn't meant for us to find?" He had a point, but maybe this was just an accident. Honestly, we wouldn't know anything until the doctor got there. I looked back at my mate.

"Let's not make assumptions right now, okay? Let's wait for the doctor to get here and then we go from there, okay?" He nodded his head. We were all disturbed by this, but we need answers, not assumptions.

We heard the door open and two sets of feet coming down the stairs. Zeus was the first to appear, then the doctor came in. I stepped closer to the doctor.

"Hi, Doctor Nina, I am Artemis, alpha of this pack. Sorry to bring you here on short notice, but we found a body on our territory, but it is too decomposed for us to figure anything out. Could you possibly solve the mystery for us?"

She just shook my hand and smiled. "Well, you sure have grown, dear. I haven't seen you since you were a child."

Now I was confused, but now wasn't the time. I could ask her later. Right now, we had to figure out what happened with this body. I didn't have to say anything because she went right over to the body. The boys and I walked into the next room to allow her to do her job. We sat there quietly, not saying a word. Honestly, I didn't think any of us knew what to say. This was the first time since my mother died that I had seen a dead body. It was starting to get to me, but right now wasn't the time to break down. I needed to be strong. I could break later in my room. We heard the door to the room open, hoping it was the doctor, but it was Daniel. He came in, looking a little sad.

"What happened, Daniel?" I knew something was wrong.

"Artemis, do you remember the family that came to us shortly after you got here? The one with the dad, mom, and child?"

My eyes got wide. "Yes, why?"

He just looked at me. "Well, they told me that their son had been missing for a few weeks, but they told him to come here before he went missing."

*Oh, God, no, please let it not be a kid.* As if Genius read my mind, he came over, placing his hand over mine.

"Princess, let's not freak out yet. Let the doctor do her work, then we can go from there." He was right and I knew it, but waiting was never my strong suit. I turned toward Zeus and Daniel.

"Go back to where we found the body and see if you can find any clues or evidence, and take James with you. He is the best tracker in the pack, boys, no offense."

They just smiled. "Hey, none taken. He is good at his job, but so are we." I just smiled at them. Those two were cocky sons of bitches and they knew it, but I didn't have to say anything else. They left immediately, leaving Alcide, Genius, and I alone in the room again. We sat there for what seemed like hours before the doctor came in. We all stood up.

"Well, Nina, did you find anything?" She walked over to a chair and sat down, motioning for us to do the same thing, so we followed suit.

She looked at us. "Well, upon doing an autopsy, I found out that this was a male in his late 20s early 30s. He has been dead for weeks, and he was tortured previous to his death. Based on the extent of his injuries, I would assume he would have been tortured for months before his death." I was shocked by what I was hearing.

This man was tortured, but before I had time to respond, Genius beat me to it: "Were you able to identify him?"

She just looked at us like she was shocked we even asked that. "No, unfortunately, the only thing I found was an article of clothing that had been embedded in his arm. His teeth were pulled, so I couldn't do a dental imprint to try and find his identity. But the clothing was from a police uniform, but I couldn't make out what department he was from." My eyes got wide and Alcide saw it.

"Artemis, what's wrong?" But I couldn't speak; tears started welling up in my eyes. I started to cry before I could even stop it; they were all looking at me.

Genius came over to me and wrapped me in his arms. "Princess, what's wrong? Why are you crying? We don't know who it is yet." I just couldn't stop the tears because I thought that it might be Officer Jacob. He was the only other one that was close enough to our family that anyone would want to hurt. I finally managed to stop the tears long enough to look at them all.

"Before I say we need to get a hold of Zeus, I need to know if they found a wallet, a badge, something." They all nodded, knowing that I wouldn't speak till I knew, so I mind-linked Zeus, "Have you guys found anything yet?"

I waited a few minutes before he responded: "No, not yet, Squirt, why?"

I took a breath. "The doctor finished her exam, and the only thing that she found was an article of clothing from a police uniform." I sat there, waiting for a reply, but nothing came back.

We sat there for about five minutes before he responded: "What do you mean a police uniform?"

"What do you think I mean? A police uniform, but she couldn't make out what department it was from."

Then Daniel piped in, "Zeus, we found something over here."

I started pacing. I needed to know. *Please, Moon Goddess, let it not be him.* "Squirt, we are on the way back. Be there in 20 minutes." This was bad; Zeus didn't say what they found, which meant it wasn't good. I turned to the boys. They heard him, but they didn't say anything. They were trying to figure out why I was freaking out. I can't believe that Genius hadn't thought about who it could be yet, but, then again, he wasn't as close to Officer Jacob as our family was.

We sat in silence for about 20 minutes when we heard the door open and three sets of feet coming down the stairs in a hurry. We looked up, and they were walking into the room.

"Well, what did you find?" I could see Genius and Daniel were upset, so James walked over to me, handing me a badge and a wallet. I couldn't read the name on the badge; it had been worn down too much. But I opened the wallet, and there it was, the news I was dreading. I dropped to my knees. "NO, no, no, this can't be happening, no."

Genius and Alcide were confused. "Artemis, who is it?" I couldn't speak. I just handed Genius the wallet. I started crying again; Zeus walked over and dropped to the ground, wrapping his arms around me. "Squirt, it will be okay. Take a breath."

Genius must have realized the name in the wallet because he punched the wall. "Who could have done this? More importantly, why? He was a great guy." I just looked at him with tears running down my face. I already knew why but I didn't know who.

"It's because of me." They all turned toward me except Zeus; he just held me tighter. He knew why I said it, but the others were confused. Alcide knelt down.

"Artemis, why do you think it was because of you?" I just started crying harder. I couldn't speak, so Zeus did it for me. Thank god for my older brother.

"Because, Uncle, he was one of the people that was helping my mother protect Artemis. He acted like he didn't know what we were, especially in front of Artemis because we asked him not to, but he knew everything. He also knew we had to protect her at all costs." Genius dropped down beside me, now understanding what was going on. Apparently, he didn't know either. I didn't know that Officer Jacob knew all about everything, but he was still one of the people I could trust and feel safe with.

Genius took me into his arms. "Princess, this isn't your fault, okay? Please don't blame yourself." Not blame myself? How could I not? He was dead because of me. We didn't know who did this. Zeus lifted my chin.

"Squirt, I am going to take the body and wallet and drop it off near the hospital. I'll make an anonymous phone call so that they can pick the body up and notify his family. His wife has my cellphone number. She will call us, okay?" I just nodded. I needed to get away from there.

"Genius, please, can we go inside? I don't want to be here. I can't." I didn't say anything else. They all just left with me. Genius stayed right beside me till we reached the house. Genius walked me in and sat me on the couch. Dream and Jade walked in. They noticed me crying and ran to me. They didn't ask questions; they just hugged me. Jade went to the kitchen, bringing me a hot cup of tea, and Dream allowed me to lay my head on her lap, just playing with my hair.

Dream looked at Genius. "We got her right now. Go finish up with whatever is going on, okay?" He just nodded. He got up and followed Alcide to the office. The more Dream played with my hair, the more relaxed I became. Soon, I found myself drifting in and out of sleep.

# Secrets

I woke up a few hours later to find that Dream and Jade were still there with me. I still had my head on Dream's lap, and I had my feet on Jade. They both noticed that I had woken up; they both looked at me.

"Artemis, are you feeling any better?"

I slowly sat up. "Not really, but thank you, guys, for staying with me. You didn't have to do that."

Dream looked at me with the softest eyes. "Artemis, you're our sister, our queen, and alpha. We would do this over and over again if that's what it took to make you feel better."

Then Jade turned toward me. "Matter of fact, tomorrow night, we are going out. No ifs, ands, or buts about it. You need a day away. You haven't had time to yourself since your mother passed, and it's starting to get to you. We can all see it." I just smiled at these two. I never thought that I would find two women that I could call my sisters ever, but I was glad that it was these two.

"Thank you, guys, but, remember, I am only 16. I can't go into a bar yet." They just looked at me and laughed.

"Artemis, we can have fun without drinking, you will see. Now go see the boys in the office. They have been worried about you."

I hugged both of them. "Thank you, girls, really, I appreciate it, and I love you both so very much."

I got up slowly and started heading to the office. What was I going to say to them? I had no clue what the hell to do. I seriously had to figure out who was controlling the Quils and who was trying to kill me. I walked into the office and all the boys were there. Zeus was the first to make it to me; he gave me a big bear hug.

"How are you holding up, Squirt?"

I just held onto him for a moment. "I am doing okay."

138

Then Genius came over. "Princess, are you okay?" I just nodded before going to sit down on the couch.

I just looked at them. "Okay, we have to figure out who is doing this. Which means, tonight, I will go back to the spirit world to talk with Mom. Alcide, you're coming with me, and no arguing.

"Then, tomorrow, Alcide will train with me more, but tomorrow night, I am going out with Jade and Dream. After that, depending on what Mother says is if we will train with my magic. But, Alcide, I need you to try and remember where that place is at in the forest so we can go into the castle. If not, we will have to go back down memory lane again." They all looked at me, letting me. "Please, don't worry, but I just can't deal with anyone else getting hurt because of me. It isn't right nor fair to anyone."

Genius walked over, grabbing my hands. "Princess, we all know the risks, but we also all know how strong you are. Never doubt your own strength, and, don't forget, you have a whole pack behind you." *I know he is right, but how can I keep letting the people I love, the people that helped protect me, get hurt? The answer is, I couldn't, so I will find a way to protect everyone, one way or another.*

"Also, Genius, while I am contacting my mom tonight, I need you and Zeus to look into the ways a mate's bond can be manipulated."

They both looked at me. "Squirt, we can't leave you alone while you go there; you know that."

I just shook my head. "I won't be alone; I have Daniel and James to look after me. If you're more comfortable with more people being in here, go get Dream and Jade and tell them to watch the door and have guards outside the window, but this really isn't up for debate tonight, boys." They both looked at one another, knowing that I wasn't going to budge. The both turned to leave, but before Genius left, he turned around.

"Baby please be careful, okay?"

I smiled at him. "Always, Babe. Now go get that information please."

I wasn't trying to be bitch or pushy, but I couldn't let anyone else get hurt; it was not fair, but I think that they all understood my moodiness with what just happened to Officer Jacob. I wondered if his wife got a hold of Zeus yet. God, what was his wife going to do without him? *I don't know what I would do if something ever happened to Genius.* But before I could get too far into my head, Daniel tapped me on my shoulder.

"Artemis, look, I know that you have had a hard day with what happened, but just know that we are all right here. Nobody is going anywhere, okay, so just breathe for a moment before throwing yourself into finding out who did this, or you will fail before you even get started." I just looked at him. Daniel had always been like an older brother to me, and with each day, since I found out who I truly was, he had begun acting like it; I didn't know whether to be worried or happy. Having two older brothers might not be a good thing, but they were great at always looking out for me in their own ways.

I just smiled; I couldn't really say much to that because I knew that he was just looking out for me, but he couldn't understand how I was feeling right now. I was not sure that anyone could at the moment.

I looked at Alcide. "I know you're not really comfortable with this, but I wouldn't ask you to go if it wasn't important. That, and I think we can agree that it is probably not best to have Zeus go with me again." Alcide looked nervous; he was fidgeting on the couch.

"Artemis, I am just nervous. I don't know what to say when I see your mother." I was shocked. Was that really what he was nervous about?

"That's really what you're nervous about with everything going on?"

He turned to look at me. "Yes, it is. I haven't seen my sister in a very long time. I wasn't there to protect her or you; she must hate me." *Now, I can understand why he is so nervous.* I never thought about that before. *It has been a very long time since he has seen my mom.* I reached over and grabbed his hand.

"Uncle, it will all be okay. Don't forget, you're not going to be alone. I will be there the whole time, okay?" He just nodded. I looked at Daniel and James. "Okay, guys, we're going to do this. So, Daniel, you already know the drill. James, just follow Daniel's lead, okay? He knows what to do. I am trusting you both, so don't let me down."

I looked back at Alcide, grabbing his hand. "Okay, Uncle, I just need you to lay back and relax. Clear your head. This is going to be new, but don't be scared. Remember, I am right here with you."

He squeezed my hand before laying his head back on the couch, and I followed suit, waiting till I found Mother's tree in my head. I focused on that tree. That is when I saw the white flash and I knew we had entered the spirit world. I turned to see Alcide standing right next to me, holding my hand, looking around.

"Artemis, this is amazing. I never knew you could do something like this."

I just smiled. "Well, neither did I, but look at me now." We both started laughing. I looked at him. "Are you ready?" He just looked at the tree for a moment.

"Ready as I ever will be." We both started walking toward the tree. The closer we got, the clearer it became. I took him with me to sit under the tree. This time, I knew I would be there for a little bit.

"Mom, it's me, Artemis. I brought your brother with me this time. Could you please come out? We really need to talk." We waited for a few minutes before she came walking from behind the tree.

She looked at me. "Artemis, I told you it's not safe for you to be coming here."

I just shook my head. "Yes, Mom, you did, but I wouldn't have to keep coming back if you would just tell me the truth and quit hiding everything from me. I have a pack to look after and people to protect."

She just looked at me with sorrow in her eyes. "I know that, Artemis, but there are some things you are not ready to know yet."

That made me angry, but before I could speak again, Alcide spoke, "Hi, Sister, I know I haven't seen you in a while, but I want to apologize for not being here for you." She just looked at him with a look I couldn't quite describe.

"Brother, you have nothing to apologize for. I am the one that sent you off."

Alcide just hung his head. "But I should have stayed; I knew what kind of danger you guys were in and I still chose to leave."

She walked over to him, placing her hand under his chin. "Alcide, you never had a choice because I never gave you one!" He just looked at her, confused.

"It was my choice to leave. I could have told you no, but I didn't."

She kissed him on top of his head. "No, Little Brother, you never did. The reason you can't remember everything clearly is because I wiped your memory." We both looked at her in shock.

"Sister, what do you mean?"

My mom backed away so she could look at us both. "Alcide, I had to wipe a lot of your memories so that they could not use them to get back Artemis." My uncle just sat there in shock. I could understand why all this time he thought he abandoned us but come to find out Mother wiped his memories, his only sister.

I looked at Mom, shaking my head. "All these people have gotten hurt because of me, yet you keep telling me that I am not ready for everything. Well, I wasn't ready to lose you, and now I have lost Officer Jacob, so please tell me again that I am not ready to hear everything."

She looked at me with shock and sorrow on her face. "What do you mean? Jacob is dead?"

I was starting to become frustrated. "Exactly what I said, Mother. He is dead. He was tortured for a long time before they killed him. They left him in the forest for months before we found him."

She just hung her head. "Artemis, I am truly sorry, but he knew what he was getting himself into. He would do it all over again, given the chance." How could she say that, like his life had no meaning?

"Mom, we came here for two things, okay? I need to train my magic, and Alcide can't remember the secret entrance into the castle. We know it is in a forest somewhere, but we don't know where."

Again, she seemed shocked. "Artemis, how do you know of that entrance?"

"Well, Mom, since you haven't been honest or been trying to help me, I had to go into Alcide's mind to try and find some of the answers, but surprise, surprise. Those have been messed up too."

She paced back and forth for a moment before looking at us once again. "Artemis, I didn't wipe those memories or mix them up. Your grandmother did for all of our sake." I just looked at her, then to Alcide whose mouth fell open at this point.

"Mom messed with my head too? How could you guys do that, did you not trust me?" I could hear the sadness in his voice as he spoke. It hurt me to hear how upset he was, but we were there for something else.

"So, Mom, are you going to answer me or keep dancing around the question?" She just let out this big breath.

"Dear Moon Goddess, why did you have to make her so damn stubborn? She acts just like her father." Alcide finally laughed when he heard her say that, but you could still see he was upset.

He turned toward my mom. "That is one thing we can agree on."

I looked at each of them. "Hey, that isn't fair because I don't even remember my dad." I could see the pained look in my mom's eyes when I said that, but it was true.

"Artemis, the forest that you saw is a long way away from the castle. We had to make it that way just in case someone tried to follow us. We made different paths that lead to different areas. The path we took was a very long way to get you safe before coming to the United States. The forest you saw was Cann Wood in Plymouth, England." She stopped a moment before continuing, "As for a trainer for your magic, there is only one person that can help you now that I am not of the living world, and that is your grandmother."

My mouth fell open with Alcide's. "Wait what? Grandma is dead, how the hell can she help us?"

I was waiting for a response, but Alcide couldn't wait, "Serena, Mother is dead. Why would you say that?"

She just looked at us. "Mom isn't dead. She can't die. That is her curse. She has just stayed hidden because of the lie we had to tell." This family had way too many secrets.

"Well, Mom, where can I find Grandmother if she is still alive?"

"She is in Plymouth, England. She stayed to guard the entrance to the castle. She knows where the entrance is and the one that can train your magic." I just looked at her. *How can this woman whom I love lie so much?* "Mom, you need to tell me everything. I can't protect anyone or myself if I don't know everything. Don't you think you owe me, Zeus, and Alcide that much?"

She squatted down so that we were eye level. "Artemis, there is one thing that I can promise you right now. If you complete your training with your grandmother and come back here before going into that entrance, I will tell you everything that you want to know. I promise you that, and when you come back, bring everyone that you trust, and I will tell everyone the truth, but I will not risk your safety no matter what."

I just looked at her. "Mom, I can only bring one person at a time, not six!"

She just smirked. "Artemis, darling, you just don't understand how powerful you truly are, do you?" I shook my head no because I honestly didn't. I knew nothing about this life because she sheltered me from it. She walked over, kissed me on my forehead and Alcide on his cheek.

"Go find your grandmother, Artemis, then you will understand. After all, you're just like her in more ways than one. My dear Alcide, look after my baby girl, and, Artemis, I meant what I said. I promise you, if you train with Grandmother and come back here before going into that entrance, I will tell you everything I know. But, now, you need to go. I can no longer keep the darkness at bay."

I looked around after she said that and I could see the darkness starting to close in. I stood up, dragging my uncle with me. I pictured a door and one popped up right next to us. Okay, that is weird. That has never happened before. I opened it, dragging my uncle through it with me. When I opened my eyes, I realized I was back in the office. I turned to look to make sure Alcide made it back, and he was sitting up.

I looked at him, placing my hand on his shoulder. "Uncle, are you okay?" He just looked at me with tears in his eyes and a smile on his face, which made no sense. He wrapped his arms around me, embracing me.

"Artemis, thank you for allowing me to go with you. That is truly amazing, but I think I am going to go lay down and let everything sink in for a while, but don't worry, I will be here in the morning, okay?" I just nodded. I knew he needed time. Hell, I needed time to process all that. Mom was actually kind of honest about something for once since she passed.

I looked at Daniel, and he was just standing there. He didn't say anything; he just stood there. "Um, Daniel, is everything okay?"

He sat down beside me. "Artemis, when you went in there this time, you glowed." I started laughing. Surely, he had to be playing a trick on me. I looked to James whose face looked shocked.

"Artemis, he is serious. You were glowing. It was weird. Are you okay?"

I stopped laughing. "Wait, are you serious?"

Daniel grabbed my shoulder, forcing me to look at him. "Artemis, I am dead serious. You were glowing like you were a lighting bug. Except it was purple. It was weird as hell because that didn't happen the last time." I could see that they were both being serious.

"I am fine, guys, I promise. Go get some rest, okay? I appreciate you watching over me. Tell the girls to head to bed too. I am about to go to bed myself. I'll fill everyone in tomorrow, okay?"

Without another word, they left the room. *I am glad that they don't argue with me as much as Genius and Zeus do.* Speaking of which, I should find out where they are.

"Zeus, Genius, where are you guys?" I stood up, stretching for a few minutes when I heard Genius, "Hey, Princess, we are in the library. Did everything go okay?"

I just chuckled. "Well, I found out a lot from Mom this time, but I will fill everyone in on what was said in the morning. You boys finish up tonight. Zeus, go lay down with Dream, and, Genius, I expect you to come upstairs. I am exhausted and would love cuddles tonight please."

I started cleaning up the office while I waited on a reply. First, it was Zeus, "Eww, Sister, I don't need to hear that, but I am heading to bed now. Genius is cleaning up, then he will be there." I just started laughing, but I went to the door, shutting the light off before leaving. I closed the door behind me, heading to bed. I really was exhausted, but I guess with each time I do this, I am not as exhausted, so I guess that is a good thing.

I walked up the stairs and opened my bedroom door. I took my shoes off and stripped down till I was completely naked, then I went and lay on the bed. *Man, this bed is really soft.* Why hadn't I noticed that before? I didn't realize that I said that out loud because the next thing I knew, I heard laughing behind me. I rolled over, and it was Genius.

"Really, Princess, you're just now noticing how soft our bed is?" I threw the pillow at him. Naturally, he caught it. He walked over to the bed, laying his naked ass right next to me. "Come here, Princess. It's time for you to get some rest; we can talk more tomorrow." He pulled me onto his chest, wrapping his arms around me. Once my head was on his chest and I heard his heartbeat, I immediately relaxed. Now I could feel how tired I truly was because my eyes became heavy, then I drifted to sleep with the love of my life's arms around me.

# Preparations

I woke up the next morning still being wrapped in Genius's arms; I looked up at him. He looked so peaceful when he was sleeping. I just admired him for a while. When I felt this intense burning between my legs, right inside of my pussy, I became increasingly wet knowing the only way that I could fix it was by having my mate. I looked at him; he was still completely sleeping. I reached up, placing my hand on his face. I just admired him for a moment before I started kissing my way down. I kissed my way down his chest and his stomach. I noticed his penis started becoming harder, and I smiled knowing that he would wake up soon. I slid the tip of him inside my mouth, rolling my tongue around the tip before slowly starting to slide him further into my throat. When I came back up to the tip, I flicked my tongue back and forth when Genius started moaning, "Baby, don't stop." With those words, I proceeded to keep teasing him by slowly sliding him down my throat and bringing him back to just the tip where I massaged it with my tongue. Once he was about to climax, I stopped and sat up, looking at him.

Genius's mouth was wide open. I know he didn't want me to stop, but I wasn't finished with him quite yet. I still had this burning between my legs that only made my pussy become wetter. So I climbed on top of him, kissing his neck, then licking all the way over to where our mark was once. I was just above our mark. I traced it with my tongue while grinding my hips across his massive penis. I slowly slid the tip in just on the outside of my pussy. When I heard him moan, I didn't want to hold back any longer, so I slowly started sliding down, pushing him further inside of me. Once I had him deep enough, I bit down on our mark. The moment I bit him on our mark, with him being so deep inside of me, he pushed further into me, making me release him, only to scream his name. He wrapped his arms around my waist before rolling me so I was on my back. I looked up at him and could see the hunger in his eyes. He pushed my legs above my head so that my hips were angled up. Once he had

146

me in the position he wanted, he pressed deeper inside of me before slowly sliding out and back in. My eyes rolled back into my head with pleasure; my pussy kept gripping his penis each time he slid in and out of me.

He bent my knees closer to my ears, leaning over to kiss my neck before he bit into our mark, causing a surge of electricity to run to my pussy. I got my legs free to wrap around him and my arms on his back. The more he pushed into me, the more I screamed. I began clawing his back; the pleasure was unbearable. I wanted to feel his release; I needed to feel his cum inside of me. But Genius wasn't ready yet because he picked me up with my legs wrapped around him, slamming me into the wall, causing me to scream his name. He wrapped his arms around my ass before slamming into me harder and faster. I couldn't do anything but moan and scream. I was reaching my climax, as was Genius; he pushed into me as far as he could. The orgasm I had ripped through my body. My pussy walls began squeezing his penis when he released inside of me, causing me to orgasm again. We collapsed on the floor beside of each other, completely out of breath; he just looked at me.

"Well, good morning to you too, Princess." I just smiled. I knew I couldn't speak nor stand at that moment. We lay down on the floor for a moment before he spoke again, "Babe, what got into you this morning?"

I just smiled at him. "Well, I got this burning sensation between my legs that caused me to become instantly wet and wanting you."

He just turned to me like he was shocked. "Princess, you're still in the heat?"

I just shook my head. "No, Genius, it's not the heat. I don't know how to explain it."

He just hugged me, kissing me on my head. "I am not complaining, Babe; that was amazing."

I just giggled. "I know it was, but we can't lay around here all day. I have to tell you and everyone what Mom told me in the spirit world." I slowly stood up, making sure that I had my balance, which just made Genius laugh. I looked down at him. "It isn't funny; I can't feel my legs."

He stood up and stood in front of me. He kissed me on my lips. "Princess, it is funny, but let me help you to the bathroom so that we can shower, okay?" I didn't say anything; I just let him help me to the bathroom. He leaned me against the counter so that he could get the shower going, then he helped me into the shower. Once the hot water hit me, my body relaxed. I closed my eyes, leaning my head back into the water, letting it run down my hair, onto my back, and down my butt. Once I leaned my head forward again and opened my eyes, I noticed Genius staring at me, licking his lips. I knew what he wanted, but we really did have to get downstairs. "Babe, we can go another round before bed tonight, but we have to get downstairs. This is important okay."

He walked over to me, kissing my lips before speaking, "I know, Babe. It is just hard to when you look so damn good with the water running down you like that." I just smiled at him, turning around in the water so that I could get the front half of me wet.

"Babe, grab my soap please?" I turned back to face him, and he handed me my soap, and I rubbed it all over my body, making sure to wash my pussy really good. Once I rinsed off the soap, I looked at him, smiling because I knew he was enjoying the show; I could see his penis was once again hard. "I am getting out, Baby. See you downstairs."

I got halfway out before he grabbed my hand. "Princess, you're really not gonna help me?" I leaned in, kissing him while stroking his penis with my hand, making sure I wrapped my hand all the way around him, going up and down for a few moments before I stopped. Releasing from the kiss, I smiled, stepping out of the shower completely.

"No, Babe, I am not. I am gonna make you wait till later." His mouth fell open. I wrapped the towel around me, walking out of the bathroom into our room and over to my closet.

I grabbed out my tight, red, short outfit that allowed my cleavage to show. I wore the boots to match. I walked over to the mirror, making sure everything was perfect before placing my hair in a high ponytail. Once I was convinced, I looked out, I turned around. Genius was standing at the bathroom door, staring at me.

"Princess, you are torturing me today. You look good enough to eat."

I just smiled at him. "Well, then this will only make it worse." I purposely bent down so he could see my ass, then I stood up, smiled at him, and walked out the door. I walked down the stairs to see some of the pack members. They all turned toward me once they noticed I was downstairs.

"Hi, everyone, did you guys have a good night?"

Paul stood up, the man who had a wife and child here. "Yes, Queen, we did, and you seem to have had a great morning." They all just smiled at me, and I began to blush. "It's okay. You just woke us all up this morning." He let out a chuckle.

"I am sorry. I never meant to do that."

Mary, his wife, stood up. "Sweety, it is okay. We have all been there. Nothing to be embarrassed by." I just smiled before walking into the kitchen to grab some water from the fridge. When I got into the kitchen, Dream and Jade were standing there. I knew they had heard me this morning, but I didn't want to say anything, so I just looked down on my way to the fridge. But Dream wasn't going to let me get away that easy. "Well well well, look who finally came out from her room."

I just looked at her starting to blush again, then Jade piped in, "Well, at least none of us needed an alarm this morning." They both started laughing.

"I am so sorry, guys. I never meant to wake anyone up."

They were still laughing when they both said, "Artemis, it is okay. We have all been there quite a few times, and it will happen again. The quicker you get used to it, the less embarrassed you will be by it."

I just smiled at them. "Well, thank you, guys. Are the boys in the office? I need to speak to them."

They looked at each other, then at me. "Yes, they are. Alcide gathered them this morning and told them that you guys needed to talk." I just started walking toward my office.

I hollered over my shoulder, "Thank you." I walked to my office door, opening it. There, they were sitting down on the couch and chairs that were in my office. I walked in, closing the door behind me. When I looked up, they were all staring at me. I held my hand up.

"Don't say anything about this morning. I already know I woke you guys up this morning and I am sorry. Genius will be down in a few minutes."

Daniel just chuckled. "I am sure he needs a few to collect himself." I picked up the pillow on the chair and threw it at him.

"Okay, so besides me waking you guys up this morning, has Alcide told you anything that had happened while we were in the spirit world with Mother?" They shook their heads no, which was good because I really wanted to tell Zeus.

I walked to my desk and sat on the edge. When the door opened, in walked Genius with a big-ass smile on his face. Zeus threw a pillow at him. "You know, you could have taken it easy this morning. You made her wake up the whole pack."

Genius threw the pillow back at him. "Nope, today is not my fault. That is all her." I just looked at the ground, not saying anything. Daniel started laughing again, falling out of his chair. I just looked at him, confused.

"Why are you laughing?"

Alcide stood up. "Well, Artemis, he is laughing because that means you were the horny one this morning." Well, they weren't lying about that, but that was not why we were there.

"Well, forget about Genius and my sex expeditions this morning. I have to tell you guys what we found out, it is really important."

Genius sat down by the boys so that I could speak to them all at once without having to turn my head a whole lot, which I appreciated. I took a breath, looking at Alcide who nodded at me. "Okay, well, when we got to the spirit world, Mom actually opened up to the both of us." I stopped for a second. "She told us that Grandmom and she both wiped Alcide's memory multiple times. That is why he can't remember everything." I looked back at Alcide; again, he nodded. "But that isn't all. She let us in on a big secret. Grandma is still alive, and she is the only one that can train me with my magic." I looked at the boys, and all their mouths fell open, except for Alcide because he already knew everything.

Zeus stood up. "What do you mean Grandma is still alive? I thought she died a long time ago." I didn't know how to answer that one, so I looked at Alcide.

"Well, Zeus, apparently Grandma has a curse, and she can't die."

He went to say something else, but I held up my hand, signaling him to stop. "Look, Zeus, we don't know much more than that. Mom didn't explain that part, but she did promise me that if I train with Grandma then come back, she would give me all the answers that we were wanting, but only if I trained with Grandma first."

Genius looked confused for a moment. "Princess, but we don't even know where your grandmother is."

I just smiled. "But we do. Mom told me that she was guarding the entrance to the tunnel that leads to the castle." The boys looked shocked, but I didn't let them ask anything before continuing, "Before you guys say anything that was another condition of Mother's, none of us are to go into the castle until I train with Grandmother." They all shook their heads.

Zeus walked closer to me. "Well, Squirt, where is she?"

I stood up looking at them all. "She is in Cann Woods in Plymouth, England."

Genius looked at me with wide eyes. "Princess, you're telling me you have to go to England for this training?"

I shook my head. "But I will allow some of you to come with me and stay nearby, but I have to do this part by myself." They all shook their heads. I knew that this was going to be a fight.

"Look, I know that you guys are not okay with it, but, unfortunately, this is how it has to go. Alcide has to be right beside me just in case Grandmother doesn't recognize me, but, Zeus, and, Genius, you will be coming along too." I turned toward Daniel. "I will need you to stay here and hold everything down while we are gone. You are the only other one that I can trust with this part. But that means you have to keep an open communication between us."

He stood up with a smile on his face. "Well, Artemis, I am honored by this, and I can promise you I will do my best to run the place while you guys are gone, but when do you plan on leaving?"

I looked around at the boys again. "I planned on leaving as soon as possible. I have to train with my magic as soon as possible or I might never get the chance to again, and I am tired of people I love getting hurt because of me. I need to be able to protect all of you."

Genius walked up to me, placing his hand on my cheek. "Princess, you don't need to be strong by yourself. I am here with you, and so is the whole pack." I knew that he was right, but I couldn't risk anyone else getting hurt trying to protect me. I just wouldn't.

"I know that, Genius, I do, but I won't let anyone else get hurt protecting me. It is that simple."

I turned toward Alcide. "Can you get the plane ready so that we can leave tomorrow? And while we are there training my magic, I will be needed you training on what to do if captured." I turned toward Genius and Zeus. "While we are there, can you guys help me with my training? I figure it not only will help me but you guys too." They all seemed nervous, I could sense it, especially coming from Genius. "I know that you guys are nervous about this, but this is what has to be done or people close to us are going to continue to get hurt, and I don't want that."

Zeus looked at me. "Squirt, I don't know how you are managing to stay so sane about all of this. You were the last to know about all of this, but you don't seem affected by it."

I guess I never thought about that before. "I honestly don't know how, but I am."

Daniel turned to me with a serious look on his face. "Ya, but, Artemis, at some point, this is all going to hit you, and you're going to break, you know that, right? You can only stay strong for so long before everything catches up to you. Trust me, I have done that before." I was confused, but that I never knew that he had been through anything that major. But I figured that it was best not to ask any further right now.

"I will be careful, Daniel, I promise. Now can we please do a little research? We still don't know if the mate mark can be manipulated or not."

I looked at Genius and Zeus. "Did you guys ever find anything?"

They both shook their heads no. "Princess, we couldn't find anything in any of the books about it."

Then Zeus looked at me. "Maybe that is one of the things we could ask Grandma when we find her." Well, he had a point there. Maybe she could answer some of the questions we had.

"Well, we can try when we find her, but I guess, today, everyone can enjoy a day off. No working today, just have fun." They all nodded before walking out the door. Genius was the only one left in the room with me.

He walked closer to me. "Princess, I really don't like this."

I kissed him on his lips. "I know, Baby, but it is something that we have to do, and you know that, right?"

He just looked at the floor for a second before looking up at me. "Ya, I know, but I still don't have to like it."

I smiled at him. "Ya, but we don't have to do anything major today, so let's make the day about me and you, okay?"

He kissed me on my lips before looking at me. "Ya, we can, but I want to plan it, so give me a little bit, then I will come and find you, okay?" I couldn't do anything but smile. *How did I get so lucky to find such a perfect man?*

"Okay, Baby, go plan our day. I'll be around the house somewhere." He kissed me on my forehead before walking out the door. I was happy knowing that he was excited. *Now let's just hope nothing pops up that can ruin our day.*

# Date Night

I had gone to the library while I waited on Genius to make our plans for the night. I had to admit; it kind of made me nervous. But he wanted to plan the night, so I would let him do it. So while he planned it, I wanted to see if I could find any information on the mate mark being manipulated. I know I told the boys no working, but I really needed to know if that man could be my father. I don't see my mother lying about that, at least not on purpose. But, then again, she had lied about everything else in my life, so I wouldn't be surprised if she had been lying. So I found myself in the library, looking through the books that Genius and Zeus had laid out on the table, but there was nothing in the books that would give me any more information then. So I got up and started walking around the library when I noticed an area of the library which did not have any books on the shelves, which seemed a little odd to have in a library as big as this one. I walked toward the area, but that is when Genius came in.

"Babe, I am ready." I just smiled at him. He walked over, grabbing my hand and leading me out the door, then outside to our massive backyard. When I looked up, I saw that he had candles laid out in a path leading to a table that had candles on it as well. He had the table laid right under the moon. He let go of my hand, letting me walk the path to the table, and it was the most beautiful thing that I had ever seen.

The closer I got to the table, I could see that he had the table surrounded with rose petals. On the table, he had a large candle that was glowing brightly, a bottle of wine, two plates, two wine glasses. I looked around at the trees surrounding us, and he had lights hanging from them, along with decorations. Genius really took his time with this. He must have noticed the shock and amazement on my face because he walked over to me, pulling me into his arms.

"Artemis, I have loved you for a very long time. The more time I get with you, the more I fall in love with you. You are truly amazing in every way

154

possible." I could feel my cheeks becoming bright. I turned around to face him, giving him the largest kiss that I could possibly give him.

"Genius, you are absolutely amazing, and this is amazing. I can't believe you did all of this."

He just smiled. "Well, that isn't all of it, Baby." He grabbed me by my hand, leading me back to the table, pulling the chair out for me to sit down. He gently pushed the chair closer to the table before sitting down himself. He clapped his hands together and the lights that were hanging from the trees dimmed down some. Then I started hearing violins playing; out from the trees appeared some violin players, then from the other side, a butler came out with a cart of, well, everything.

I turned back toward my mate. I was smiling from ear to ear. He really planned this evening down to every little detail. The butler came over, pouring us both some of the wine that was on the table, then he placed our food on the table. He took the tops off of both plates, allowing us to see what was underneath and it smelled so good. We both had steak, mashed potatoes, and fresh green beans. The smell was intoxicating; my mouth started watering as soon as the smell hit me. Genius started laughing at me. I just smiled.

"Genius, this is amazing. I can't believe you pulled all of this off out of nowhere."

He just smiled at me. "Well, I would do anything for you, Princess." We both started eating, not saying much, just enjoying our meals and each other's company. When we were done with our plates, the butler took them away.

"That was absolutely amazing." Genius stood up, walking around the table. Pulling my chair out, he grabbed my hand, leading me away from the table. The violinist followed us. Genius grabbed my hands, placing one around his neck, and the other one, he intertwined with his hand, then we started dancing to the music that they were playing.

We were just spinning around for what seemed like an eternity. Before we stopped, he sent everyone away, then turned back toward me. He got this mischievous smile on his face; I knew he was up to something. He picked me up, allowing me to wrap my legs around him.

"Princess, will you go skinny dipping with me?" I just smiled at him. How could I tell this man no after all of this?

"Lead the way, Baby." With that being said, I got down, walking hand in hand, allowing him to lead me to the lake. We were just standing on the outside, but it looked beautiful from where we were standing. The moon was bright and full, shining down on the lake. I turned to look at Genius, and he was just staring at me. I started blushing again. *I don't know why, but each time he stares at me like I am the only thing that matters in the world, I immediately start to blush.* Genius started stripping his clothes off before running and jumping into the lake. He disappeared for a moment before appearing above the water again. God, did he look amazing right now. The water was glistening down his abs and running back into the water. I didn't realize how hard I was staring until, "Hey, Princess, if you like what you see, why don't you come and join me?"

That snapped me back to reality. I just smiled before stripping my clothes off and running in to join my mate. When I came back up, he pulled me closer to him, turning me so that my back was against his chest, allowing me to get a good glimpse of the moon. The moon was always calming to me no matter what, but being there with Genius, watching the moon together while my mate held me, things couldn't be more perfect than what they were then. Genius gently turned me around so that we were facing one another. He gently placed the hair that was in my face behind my ear.

"Babe, you are the most beautiful woman to ever walk this earth, you know that?" I just smiled at him. He placed his hand under my chin, gently lifting it up before placing his lips upon mine. I melted into him, allowing his kiss to consume me. I wrapped my arms around his neck when he lifted me up, allowing my legs to wrap perfectly around him. We finally broke our kiss. Looking into each other's eyes, I could never love a man more than I love Genius.

Genius walked up to the grass shore with me wrapped around him still. I hadn't noticed that he had a blanket laid out for me. Genius gently laid me on top of the blanket, allowing me to lay flat; he just looked me up and down.

"Babe, you truly are beautiful." Genius bent down to kiss me before he kissed his way down to my neck right where our mark sat. He gently nibbled our mark; my eyes rolled into the back of my head. But he didn't stop there. He kissed his way down to my nipples, gently sucking and nibbling on them before kissing his way down to my lip. He gently opened them up before licking my clit, sending a shock through my body, causing me to moan with anticipation. He gently sucked on my clit while sliding two fingers inside of me, causing me to grind against him. He started licking my clit like it was like an ice-cream cone that he couldn't get enough of. Right when I was about to climax, he stopped, kissing his way back up to my lips. But he didn't kiss me; he just stared at me for a moment before he started rubbing his big, hard shaft against my pussy lips. He grabbed one of my legs, gently lifting it up. He slid into me, causing me to arch my back and moan with excitement.

But this time was different. He wasn't going rough and fast like he normally would. No, he was taking his time this time. He was sliding in and out of me, causing me to moan each time. He started kissing me while he grabbed my hips, pushing deeper and deeper into me. I wanted to scream, but I could not with his lips right there. His pace started to pick up speed, letting me know that he was reaching his climax, just like I was. I finally broke the kiss, only to kiss my way down to our mark. When he shoved into me deeper, I bit down on our mark, allowing my canines to break his skin, causing him to scream while he climaxed, but I didn't let him pull out. I wrapped my legs around him, forcing him deeper into me while I let my orgasm consume me. We stayed like this for a moment before he collapsed on top of me. We were both panting from what we just did. Genius turned his head toward me.

"Baby, I love you!"

I turned toward him. "Genius, I love you too." We just cuddled up under the moonlight, laying there for a long time. We lay there till the sunset, just enjoying each other. I sat up on my elbow, turning toward my mate.

"Genius, you know we have to head back, right?"

He just smiled at me. "I know, Babe. We really have to get our bags packed for the trip in a little bit." We both stood up, getting dressed. Once we both had our clothes on, I followed him back to our home. I was nervous, but I knew that this was what I had to do to protect my pack.

# Leaving

Genius and I walked into our room. Genius went and grabbed the suitcases from the closet so that we could pack our things. I was becoming increasingly nervous about this. I never got the chance to meet my grandmother, and, now, I not only have to meet her. She has to train me on something I never thought existed. Genius realized I was just standing there and walked up to me, wrapping his big arms around my tiny body.

"Artemis, I know that you are nervous. So am I, but you are the strongest woman I know. If anyone can make it through this, it's you."

I turned my head just enough to look at him. "I know, but what if my grandmother doesn't recognize me or Alcide?"

Genius spun me around to look at him. "Princess, I don't believe that she could have forgotten about her own son, and even if she doesn't recognize you guys, you will make her believe. That's just who you are." I guess he was right.

"Go make sure the boys are ready, and can you carry the bags down to the office? I will meet everyone down there in a second. I just need a minute." Genius, without saying anything else, kissed me on top of my head before grabbing our suitcases and heading downstairs.

Now, I just needed to talk to Violet; we hadn't spoken much here lately. "Violet, can you hear me?" I waited a moment before she said anything.

"Well, well, well, look who knows how to talk now." I knew she was upset with me. I had been neglecting her without realizing it.

"I am so sorry, Violet. I just forgot, with everything going on. I truly am sorry for not speaking to you more." I heard her laugh in my head.

"Artemis, it is okay. I was just messing with you. I know that you are still getting used to hearing me and being in a pack. This is all new to you. I don't expect you to talk with me all day and ignore your duties as queen."

I just smiled. "I know, but, still, we are one, and I need to be a little bit more considerate when it comes to you. Can you forgive me?" I waited a moment.

"Yes, I forgive you." Thank the moon goddess for that.

"Violet, I am really nervous about this training that I have to do. What if I can't catch onto it?"

"Artemis, you are stronger than you give yourself credit for, and, don't forget, I will be here with you the entire time. We will become closer and more bonded together through the training; it is just natural for us to do so."

I just smiled. "Well, I guess it is time for us to go downstairs."

With that, I turned around, walking toward my bedroom door, but before I opened it, I felt a sharp pain in my stomach.

I heard Violet, "Artemis, something is wrong with Genius." I flung the door open, running down the stairs and into the office. When I opened the door, what I saw, I wasn't sure what to do, laugh or punch the shit out of those dumbasses. They were wrestling a little too hard in my office, because the whole office was destroyed. Zeus had a hammer in his hand, and Genius was hunched over, holding his stomach. They both turned toward the office door, and when they saw it was me, their eyes got very wide.

"Squirt, let me explain first." I didn't give him time to speak. I walked over, grabbing the hammer from his hand and hitting him right in the lower right side of his stomach where I felt the pain, causing him to hunch over in pain.

"Now, we're even, you ass." Alcide and Daniel fell out of the chairs, laughing. Genius walked over, kissing me on the forehead, but he wasn't getting off that easy. I dropped the hammer on his foot, causing him to jump up and down on one foot. Yes, it hurt me, but not as much as it hurt him.

"Now do you two want to explain why the hell my office is destroyed and why you had a hammer in your hand?"

Alcide got up from the floor. "Well, we had a bet on whose stomach was stronger out of Zeus and Genius."

I just shook my head. *Did he really just say what I think he said?* That is when I heard Violet laughing. "Yes, my dear, he did in fact just say that."

I turned toward Zeus and Genius. "So you two thought it was a great idea to hit one another with the hammer to see whose stomach was stronger?" They both nodded in agreement. I wasn't sure whether to hit them again or laugh, so, instead, I did nether. "Okay, well, I guess you both lost then, because I felt the pain and didn't even buckle." Their mouths fell open. Alcide and Daniel again fell over, laughing.

Daniel was the first to say something, "You two just got your asses kicked by a girl."

Genius just looked upset. "Well, how about you come over here and let her hit you with it and see if you can do better."

Daniel started shaking his head. "I am not that dumb."

That caused me to laugh. "He does have a point, boys." They just both looked down at the ground. "Okay, enough horsing around. We have a long flight ahead of us, you know that, right?" I turned toward Alcide. "Did you get the plane ready to go?" Alcide stood up, wiping the tears from his face. "Yes, the plane is fueled and ready to go, with our most trusted pilot waiting on us."

I turned toward Daniel. "Are you sure that you can handle this while we are gone?" Daniel acted offended after I said that.

"You don't trust me to handle the pack?"

I punched his arm. "It's not that I don't trust you. I just want to make sure that you're okay with all the responsibility that comes with it."

He just smiled. "Artemis, I got this. You don't have to worry, and I have Dream and Jade here to help me if I get lost along the way."

I had forgotten all about their mates for a moment, so I mind-linked them, "Dream and Jade, can you come to the office please?"

I waited a few moments before I got a response, "Yes, Queen."

I looked at Daniel again. "Okay, Daniel, but I am so serious. If anything goes wrong, I need you to get a hold of one of us immediately or have the girls or James do it, but please just promise me you will keep everyone safe while we're gone, because I don't know how long we will be gone."

Daniel walked over to me, wrapping me in a hug. "Artemis, I promise you that if something happens. I will get a hold of you immediately, and if it gets really bad, I will send James to find you, okay?"

I just smiled, then I heard a knock on the door. "Come in."

In walked Dream and Jade, my two, lovely, older sisters. I walked over to them, giving them a hug which they reciprocated.

Dream pulled me away a little. "Well, not that I don't appreciate the hug, but why did you call us in here? You guys have to get going, don't you?"

I just smiled at them. "Well, a couple of things actually. One, I wanted to see you before we take off, and, two, I have a really big favor to ask you." I turned toward Daniel, smiling. He just nodded, knowing what I was going to do next. "Will you guys be Daniel's beta and delta while we are gone so that he has people he can trust to help him while we three are away?"

They both looked shocked; Jade just smile. "Artemis, are you sure that you don't want James to have one of those positions? He would be better suited for that."

Dream looked at me. "Ya, I have to agree with Jade on this one."

I just shook my head. "You guys don't give yourselves enough credit. You guys already know how everything operates around here. As for James, no, he is the bodyguard for you guys while we are away."

They both smiled, giving me a big hug, and, in unison, they both spoke, OMG, thank you, Artemis. "We won't let you down, I promise."

I just smiled. "I know you guys won't. Now go say your goodbyes. We will be leaving in a moment. It is a long flight and we have to go." They let go of me before heading over to the guys. I turned to look at everyone. "Violet, how did we get so lucky to get a family like this?"

I heard her chuckle. "I don't know, but I am grateful we have them to count on. With all of this going on, this is more than enough reason for us to fight through and become stronger so none of them get hurt." With that, I had to agree with her. We had to become stronger so that we can protect all of them and the rest of the pack. I wasn't sure what was coming, but I knew it was going to be bad. They are our family, and I will protect them with every ounce of my strength.

"Okay, Daniel, Dream, and Jade, while we are gone, make sure everyone is taken care of. You know where the safe room is. If anything goes wrong, to get everyone inside. The barrier should be okay while I am gone. If I sense anything around it, I will contact you guys immediately. Daniel, have James see if he can find any more of our pack or anyone that has been kicked out of theirs, and if you guys feel you can trust them, then bring them back here, but, remember, everyone, trust your instincts no matter what. If your gut is telling you something, listen to it. I won't be here this time to help."

They nodded, letting me know they all understood. Jade and Daniel left the room first. Dream gave Zeus a kiss before leaving.

I turned toward the boys. "Are you guys ready for this trip?" They all nodded. We left the office, heading to the airport not too far from our home. I was getting more nervous the closer we got to this plane.

But before we got on the plane, Genius came up behind me, wrapping his arms around me and leaning in to whisper, "Babe, everything will be fine. You are strong, and you have a family with you." I just smiled. I knew he was right, but I was still nervous. We all boarded the plane, getting in our seats. We sat there for what seemed like an eternity before the plane took off. Now, reality was setting in. We were actually on our way to meet our grandmother. I hoped she remembered Alcide, because, if not, I didn't know how well this would go, because Mother said Grandmother was strong which makes me nervous. If she doesn't recognize him, will she try to fight us? I turned to see what the boys were doing. Alcide and Zeus were already asleep in their seats. I turned toward Genius who was sitting next to me; he just looked at me at smiled.

"Princess, you need to rest. Tomorrow is going to be a busy day. Come here and lay on my chest." I couldn't argue with that. I needed to feel his body against my own. Maybe it would help me relax a little bit, and as if he knew exactly what I needed, he wrapped his arms around me, waiting for me to relax my head on his chest, and I somehow became instantly relaxed, causing me to drift to sleep in his arms.

# Cann Wood Forest

## Part One

I woke up when the plane started to shake a little more than normal. I looked up to see Genius awake; the turbulence must have woken him up as well. I turned to see if Zeus and Alcide were still asleep, but they were wide awake too. I had never been on a plane with this much turbulence before; it was making me really nervous.

I turned my head up toward Genius. "Babe, what's going on? Why is there so much turbulence? Are we in a storm?"

He looked down at me. "I honestly don't know. We haven't heard anything from the captain."

I sat up, turning toward Zeus and Alcide. "Do either of you two know why there is so much turbulence?" They both shook their heads no. Great, nobody knew what was going on. I got off Genius, fixing my shirt before turning toward the captain's pit. Once I reached the captain's pit, I knocked on the door once, but he didn't answer, so I knocked again, still no answer. So I tried to open the door, but it was locked. *O, boy, this isn't good.* I turned toward the boys. "Umm, he isn't answering, and the door is locked, so what are we supposed to do exactly?"

All of their eyes became wide, but Alcide was the first to speak, "Well, we are gonna have to open that door." Without hesitation, Genius walked over there, grabbing the door and ripping it off of its hinges. *What the hell? I didn't know he could do that.*

But I didn't have time to gawk over Genius. I walked into the captain's pit, but what I found wasn't what I expected. Our captain was unconscious which meant that nobody was flying that plane.

163

I turned toward the boys. "Um, we have a problem." They all came into the pit slowly. When they saw the captain wasn't conscious, Daniel turned toward me.

"What do we do now?" That was a good question.

"Alcide, can you tell if we are over the Cann Wood forest in England or not?"

Alcide stepped forward, looking around before he turned back toward us. "Ya, we're directly over it, which would explain quite a bit actually."

We all looked at him, confused. "What do you mean?"

He looked at me. "Well, Artemis, if you think about it. If my mom is still alive and we're flying over the forest and now our pilot is unconscious and we have a crap ton of turbulence, wouldn't that mean that she has some sort of barrier or something up to protect that entrance?" Honestly, that made a lot more sense than I thought it was going to.

Genius turned toward me. "Well, if she put up a barrier, shouldn't you be able to create a hole or something in it, allowing the plane to go through it?"

That was a good question, one that I didn't have the answer to. "I honestly don't know, Genius. I am not as powerful as my grandmother, so I don't see how I could break through the barrier at all."

That is when I heard Violet laughing in my head. "Artemis, do you really think that our grandmother is stronger? No, sweetheart, she isn't."

That shocked me. "What do you mean? She is a lot older than me, with a lot more experience than me."

I heard Violet start laughing again. "None of those reasons mean she is stronger than you. It just means that she has the experience. Artemis, we are one of the strongest beings of our kind. Why do you think that everyone was hiding us and protecting us?" I thought about it for a moment. *Is she right? Are we the strongest of our kind right now?* Alcide must have known something because he walked over to me, placing an arm on both shoulders.

"Artemis, you are stronger than you think you are. Just try it because, honestly, you're our only hope at this point." Great, no pressure. Zeus and Genius just gave me a warm smile. I guess I could try.

I looked at them. "Okay, I can try, but you know, once I do this, it will let her know that we are here." They all nodded, so I stepped closer to the front windows of the plane, placing my hands on them. Then, I closed my eyes, concentrating, trying to find the energy from the barrier. Once I located the

164

barrier, I focused on a hole appearing in the barrier big enough to allow the plane through. I focused as hard as I could, then I could feel Violet there helping me, guiding me. After what seemed like forever, I managed to open a hole in the barrier, allowing the plane to start inching through. I kept concentrating Violet and my energy till the plane was through. Once the plane was completely through, I allowed the barrier to close behind the plane. I opened my eyes, turning back toward the boys. They were all smiling from ear to ear. Genius walked over to me.

"See, Princess, we knew you could do it." I just smiled before turning back toward our captain. He was slowly waking up. So I kneeled next to him, placing my hand on his shoulder, allowing my energy to pass into him. Once I did that, he fully woke up.

"What's going on? Why are you guys in here?" I just looked at him. I felt horrible that this happened to him.

"A lot has happened, but you're safe. We will grab our parachutes and jump out the plane now. Once we do, I want you to continue to the airport and then go to the hotel that we picked out. We will call you when we are ready."

He looked confused but nodded. I stood up, looking at the boys. "Well, let's get our things. We have a long adventure ahead."

Zeus laughed. "You would call it an adventure, Squirt, but ya, let's get going." With that, we all headed back to the back part of the plane. We started grabbing everything we needed. Genius walked over to me.

"Are you ready to strap onto me?" I just nodded; I had never sky-jumped before, so I felt safer jumping with Genius because he had done that before, so I knew I would be safe.

Alcide opened the back part of the plane before shouting at us, "Okay, everyone, this is it." Then he just ran and jumped out the plane, then Zeus followed, but Genius walked us over to the edge before looking down at me.

"All right, Princess, let's go." Then he jumped. We were falling straight down, and it was the scariest, most exciting thing that I had ever done. I looked up, and Genius pulled our parachute, allowing us to safely drop to the ground so we weren't injured. Alcide and Zeus were already on the ground, stripping their parachutes. Genius unbuckled me from him before he stripped off our parachute as well. I got my backpack situated on my back, then I turned toward Alcide.

"Do you remember any of this?"

He looked at me with a serious face. "Artemis, I only remember bits and pieces, so I don't know how much help I will be."

I just smiled. "Alcide, you forget you're a wolf sometimes, don't you?" He just smiled, then started laughing.

"That is the same thing Dominic just said in my head." I had never heard my uncle say his wolf's name, but I was glad that he was opening up.

"Well, ask Dominic if he smells a familiar scent anywhere around here." Alcide tilted his nose up, taking a big breath of air before looking back at me.

"I know which direction to head, but I don't know how far we are going to have to walk before we reach the entrance."

Genius turned toward me. "Well, I guess we can start walking in the direction, then when it gets dark, we can set up camp until morning." I nodded, knowing that was probably what was best, even though I didn't want to stop, but I knew I would need the rest once we met up with Grandmother.

I turned toward Alcide. "Well, lead the way." Alcide started walking to the right of us and continued straight. I didn't know what path was ahead of us, but I knew, with these three beside me, we would get through anything together. We started following Alcide for what seemed like hours when he came to a stop. He turned toward us.

"It is getting dark. We will set up camp here, then continue in the morning." We all nodded; the boys got the tents and fire going while I looked around at everything. It was beautiful out there despite the reason we were there. Once everything was set up, Alcide and Genius went into their tent. Genius walked over to me. "Princess, we need to lay down. You need all the rest you can get."

I allowed him to lead me to our tent, then we lay down on our sleeping bag. "Genius, do you think my grandmother will remember us?"

He sat up on his elbow, staring at me. "Artemis, I honestly don't know, but if anyone can convince her that you guys are family, it is you. Now get some rest please." With that, I lay against Genius, and he wrapped his arms around me. I stared at the top of our tent for a long time before my eyes finally became heavy. I allowed myself to succumb to the darkness behind my eyes, drifting off into a deep sleep.

# Cann Wood Forest

## Part Two

I woke to hearing the leaves rustling outside of our tent. I looked over at Genius, and he was still sound asleep. So, I lay there, hoping that maybe it was just an animal passing by, but the leaves began to rustle more and more which made me worry a little more. So, I nudged Genius, and he slowly opened his eyes.

"What, Princess?"

I just stared at him. "Do you hear that?"

He lay there for a moment before sitting up. "What is that?"

I sat up. "I don't know, Babe, but maybe we should check it out together." With that, we both unzipped the tent. Peeking our head out of the tent, we didn't see anything, so we got out of our tent and walked over to Zeus and Alcide's tent.

"Zeus, Alcide, are you in there?" We heard moving around in the tent when we saw two heads pop out of the tent.

"What's going on, Artemis?" Zeus and I looked at one another before looking back at them.

"We heard the leaves moving outside of our tent." They both walked out of the tent and started to look around, but they couldn't see anything either.

I wasn't sure what that noise was, but it made me nervous; I was feeling uneasy for some reason.

"Well, I guess we should pack up and start walking toward the entrance." They all nodded in agreement, so we all packed up our tents and covered up the fire that we started last night.

Genius turned toward Alcide. "Well, you have to lead the way, remember?" Alcide nodded, tilting his nose up in the air to get a whiff, then he started walking straight forward. He continued on this path for what seemed

167

like forever before he took a sharp right turn. We followed him for hours before we came to a complete stop.

He turned toward me. "Artemis, we're here, but I can't see anything. Do you feel anything around us that could be stopping us from seeing it?" I just stood there for a moment before closing my eyes, trying to feel out around us, but the only spot I sensed something was right in front of us. So I walked forward, placing my hands in front of me until they rested upon an invisible barrier. I sent out an energy to open a door, but it wouldn't budge.

I looked back at the boys. "There is a barrier here, but I can't get through this one right now. Maybe my magic isn't strong enough to penetrate this one." They looked at each other before turning back toward me.

"Well, if you can't get through, that means your grandmother has to be somewhere around here, right?" I just nodded. I knew that she was here, but I had no way of knowing where or if this would be a good thing or a bad thing.

I turned toward Alcide. "Alcide, can you come here real quick? I want to try something." Alcide did without hesitation. I grabbed his hand before grabbing the knife out of my pocket. His eyes got wide.

"Artemis, what are you doing?" I just ignored him before slicing his palm, then I placed his hand on the barrier with mine on top. This time, I was trying to send a signal, not open a door. I was hoping that with her son's blood, she might be more keen on talking rather than fighting. I closed my eyes, focusing on sending a signal around the barrier, allowing Alcide's blood to pool around the outside of the barrier before sending it around the barrier. I followed through the barrier when I hit something or someone, causing me to jump back to where I was. I opened my eyes, letting Alcide's hand go.

I turned to all three of them. "Well, if she didn't know we were here a moment ago, she knows now."

They all looked at one another before Zeus turned toward me. "What do you mean, Squirt?"

I just looked back at the barrier. "Well, I sent out a signal using Alcide's blood around and through the barrier, but I got sent back when I hit someone or something with the energy I was using to do this. So I can only assume that this is Grandmother." I turned back around to see them all just staring at me.

Alcide was wrapping his hand up. "Artemis, does that mean we have trouble coming our way?"

I just stood there for a moment. Would she really try to fight us? "I honestly don't know, Alcide. Maybe we should just wait here and hope that she wants to talk with us instead of hurting us." I honestly didn't know if the blood thing would work, but I knew I had to try something to get her attention. I was just hoping I didn't make things worse before they even got started.

I stood there for a moment before speaking into my mind, "Violet, did you sense the same thing I did?" I stood there, waiting for a reply from her. It took a few moments before I heard anything.

"Artemis, we really do need to work on you sensing abilities, don't we!?"

I just shook my head. "I know that. Why do you think we're all the way out here? For me to train more. But you didn't answer the question." I sat there for a few moments.

"Artemis, whatever you touched with our magic is very old and powerful. I don't know if it was your grandmother, but she knows we're here now." Damn, I knew I was right, but I couldn't sense her power or that she was old. I just bumped into something with my power and it got sent back.

I turned toward Genius. "Babe, whatever happens next, you are to just sit back. Do not try to get in the middle of it. I don't want you getting hurt. Promise me."

Genius walked up to me, wrapping his arms around me, pulling me closer. "Princess, I will not make that promise because if you're in danger, I will do what I have to." I just shook my head. I knew he would say that. I don't know why I tried to convince him otherwise.

Zeus looked at me. "Artemis, what should we do now?"

I looked at him. "The only thing we can do right now is wait."

Alcide looked at me. "Well, we should set up camp. We don't know when she is going to come, but we do know that she will." We all nodded in agreement; we all sat our tents up.

Genius looked at all of us. "We should go hunting so that we can get a good meal in before this whole thing starts." We all started stripping our clothes off. Before shifting into our wolves, we ran as a pack through the forest until we all spotted some deer. Alcide and Zeus were the first to take off, then Genius and I followed. We each caught our own deer, carrying it back to the campsite with us. Once we dropped all of our kills, we all shifted back.

Getting dressed, I turned toward all of the boys. "Well, you guys better get stripped and everything. Looks like we're going to be having deer for a while."

169

They all started laughing, but they did. They got the deer ready to be cooked. Genius cooked for me. I was sitting down on one of the logs that they had dragged over, zoned out.

I wasn't paying much attention to the boys. I was more focused on when she would show herself. I had a feeling she was watching us, but she probably wasn't going to make a move until we least expected it. Which is what made it so much worse. I sat there for hours, trying to figure out how or when this would happen. But I was giving myself a headache, trying to figure that out. That is when Genius tapped me on my shoulder, snapping me out of my head.

"Princess, are you okay?"

I just smiled up at my mate. "Yes, just got lost in thought." He handed me a stick with a leg from one of the deer on it. I took a bite out of it, not saying much at all. Genius placed his hand on my thigh, causing me to look at him.

"Artemis, please don't worry. There isn't anything we can do right now, but wait for her to come to us." I knew he was right, but I had a bad feeling this wasn't going to be the reunion we wanted it to be. I ate my food in silence before laying by the fire, staring up at the sky. I didn't notice that the boys had did the same.

Zeus finally spoke, "Do you think she will try to kill us?"

Alcide closed his eyes. "I honestly don't know. I haven't seen my mother in so long, but if she is anything like my sister said, then we should just be prepared for the worst just in case." I knew it was true, but I couldn't help but be hopeful that that wouldn't turn out as horrible as it felt.

We just lay there for hours, waiting, but nothing happened. It started to get dark, so we all sat up and just started joking and laughing. I sat there and watched all of their smiles, and it made my heart skip a beat. *I love every one of these boys, and I will do whatever it takes to protect them.* I would die if something happened to them…

# Cann Wood Forest

## Part Three

We all drifted off into a sleep after joking around with one another for a while. That's when I could sense a powerful aura swirling around us. So I woke up and turned to see if the boys were asleep, but, to my surprise, they were already awake.

"Guys, do you feel that?" They all turned toward me, nodding. I stood up, and that is when I noticed her. My grandmother was walking from behind the barrier toward us. She had white hair with deep-violet eyes. She stood just as tall as I did, but she was a lot more intimidating than I was. I wasn't entirely sure what to do. So I walked a little closer, but when I did, she held her hand up, sending me flying backward into the tree behind me.

Genius rushed over to me. "Princess, are you okay?" I just nodded, standing up. I looked over to my uncle, and he seemed to be frozen in place. I walked over to him, placing my hand on his shoulder.

"Alcide, try to talk to her before this goes south really quickly?" I could see that he was shocked to see his mother, but this wasn't the time for this. I knew this could go south really quickly if we didn't convince her of who we were.

So I turned my uncle around so that he was facing me. "Alcide, I know this is a shock, but I can't lose you guys, and you know what will happen if we can't convince her of who we are. Please try."

He just nodded before turning around and walking toward his mother. "Mother, it's me, Alcide. Do you not recognize your own son?"

She turned her head to the side before sending Alcide flying through the air. "My son is dead!!!"

I stood there in shock of what just happen, but I didn't have time to process anything before Zeus started walking forward. "Grandmother, it's Zeus, your

171

daughter's son. Please tell me that you remember me." Again, without batting an eyelash, she flicked her hand, sending my brother flying right on top of my uncle. This is going very badly. Genius stepped forward. I went to stop him, but he wasn't listening as always.

"Look, calm down a minute. I know that you don't remember them, but you remember your daughter, right? Athena Cage." You could see something in her eyes soften a little bit, but then they were back to being bright violet. She lifted her hand up again, sending Genius in the air and on top of the other two.

I stood back up, slowly walking toward her. That is when I heard Violet, "Art, you're going to have to show her your eyes. I don't think she is going to recognize anyone right now. She has been by herself for so long." I knew that she was right, but what if I couldn't get my eyes to do it? They seemed to only do it when I was angry or fighting. I walked up, focusing on the aura around my body, allowing that powerful energy that coursed through my body to take over. When I opened my eyes, I could tell they had changed. I didn't know how, but I could feel it. I walked closer.

"Grandmother, it is me, Artemis. I am your granddaughter, child of your daughter, Athena Cage. I ask that you please look at me and see that what I am saying is true." I held my hands out to the side to show her that I held no ill will toward her. She walked closer to me. I flinched for fear of what might happen, but she grabbed my face, looking me in the eyes.

"Athena, is that you, my sweet girl?"

I wanted to cry; she didn't even know that her daughter was no longer on this earth with us. "No, Grandma, it's your granddaughter, Athena's daughter."

I could see the tears welling up in her eyes. "This cannot be true. You guys shouldn't be here. No no no, this isn't possible." I turned to see that all three boys were walking our way. Alcide was on the verge of crying; I could see it in his face and it broke my heart.

"Mom, it's me, Alcide." She started to get angry again, but I placed my hand on her face, closing my eyes, allowing my memories to drift into her mind. I didn't know how the hell was I doing that, but it was like that was something I had to do to get her to see. When I removed my hand from her face, she was in complete tears.

"My son, how, how are you here?" They both were in tears, but before they could completely break, Zeus stepped forward.

"Grandmother, do you remember me? It's Zeus, your grandson." She looked him up and down.

"Zeus, you have grown so much." She engulfed Alcide and Zeus into a hug. Once she released them, she turned toward Genius. "And who might you be? I don't recognize you."

Genius stepped forward, lowering his head. "Ma'am, I am your granddaughter's mate."

Her eyes became wide before turning toward me. "Artemis, is that you? This cannot be; I really thought you were Athena." I just shook my head, trying to keep myself from crying because I had a feeling the next question wasn't going to be a great one. She turned toward all four of us. "Well, where is Athena? Where is my daughter?" Everyone became silent; I couldn't bring myself to tell her, I just couldn't.

But as if Alcide could read my mind, he stepped a little closer to his mom. "Mom, Athena didn't make it. She was attacked by a wolf that meant Artemis harm." I could see the anger and the hurt in her eyes.

She turned back toward me. "What is the meaning of this?" Again, as if something pulled me toward her, I stepped forward, placing my hand against her face, closing my eyes and allowing the memory of that horrible day pass between us. When I removed my hand, I could see her start to cry. She wept for her daughter, and there was no amount of comfort that I could offer her to make her feel better.

We sat in silence for what seem like hours before she spoke again, "Alcide, why have you come? How did you remember this place? We wiped it from your memories so you couldn't come back here."

He turned toward his mother. "Mom, I wouldn't have remembered if Artemis hadn't helped me."

She turned toward me. "How? There is no way you have come into your powers that quickly." I didn't know how to answer that because I wasn't sure of the answer myself.

"I don't know. I just knew how to help, just like I know how to speak to Mother in the spirit world." Her eyes seem to enlarge after I spoke.

She turned toward the boys. "Is what she saying true?" They all nodded.

Alcide stepped a little closer to his mom. "Mother, Artemis took me to see my sister. If it wasn't for her, I wouldn't have even known you were still alive. I thought you died a long time ago."

She placed her hand on Alcide's shoulder and lifted his head with the hand. "My son, I never meant to cause you so much grief, but we had to protect her and him from what was coming. Yes, Artemis was the main focus, but, Zeus, you are connected to your sister in a way that we cannot totally grasp, so, because of that, it puts you in danger as well." We looked at one another, confused.

Genius beat everyone to the punch, "Excuse me, ma'am, I don't mean to interrupt, but what do you mean that they are connected?"

"First of all, quit calling me ma'am. My name is Hera. Second off, how could none of you know any of this? Didn't Athena tell you this?" Everyone looked down at the ground.

Zeus looked up at our grandmother. "No, she kept much away from us, but she never even told Artemis about any of this. She didn't learn about us till the night Mother died."

Her eyes became wide before turning to me. "Child, is what your brother saying true?" I lowered my head, not sure how to answer, when I felt Genius's hand on my back.

I looked up at my grandmother. "Yes, it's true. I knew nothing about any of this till the night she was killed, but I didn't find out most of it till the first full moon. Mom never told me anything. I didn't even know anything like this existed till that time." My grandmother was furious after hearing this. She started cussing and then she said something that we didn't quite understand, but after she said it, my mother's spirit appeared above the fire.

We all let out a loud gasp before my grandmother spoke, "Athena Raine, why on this earth have you withheld so much information from them and then have the audacity to send them here?" I could see the shame on my mother's face. You could see how disappointed in herself she was.

"Well, hello to you too, Mother. I didn't feel it was necessary at the time to tell them anything because she wouldn't come into her powers again until she was 16, but I see now that my mistake has caused a lot of trouble."

My grandmother started pacing back and forth in front of the fire. "Athena, you know you have not properly prepared any of them, they know nothing of what is to come, and you didn't even properly train Artemis and Zeus before you left this earth. They didn't even know about their connection."

My mother's eyes became wide. "Please, Mother, tell me you didn't mention that."

My grandmother rolled her eyes. "Yes, I did, of course, but I hand no clue how much you have sheltered them from and hid from them. How the hell are they supposed to properly protect themselves and their pack if you lied to them there whole life?"

With that, my grandmother didn't even give my mother time to speak before waving her arm and causing her spirit to dissipate. My grandmother turned toward all of us. "Let us go beyond the barrier. I have a home. There, we will rest and then discuss everything in great detail tomorrow, okay?" We all nodded. We knew better than to question her. I didn't want to see her when she was angry and, apparently, the others agreed.

We followed her through the barrier deep into the forest before walking up to a small cottage in the middle of nowhere. My grandmother recited some sort of incantation, that I was sure, but I had no clue what she said, but after she said it, her cottage grew a whole lot bigger. She turned toward us and said another incantation.

"Now off to bed, all of you. I will wake you in the morning. We have much to discuss." With that, she disappeared, and all of our bodies started moving on their own, causing us all to go into the house and in different directions. Genius and I were in the same room, and then we both were in bed, drifting off to sleep quicker than we ever had before.

# Hera's Words

The next morning, I had awaken to hearing my grandmother's words. I sat up to find Genius was still fast asleep. I thought maybe I was dreaming, but I heard her again. My body started moving on its own, opening the door before heading down the hall and into the kitchen where my grandmother sat with a cup of coffee in front of her and one sitting on the table across from her. I pulled the chair out and sat down.

"Grandma, are we the only ones up?"

She looked at me. "Artemis, right now, you and I need to talk before I wake your brother. There is much to discuss before I wake him." I nodded. I had a feeling that I wasn't going to like what she was about to say, but I knew it was important.

She let out a breath before speaking, "Artemis, I want to apologize to you first. Had I know that your mother kept all of this from you, I would have had her bring you to me."

I just looked at her, confused. "It isn't your fault that my mother hid things from me and lied."

She just shook her head some more. "That is where you are wrong. If I had kept in touch with her over the centuries, then I would have known, but I focused so much on protecting her that I left her alone in all of this. Artemis, do you realize how important you are?" I just shook my head no, fearing my voice wouldn't remain strong if I were to speak; she looked upset. "Artemis, you are stronger than you think you are. You are stronger than your mother, and, eventually, you will be stronger than me. Yes, you have the power of an enchantress in you but also the power of an alpha in you. Those two make a very strong connection, but your weakness is your brother. Always has been, always will be."

I was confused. "How can Zeus be my weakness?"

She sat back in her seat for a moment before speaking, "Do you remember how I said that you two have a connection but we weren't sure exactly how you were connected?" I nodded. "Well, your brother has blood of an enchantress in him as well. Males are known as enchanters, but because you guys share a close bond, it can be dangerous if one of you were to be harmed."

I was even more confused now than before. "Okay, but how I still am not understanding?"

She held her hand up, instructing me to stop. "Let me finish before you start asking questions. Your brother and your bond is unique. Not a lot of half siblings have this bond; it is rare. You have the ability to share energies among other things. Like I said before, I haven't seen a bond like this between siblings ever." She paused for a moment before speaking again, "There is much to learn about the bond between you guys, but that will require training from both of you, but we will get to that in a moment. How much has your mother told you about your powers?"

I looked at her. "Honestly, not much. My wolf, Violet, has helped me more than anything."

My grandmother raised her eyebrow. "Your wolf has been the one helping you?" I nodded, then my grandmother spoke a few words, then I started feeling funny, then this purple haze formed beside me in the chair, and I could see a human with deep-violet eyes sitting next to me. She was beautiful. She had light-purple hair, porcelain skin, and the most beautiful smile I had ever seen.

The lady turned toward me. "Well, Artemis, nice to see you. I am Violet."

My mouth fell wide open. "But you're not my wolf; you're human."

My grandmother started laughing. "I can see your mother failed to tell you a lot, huh."

Violet started chuckling. "Hera, she hasn't taught this child anything. I have been doing my best, but, unfortunately, I can't do much with her not knowing everything either."

My grandmother nodded. "Violet, you have grown much since I had seen you last!"

I was so confused. "Wait, how do you know her? How is she appearing in human form? What is going on?"

My grandmother turned toward me. "Sweet Child, your wolf can change forms just like you. You can turn into her wolf form, correct? She can take over your body in human form if need be."

Violet turned toward me. "As for how she knows me. Well, when you were a child, before either of us knew how to control our power, we had an outburst one time, and, well, Hera here brought me out to inform me of what was going to happen with them sealing your powers away. It meant that they had to seal your wolf side away too." That actually made a lot of sense now.

Hera turned toward me. "Child, I want you to know that you and Violet have a lot to learn before you're fully ready to protect yourself and your pack.

"But before we can train, I must tell you, Artemis, you are the strongest from our family. That is why we had to seal Violet and your power away till you were older. Your mother was supposed to sit down and let you know about all of this, but I see she has not, and you two have been struggling." She spoke a few silent words. That is when my brother appeared from behind her, rubbing his eyes. He came and sat down at the table.

"What's going on, and who is that?" He was pointing at Violet.

She just smiled at him. "Hi, Zeus, nice to meet you. I am Violet."

Zeus's mouth fell open before turning toward me. "That is your wolf? She is wow." I started laughing. "Okay, what is going on, Artemis? Why are we the only ones up?"

I looked at him, placing my hand on his. "Well, Grandmother has some information she is trying to share with us and felt that it was a good time to wake us to share it."

He turned toward our grandmother. "Well, what's going on?"

She lowered her head. "Zeus, you and your sister are connected in a way that I am not even sure how to explain at the moment. You have a bond that most half siblings don't share. Hell, not even full-blooded siblings have—"

Zeus cut her off, "I know we have a bond. She is my sister, and I will protect her with my life."

My grandmother held up her hand, silencing Zeus. "My dear boy, have you not felt the connection you have with your sister? How can you not notice? Zeus, have you ever noticed that you are the first one to always know where your sister is and what she is feeling? Kinda like her mate does, but not on that level."

Zeus hung his head. "Ya, but I thought that was just because we were family."

My grandmother grabbed his hands. "No, that is only part of it. You two have a deep connection. I am not quite sure what it is or how it fits into all this,

178

but I am hoping once we start training, we can figure it out together." She released his hand before turning toward us both. "But there is a prophecy that speaks of the battle to come as well as two siblings. One will give their life to save the other. It also speaks of the sibling that passes will give its strength to the other in order to save the pack." She stopped speaking.

"Wait, you're telling us that one of us will die during this battle?" Zeus placed his hand on mine before closing his eyes to speak, "So what you're saying is one of us won't make it through the battle but gives the other the extra strength needed to survive."

My grandmother spoke again, "Yes, but just because this is said in the prophecy doesn't mean that it has to happen. Yes, most prophecies do come true but not always. I am hoping we can avoid this one at all costs.

"We still have much to discuss, but I will allow you time to process this little bit of information before telling you everything later tonight." She went to get up from the table, but I had to ask her something before she left.

"Grandmother, I have a question." She sat back down, looking at Violet, then to me. "Is there a way to mess with the mate mark and bond?" She looked surprised. She said a few silent words, sending Violet away.

"Why do you ask, Child?" I looked down at the table. That is when Zeus squeezed my hand.

"Well, I was in the forest one day back at home, and a man appeared, telling me that he was my father, but Mom said our father died when we tried to escape, and she felt the bond break, so I am confused."

My grandmother let out a breath. "Yes, Artemis, there is a way to manipulate a mate mark and bond, but it takes a powerful enchantress or enchanter to be able to do something like that."

I looked at Zeus. "So is there a possibility that was our father?"

My grandmother sat there for a moment. "I cannot say for sure at the moment, but I will do some digging and see if I can come up with anything. In the meantime, I want you guys to go back and rest for a while before we wake everyone up to eat before we speak some more." We went to protest, but she held her hand up, speaking this language I had no clue, causing me and my brother to start walking to our room again and then to bed we went.

# Relax

I woke up because of the bright light emanating from the window. Genius had wrapped his arm around me sometime in the middle of the night. I could hear him breathing in my ear, so I didn't move because I didn't want to wake him. Genius nuzzled my ear before kissing my neck. He gently rolled me onto my back. While he balanced on his elbow, he looked at me.

"Morning, Beautiful, how did you sleep?" I just smiled up at him. This man couldn't be more perfect.

"I slept well. How about you?" He didn't speak. He just pressed his lips against mine, sliding his tongue into my mouth to allow our kiss to deepen. He broke the kiss but only to kiss his way to my neck. He started nibbling on my neck all the way down to our mark. My eyes rolled back into my head. The electricity that shot down to my pussy was amazing. Genius helped me out of my shirt and shorts before he started kissing his way down. He stopped at my breasts and gently started sucking on them, then he started to nibble on them while sliding his hand down to my pussy. He started flicking my clit with his finger while he was nibbling on my nipple, causing me to let out a moan. I could feel myself becoming wetter and wetter by the second. But Genius didn't stop there. He started kissing his way down till his lips were just within reach of my pussy. He opened me up with his hands before he started flicking his tongue across my clit. He grabbed my thighs, pulling me closer to his mouth. He was licking and nibbling on my clit, causing me to let out a deep moan while I started moving my hips up and down on his tongue. I knew I didn't want him to stop, but he wasn't letting me cum that way, because he stopped, then looked at me, smiling, before kissing his way back up to where our mark was.

I could feel his hard penis at the entrance of my pussy, but he wasn't sliding in just yet. He looked at me, placing a kiss on my lips. "Princess, I love you."

I just smiled at him. "I love you too, Genius." He tried going in too fast, but I was so tight that he had to gently press his way into my pussy, but once he was in, I let out a scream of pure pleasure. Genius wasn't just fucking me; he was making love to me. He wrapped his arm around me as if he was embracing me while he was sliding in and out of me the whole time, looking at me in my eyes. But I couldn't take it anymore; I needed him deeper inside of me. I wrapped my legs around his waist while my hand grabbed his ass, forcing him deeper inside of me. But it still wasn't deep enough, so we rolled so that he lay flat on his back. He was still inside me, but, now, I had him deeper than I could imagine, and it felt amazing. I started going back and forth, rocking my hips before bouncing up and down slowly. When I would come down, he would push in deeper, causing me to throw my head back in pure ecstasy. He sat up, wrapping his arms around me so that he could grab my shoulders and then started pressing into my pussy harder and harder, causing me to start gushing everywhere.

"OMG, GENIUS, DON'T STOP!" I could feel myself about to climax, and Genius was too, because his pace quickened, and he started pushing me down more with his arms while his penis crashed deeper into my pussy. I could feel my climax coming; he thrusted into me one last time as deep as he could go, causing me to release all over his penis. I could feel that he released inside me too and it felt amazing.

I collapsed down on top of him; he started rubbing my back. "Princess, you're amazing, you know that?"

I just looked up at him. "You were pretty amazing yourself." He just smiled at me, holding me on top of him. We sat like this for a moment. I looked up at him. "Genius, we have to get up so Grandmother Hera can speak to all of us."

He kissed me on top of my head. "Well, Princess, let's get up so we can figure out what are next move is supposed to be." I rolled off of him onto the other side of the bed. Genius stood up. Walking over to our bag, he reached in, grabbing himself some boxers before throwing me my workout outfit.

I just chuckled. "Are we training today or something?"

While he was sliding his pants on, he looked at me. "I honestly don't know, Babe, but it wouldn't surprise me if your grandmother didn't make us train today." I started laughing because he made a good point. I stood up out of the bed before getting myself dressed. I pulled my hair up into a messy bun so that it was out of the way just in case.

I turned back to Genius. "You ready, Babe?"

He just smiled. "Ready as I ever will be." We walked out of our room, heading toward the kitchen. When we got closer, we could hear Zeus and Alcide laughing. We walked into the kitchen, but Grandmother wasn't in there yet. *Hmm, I wonder where she is at.*

My uncle, Alcide, was the first to notice that we were in the room. "Well, morning, guys. How did you sleep?"

We just started laughing. "We slept pretty good." I turned toward Zeus. "Hey, where is Grandmother? She was supposed to be here in the morning so we could talk some more, remember?"

Zeus just stared at me for a moment before speaking, "Artemis, I don't know where she is. Maybe she is just running late." He was right, but I was anxious to talk more about everything. I needed to know more.

Genius walked up behind me, placing his arms around me before whispering in my ear, "Sit down, Princess. I will get you something to eat while we wait on your grandmother." I hadn't noticed how hungry I was until he mentioned food, so I sat down. Genius went back to the fridge and started pulling things out to cook us for breakfast.

I turned toward Alcide. "Well, Grandmother woke us up last night, and she did say that the mate mark can be manipulated, but it can only be down by a powerful enchantress or enchanter."

Alcide looked up from his plate. "What do you mean the mate mark can be manipulated?"

Zeus just shook his head. "Exactly what she said. So, basically, people can use their mate mark or bond to manipulate one into thinking their mate is dead when, in fact, they're actually not." I nodded in agreement with what Zeus had just said.

Alcide looked back at me. "Well, what else did she say?" I turned toward Zeus, Zeus looked at Alcide.

"Well, it is a lot to explain and kinda difficult for me to explain, so why don't we wait for Grandmother to get here, then maybe she can explain it to you two." Alcide nodded, knowing not to press the issue. Genius came over with a plate of eggs, bacon, and toast for everyone before sitting down.

It was good. I ate almost all of mine. We just ate in quiet before Genius spoke up, "So when is your grandmother supposed to be here?"

Zeus and I looked at each other. "I am not sure; she didn't really say what time to meet for us all to talk, but I think she said it would be later tonight."

Alcide turned toward me. "Well, do you want to get some training in while we wait, or do you think we should explore some while we wait?"

I thought about it for a moment. "Let's explore for a while before we decide on the training. I think we deserve to relax for a little bit, don't you?" All three boys just smiled at me. We finished our breakfast before getting up from the table, we all walked outside.

Grandmother had this place made, it was beautiful outside. Over to the right of the house, she had a hot pond. To the left, she had a fire and a chair set up; the view was beautiful.

Genius looked at me. "Princess, you want to get into the hot pond and relax?" I just smiled because that sounded amazing, but before I could answer, the boys were already stripped and running toward the pond. All I could do was laugh at them. I started stripping my clothes off before walking over to the pond and slowly easing myself into the water. Once I was submerged, Genius pulled me closer, wrapping his arms around me.

I looked at Alcide. "So is any of this bringing back any memories?"

Alcide lowered his head. "Unfortunately, no, it isn't. I still don't remember much about this forest at all."

Zeus placed his hand on our uncle's shoulder. "It's okay. It might just take some time to get the rest of your memories back from that time." We just sat in the pond for hours, talking and joking. It started to get dark, and Grandmother still hadn't met us, but the fire and lanterns around the house immediately lit up once the sun went down. I knew that she would be coming soon, but I wasn't sure whether or not I should be nervous or not. One thing that I did know was this was going to be a great experience, but a scary one, and I was excited to get started.

# Discussion

As we sat in the pond at night, admiring our surroundings, the torches and lanterns were all on. I was expecting Grandma Hera to appear soon. I don't understand why she wanted us up early if she wasn't going to be here to speak with all of us. I looked around at the boys; they were all laughing and having a good time. It made me love them more than what I already had. Out of the corner of my eye, I saw a figure coming through the barrier. The boys must have noticed too because we all stood up, waiting to attack if we needed to, but the closer the figure got, we still couldn't quite figure out if it was Grandmother.

"Grandma Hera, is that you?"

It took a few moments, but we finally got a response back, "Yes, dear, it's me. Now will you guys sit down? You're all stark naked out here and I would rather not see it." You could see all the tension release from the four of us, so we all sat down and immediately started laughing. Alcide got out first, drying off with the towel before putting his pants back on. He turned toward his mother.

"Where have you been? We have all been waiting for you to return so that we could talk."

She just looked at her son with a blank expression. "You do realize, just because you're here doesn't mean that I will stop doing my rounds around the forest to make sure everything is okay." We had all gotten out the pond at this point. Genius started walking toward me. He grabbed my hand and wrapped his fingers around mine. We walked over to where my grandmother was. I looked at my grandmother.

"Well, Grandmother, did you want to explain to Alcide and Genius what you told Zeus and me last night?" She nodded yes, then started walking to the house. So we all followed her and she led us into a den-like area where there was a lot of room to sit. She sat down in one of the chairs before she looked at us. We all sat down in different areas. Genius and Alcide sat closer to Grandmother.

"Okay, so while you guys were asleep last night, I called upon Artemis and Zeus to come to the dining room. There was some information that they needed to know before you guys did, and that was just simply the right thing to do at the time." They both nodded. "Now, I don't know if you guys have ever realized how close Zeus and Artemis are actually—"

Genius cut her off, "Well, I have noticed that no matter where she is, Zeus knows without even looking for her too much."

Then Alcide, "That, and ever since they were younger, it's like they can share energy."

My grandmother smiled. "Well, it seems at least the two of you pay attention better than they do at least. Okay, so you know that much, but what you don't know is that there is a prophecy that speaks of the battle to come as well as two siblings. One will give their life to save the other. It also speaks of the sibling that passes will give its strength to the other in order to save the pack." Hera held her hand up, silencing them before they could speak. "That is not all, so let me finish before you interrupt. Zeus has the blood of an enchanter which means that yes, he has powers. They just aren't as strong as Artemis because their bond is unique. It can be dangerous to them as well as those around them. They have a bond that nobody has seen before, and we don't quite understand how it works yet, but just because there's this prophecy does not necessarily mean that it will come true. Prophecies can be changed and have been in the past." My grandmother paused.

Alcide was the first to speak out of the two, "So you're telling us that Zeus has powers, they are bonded uniquely, as well as one of them is most likely going to die to save the other basically."

Genius spoke next, "That can't be right. How can two half siblings have a bond that you don't understand, and how can they put into that situation in the first place? There has to be something we can do to change the outcome."

Grandmother held her hand up once again, silencing them. "Now now, calm down. Yes, there is a lot that we still don't understand about them, but one thing is for sure. We have a lot of training to do."

Zeus stood up, walking closer to Grandmother, "Grandmother, we asked you last night about the mate connection. Have you found anything else out about it or at least some information that can be shared?" We looked at her, eagerly awaiting her answer, but she fell silent, not speaking at all.

So I stepped closer to her, "Grandmother Hera, please answer Zeus. This is important." She got up from her chair and walked to the bookshelf behind her. She pulled out a large book with leather binding; it looked old. Then she walked back to her chair, sitting down once again.

"In this book will be the answers you seek, Artemis, but I must warn you, you are not ready for anything in this book, so please do not attempt anything in here before we train you properly." She went to hand me the book, but before she could, Genius took it from her, then he looked at me.

"No offense, Princess, but you're not good at following directions. Alcide and I will ready the book, then once you do some training with your grandmother and she feels a little bit more comfortable with you reading it, then I will give it to you."

I was getting angry. How could my mate not trust me with reading the book and not doing anything?

But before I could speak a word, I heard Violet in, "Well, Artemis, he has a point. You never have been good at waiting, especially on reading." Well, I guess they did have a point, but I didn't have to like it.

"Fine, Genius, but I do not like that you don't trust me."

He touched my shoulder. "It's not that I don't trust you. I don't trust the curious part of you; there is a difference."

At this point, my grandmother started laughing. "God, do you sound like your mother." Seriously, how can she be laughing at me?

"Really, Grandma, this isn't funny."

She, still laughing, looked me dead in my eyes. "O, my child, it is. If you only knew your mother at your age, you would understand more."

I looked over, and Alcide was laughing too. "She has a point. Your mom was really bad about being way too curious too soon." Well, I was glad that they all thought this was funny, because I didn't.

My grandmother stopped laughing at me. "Okay, so, tomorrow, we will start your and Zeus's magical training, but, Alcide and Genius, you will be training physically and mentally tomorrow. There is one person I trust to train you and has been alive just as long as I have."

We all looked at each other before speaking in unison, "Well, who would that be?"

She just shook her head. "You will find out tomorrow, but, for now, we need to talk more before we all get some rest."

She turned toward me specifically which just made me uncomfortable. Artemis, you remember when I told you that you had a long way to go before you could properly protect your pack?" I nodded. "Well, I was not exaggerating. This road will not be easy; you have much to learn, but I can tell you that you will learn a lot from our past, things that you will need to help your future. There will be a lot of things that you have to read as well." She stared at me for a moment.

"I know this. This is why Mother sent me to you!"

She just shook her head. "No, your mother sent you to me because she was a damn idiot who didn't tell you shit about who you were and what was coming!" My mouth fell open. I never thought I would hear her speak this way of my mother. Alcide seemed to be shocked too. He placed his hand on his mother's leg.

"Mother, don't speak ill of Athena. She did what she thought was best at the time." I could see the anger boiling in my grandmother's eyes. I knew this wasn't going to be good.

"NO, ATHENA DID WHAT WAS BEST FOR HER, NOT WHAT WAS BEST FOR HER CHILDREN. SHE MAY HAVE THOUGHT SHE WAS PROTECTING THEM, BUT LOOK AT WHAT HAS HAPPENED. ARTEMIS IS NOT FULLY TRAINED ON ANYTHING, AND ZEUS DIDN'T EVEN KNOW HE HAD POWERS LET ALONE HOW TO USE THEM. MY DAUGHTER WAS AN IDIOT. I TOLD HER EXACTLY WHAT TO DO AND SHE DISOBEYED ME."

We were all shocked by how angry she was about that. I mean, I know Zeus and I had been angry with just cause, but what I couldn't understand was why she was so angry. But before I could ask, she looked back at Alcide.

"My son, your sister was supposed to return your memories before your niece turned 16. That way, you knew exactly what had happened and what was going to happen, but she didn't do that. Artemis had to help you and even then because she isn't properly trained. She couldn't even fully return them to you, so, now, I have to return them to you so you know what is going to have to happen after this." Alcide went to speak, but she held her hand up again.

"We will not do this tonight. Tonight, everyone rest, because, tomorrow, we have a long day." Before any of us could object, she spoke a few words silently. I already knew what was going to happen. She raised her hand, sending us all back to our rooms and straight to bed. I lay in bed, looking at the ceiling. What was going to happen, I had no clue, but one thing that I did know was that was not going to be an easy path for me, and I wasn't sure whether to be scared or excited. I looked over to look at Genius, and I noticed that he was sound asleep. Why did what she whisper always put him straight to sleep but it took me a while to do so? No matter, I would just lay, staring at the ceiling until I did.

# Information

The next morning, I woke up to find that Genius was no longer in bed. I sat straight up and started looking around the room, but he wasn't in here. *That must mean he is out in the kitchen.* So I got up and went into the bathroom. I took a shower, then got dressed and walked to the kitchen. When I walked into the kitchen, everyone was there, and there was a new face. I stood at the door, just watching everyone laugh and giggle. They were enjoying themselves, and that meant a lot to me because I knew this wasn't going to be an easy road to take now that we were here. My grandmother looked up and noticed me standing there.

"Artemis, there is someone I think that you should meet." So I walked over to the table and sat down beside Genius. He placed his hand on my thigh, giving it a slight squeeze. I suddenly began to feel uncomfortable; he never did that unless he was trying to comfort me. The man that I couldn't recognize was just staring at me, which wasn't helping matters any.

My grandmother looked at me. "Artemis, I would like you to meet your granduncle, Ares!" I must have looked shocked because my uncle, Alcide, walked over to me and kneeled down beside me.

"Artemis, she isn't lying to you. This is her brother. I just couldn't remember him till this morning when your grandmother returned the rest of my memories." I was confused.

"Umm, I didn't even know you had a brother; nobody ever told me that."

My grandmother started laughing. "Sweet Child, your mother failed to tell you a lot. So are you surprised by her withholding that I had a brother?" She had a point. Apparently, there was a lot that my mother hadn't told me and Zeus.

"So why is he here? And why are we just now hearing about him?" But my grandmother wasn't the one that spoke.

Ares stood up. "I am here to train my nephew and your mate. That way, they are properly prepared for the battle to come while you and your brother train with my sister." So that was who she was talking about last night. Why was I not surprised?

My grandmother stood up. "Now let's get this straight. Yes, Zeus and Artemis will be training with me, but you will also be training with Ares as well as Alcide and Genius will be training with me. I want you guys properly trained. That way, you're better off to defend yourself."

Genius looked confused just as much as everyone else, so he looked at my grandmother. "Um, no offense, but why do Alcide and I need to train with you? Neither of us has magical capabilities." My grandmother and her brother just threw their heads back and started laughing.

Ares turned toward my grandmother. "Hera, these children really don't know anything, do they?"

She just started chuckling. "My dear brother, they have no clue about anything because their history and ours were never explained to them."

I stood up, slamming my hand on the table, trying to get their attention, "Well, then, maybe you should enlighten us instead of laughing at us."

Ares was taken aback by what I did. "Hera, I do believe we have our fighter out of the bunch. God, she reminds me of my niece."

Hera turned toward her brother. "Yes, we do, and, yes, she is almost completely like her mother, but not." He just shook his head as if he understood what she meant by that, then she turned toward the group. "Alcide is my son, so, of course, he has magical abilities, but he does take after his father more so then me, but he does have some magic in him that he hasn't used since he was a child."

We looked over to my uncle. Why wouldn't he tell us any of that? He must have known that. Before I could speak, he stood up.

"Before you say anything, please remember, I couldn't remember my past, so, of course, I wouldn't remember me having powers." Well, he had a point there, so I couldn't be angry with him for that because it wasn't his fault. I just stared back at my grandmother, but she wasn't the one that spoke this time, which was becoming irritating because none of us knew him at all.

"As for your mate, Genius, you do realize that you two are mated now, and, Artemis, you share your power with your mate, so he now has the ability to use some magic if he chooses, and with the battle to come, we want him trained just in case he needs to use those powers."

But before I could speak again, my grandmother held her hand up. "Look, Child, other than Ares and myself, you are the most powerful in the room. Actually, by the time you have completed all of your training, you will be stronger than us, but, remember, we have been around a long time, so we know a lot of things that will help you along the way, so please don't argue, just listen."

I went to argue with her, but Genius just placed his hand on my shoulder. I turned toward him, and he just shook his head no. *Why is everyone taking this so easy? I am so damned confused as to what is going on, and they are just sitting here like everything is okay.*

As if my grandmother read my mind, "Artemis, look, I know this is all hard to understand right now, but I promise you will learn all about our family and what that means. Once you're mated, you share a lot with one another. I don't expect you to understand because none of you have been properly trained on your histories as a wolf or as an enchantress and enchanter." I sat back down. I wasn't sure if I should say anything else at that point because I didn't think it would do a lot of good to talk.

But Zeus stood up and looked at Grandmother. "So when does all of this training begin?"

She walked over, placing a hand on each of his shoulders. "My dear Zeus, the training that we will be doing will be starting tonight, but I do have books for you and your sister to read until then so that maybe you guys can better understand everything."

She turned toward Alcide and Genius. "As for you two, your training starts right now."

Ares just smiled. "Follow me, boys. We will be going outside for some physical training today."

Genius stood up, kissed me on top of my head. "I love you, Princess. Remember, you can do this no matter what." I just smiled at him, then he turned and walked out the door with Alcide and Ares.

I turned toward Grandma Hera. "Will they be okay?"

She just smiled. "O, they will be okay. A little beat-up, but okay, nonetheless. Now, you two, follow me to the den. You have a lot of reading to do before tonight."

I turned toward Zeus. "Squirt, it will be okay. There is a lot that none of us understands right now, but the only way to understand it all is to do what she says. Mom wouldn't have sent us to her if it wasn't important." I knew he was right, but that was just a lot to take. Couldn't she give us some time to process all of the information she just gave us before she started piling more into our heads that could confuse us more than we already were?

But there was no use in arguing because she was already heading to the den with Zeus right on her tail. *I don't understand how he is remaining calm about all of this. Now is the perfect time for him to freak the hell out, but he isn't. He is just... I don't know.* But I got up and followed them to the den. When I entered the den, there had to be like a hundred books just piled up on the table.

I looked at my grandma. "You want us to read all of those before tonight?" She just turned and smiled, then walked out the door. *She has to be out of her mind. That's it, completely out of her mind.* I looked at Zeus. "There is no way in hell we are reading all of this by tonight."

He just shook his head. "Artemis, you are such a pessimist. If you would quit talking and get over here and sit down, we could get started." I just shook my head, but I walked over to the table where all the books were. She had paper and pencils everywhere. Apparently, she wanted us to take notes too. This was going to be exhausting. This was a lot to read; I am looking at some of the titles on the books, but one caught my eye more than the other, so I picked it up and, on the front of the book, it said, 'Cage Family History.' Maybe this wouldn't be so bad after all. I pulled the chair out and began to read the book, zoning out anything else around me.

9 781647 505158